THE MAN IN THE RIVER

First paperback edition September 2020.

www.indiecrime.com
Facebook.com/ChrisCulverBooks

THE MAN IN THE RIVER

A Joe Court Novel

BY

CHRIS CULVER

ST. LOUIS, MO

Other books in the Joe Court Series

1

An icy breeze blew through the vehicle's open windows, and gasoline sloshed in the red five-gallon container in the footwell of the front passenger seat. Luke Glasman had draped a thick blanket over his infant daughter's car seat to keep her warm, but he shivered as he drove. Luke had thought about killing people often, but he had never done it. In just a few minutes, though, he would torch an asshole's house and burn him alive. Even the thought made him smile.

He glanced in his rearview mirror. Though Kendra's seat faced the rear of the SUV, he had installed a mirror above the backseat, allowing him to see her face while he drove. Her eyes were closed, and she bounced along with the car as he passed over the rough pavement. She oftentimes had a hard time falling asleep, but once Kendra yawned and stretched and closed her beautiful blue eyes, she'd sleep for hours at a time as long as no one interrupted her. He didn't need to worry about her, safe and sound in her car seat. It made the work in front of him much easier.

He didn't know the name of the street they were on, but that didn't surprise him. Even after living in St. Augustine for six months, Luke still didn't know the area well. Moving had been Irene's decision. She thought it was sensible, which meant he hadn't had a choice in the matter. Still, he and Kendra were making the best of it, enjoying the parks in good weather and the restaurants and shops on cold days.

Irene Glasman, Luke's spouse, made a lot of money as a corporate attorney in St. Louis, but she had almost two hundred thousand dollars' worth of student loans and an inexhaustible need for new clothes, shoes, and furniture. With her spending habits, they couldn't afford a home near her work in St. Louis, so they had bought a sprawling ranch in St. Augustine, and she commuted an hour to the city and an hour back every day. That was just as well. Had she been around more often, Irene would have killed him in his sleep by now.

The day had started as Luke's days often did. His wife had left for work at seven, but he had woken up at eight, having taken care of the baby the previous night. For an hour, he drank coffee and answered emails from old friends and potential clients. Luke had a master's degree in theater and specialized in set design and construction. He was good at his job, so he could have secured a full-time position with a professional theater company in a larger city. Barring that, he could have landed a teaching job in a university. Irene loved St. Louis, though, and he had yet to convince her she'd love Chicago or New York just as much.

At nine, Luke finished his cup of coffee and walked down the hallway to Kendra's nursery. Kendra was their miracle baby. She had been born with a heart defect and had undergone major surgery shortly after her birth. Her recovery had been tough, but she was still with them, and it didn't seem that she'd have too many complications down the line. Still, he was a germophobe around her because of it, so he washed his hands in the ensuite bathroom before picking her up from her crib.

Irene treated Kendra like a status symbol. By dressing the baby in designer clothes and ensuring that she had the most expensive stroller and car seat available, she showed the lawyers at her firm and her superficial friends that she could have it all—a high-powered job, a family, and a home all her own. She barely knew Kendra and rarely took care of her, but that didn't matter. Irene wanted a life that was outwardly beautiful and didn't mind that it was hollow inside.

After changing Kendra's diaper, Luke fed her baby oatmeal and a bottle. They then spent the rest of the morning in the park and the grocery store. Even in the grocery store, he kept her covered so she wouldn't pick up any aerosolized germs. After the grocery store, Kendra fell asleep, giving Luke a welcome moment of silence. The car often lulled Kendra to sleep. It was his place of respite, and he would have normally driven around for an hour or two to take advantage of her nap, but he needed gas, which meant he had to go to the BP station.

The station was quiet at first, but then a faint buzzing filled the air. Then the buzz turned into pulsating, loud music as a white Pontiac Grand Am pulled into the station. Bits and pieces of the car rattled as the bass shook the late-model sedan. In the back of Luke's SUV, Kendra stirred and stretched. If she woke up, she would become cranky, and his quiet morning would be ruined.

The Pontiac parked at the pump nearest him, and a man in his early twenties stepped out, the car still vibrating with its loud music. The man wore a diamond stud earring in his right ear, and he had dirty-blond hair with dark roots and bushy eyebrows. His baggy jeans looked frayed but clean, and his white T-shirt hugged his fit torso. A pair of tattooed wings adorned his neck, and mutton chops covered his cheeks. The look hadn't been attractive, but maybe it was trendy.

As Mutton Chops walked to the convenience store, Luke called out.

"Hey, buddy! If you're going to leave, can you turn the music down?"

Luke had hardly heard himself shout, but Mutton Chops stopped and considered before flipping his ear forward with his middle finger.

"Turn off your car!" Luke shouted. "Your radio's so loud it's shaking my car, and I've got a baby sleeping. Please."

Mutton Chops sighed then and returned to his car to turn off the radio.

"You happy now?" he asked, standing.

"Thank you."

Mutton Chops rolled his eyes and walked away. Luke had expected that to be the end of things, but it wasn't. Luke's Suburban had a thirty-one-gallon tank, so it took a while to fill up. Had it been up to him, he never would have sold the Subaru he had driven throughout college and graduate school, but Irene thought they needed something bigger and fancier. They had fought about it for weeks, but then, one day, the dealer dropped off the new SUV in the driveway and picked up the Subaru while Luke napped. That was typical Irene.

Luke watched the numbers fly by on the pump before the pump's handle popped as it sensed the gas tank had filled. At the same moment, Mutton Chops stepped out of the convenience store carrying a package of white powdered donuts and a soda. Instead of walking to his Pontiac, he sauntered to Luke's SUV.

"Can I help you?" asked Luke.

"Your daughter still asleep?" Mutton Chops asked.

"Yeah," Luke said, wondering why Mutton Chops was still talking to him. "I'm heading out now, so I'll be out of your hair."

Mutton Chops pressed his face against the window before straightening and looking to Luke. Then he pounded on the glass with his knuckles.

"What are you doing?"

Instead of answering, Mutton Chops smirked and reached into his pocket for a pack of cigarettes. As Kendra started crying, he lit up.

"Your wife a screamer, too?"

The asshole then walked toward his Pontiac, and Luke's face grew red.

Spray him with gas. Light him up.

The voice sounded reptilian, almost. Luke removed the nozzle from the gas pump. Mutton Chops paused before getting in his car. Then he laughed.

"Fuck you, Grandpa, and fuck your kid."

The pulsing beat of the music began. Kendra cried. Luke hated hearing his daughter cry and wished he had sprayed Mutton Chops with gasoline. With the cigarette dangling from his lips, that would have killed him. *He deserves it. Follow him. Burn him. Hear him scream.*

Intellectually, Luke knew that the voice was likely the wind and that his subconscious mind had ascribed to it meaning it didn't have, but that didn't matter. He had slept five hours last night after getting four the night before. His eyelids felt heavy, and muscles all over his body ached. Fighting that voice would have taken strength Luke didn't have.

So he reinserted the nozzle in the gas pump and followed Mutton Chops across town to a single-story brick home with a detached garage. The younger man parked, and Luke drove past before stopping on the side of the road.

Burn it to the ground. He doesn't deserve to live.

"No, he doesn't," said Luke.

After learning where Mutton Chops lived, Luke and Kendra drove to Walmart, where they purchased a red five-gallon gasoline can. Then they filled it at a different station than the one they had just visited. Kendra woke up for part of that, but she fell asleep on the drive back to Mutton Chops's home. That was just as well.

This was Daddy's time, and Daddy intended to have fun.

2

I paced the length of the windowless corridor outside the conference room in my attorney's suite of offices. My right thumbnail throbbed, having been picked at enough over the past week to have been worn down to the quick. I hadn't done anything wrong, but my heart palpitated, and my lungs felt tight. I had interrogated and interviewed hundreds of people over the years, but none of that experience made what lay ahead of me any easier.

In just a few short minutes, two detectives planned to interview me about the murder of George Delgado, a former colleague. They had found his body floating along the banks of the Mississippi River near Cape Girardeau, a town of about forty thousand people a hundred and twenty miles south of St. Louis. Someone had shot him in the chest six times with a .40-caliber pistol. Since I owned a .40-caliber pistol, and since George and I had fought constantly over the years, they suspected me. I hadn't killed him, but these cops were more interested in finding someone to blame than in finding the truth.

Eventually, my attorney stepped out of her office. She had brunette hair that shone even in the office's dim light, and she wore a tailored navy blazer and skirt. The diamond pendant on her tanned neck swung with every step. Her calm smile should have put me at ease, but it didn't.

Alexa Swaine was the senior partner of Swaine,

Hollander, and Associates. As a detective, I had met and talked with a lot of defense attorneys over the years. Few were naïve. They knew the vast majority of their clients were guilty, but they also understood that good people sometimes made mistakes. They fought for their clients not because they thought they were innocent but because they recognized the important role defense attorneys played in our justice system. They kept the government in check and made sure cops followed the rules.

Alexa Swaine was an exceptional attorney. In the past year, she had gone eleven and three in jury trials. That'd be an impressive record for a prosecutor who could pick whether or not to take a suspect to trial, but it was an incredible record for a defense attorney. She specialized in major felonies, but she never touched sex crimes. I wouldn't have hired her if she had.

"My assistant told me they're in the building," said Alexa. "Are you ready?"

"I'm not sure my readiness has much bearing on what'll happen."

My attorney smiled.

"This is a voluntary interview," she said. "We can end it before it starts."

I thought about taking her up on that, but then I shook my head.

"No. I did nothing wrong."

Alexa's smile waned, and she crossed her arms.

"This isn't about right and wrong. The men on their way to talk to you are trying to send you to prison. My job is to keep you out of it. In this office, the truth will not set you free. It's a tool, and so is silence. If it's in your best interest, I'll end the interview immediately. If that happens, you can't speak. Okay?"

My stomach churned, but I forced myself to nod.

"I hired you because I trust your judgment."

"Good," said Alexa. "Let's get to it, then. They should be here any moment."

We walked to the conference room. Floor-to-ceiling windows filled the western wall, and a long wooden conference table dominated the center of the room. A dozen black leather office chairs ringed the table, while coffee brewed in a pot on the credenza beside the door. A neat pile of danishes rested on a plate beside the coffeepot. Since I was paying for everything, I figured I might as well enjoy the snacks while they were out. I poured myself a cup of coffee and grabbed a pastry and napkins.

"Myles can bring in milk and sugar if you'd like," said Alexa. "My staff rarely puts it out when I interview police officers. They usually just drink their coffee black, so it goes to waste."

"Black is fine," I said, sitting at the table with my back toward the windows and my face toward the doors. Alexa poured herself a soft drink and sat beside me at the table. Within five minutes, Myles—Alexa's assistant—led Detectives Roger Vega and Jim Hargitay of the Cape Girardeau Police Department into the room. Vega wore a navy suit, light blue shirt, and dark blue tie. Hargitay was a study in earth tones and wore a brown suit, cream-colored shirt, and brown corduroy pants. Both wore firearms at their hips and badges on their belts.

"Morning, gentlemen," said Alexa, standing. I stood beside her and smiled. "Get yourself some coffee, and we'll get started."

"Thank you, but no," said Hargitay, not taking his eyes from me. His partner pulled out a chair but said nothing before sitting down. Their responses were coordinated and brusque. I wondered whether they had talked about them beforehand. "Please have a seat, Ms. Court. We've got a lot to cover."

Alexa put a hand on my forearm so I wouldn't move. She smiled, but the good humor ended at her lips.

"Thank you for coming out here, detectives," she said, "but I'm afraid an emergency's come up, and we need to reschedule the interview. How's next week sound?"

"Excuse me?" asked Detective Vega, raising his eyebrows. Hargitay crossed his arms.

"We drove for two hours to get here," he said. "We're not leaving."

"And that's a problem," said Alexa. "You ordered my client to sit down as if she were already convicted of a crime, but since you need a reminder, you've not even arrested her, and this is a voluntary interview. You have no authority to order her around. This is my building, so if I want you to leave, I can kick you out at any time."

I closed my eyes and held up a hand before either

detective could speak.

"Nobody's going anywhere," I said. "Detectives, I will answer your questions to the best of my ability, but I didn't kill George Delgado. If I'm your primary suspect, you suck at your jobs. Ms. Swaine is my attorney, and I trust her. If she says the interview is over, it is. I'd advise you to be polite."

The two detectives shifted. Vega looked to me.

"May I have a cup of coffee?"

I looked to Alexa, who smiled.

"Sure, Detective," she said. "Help yourself."

The two men got coffee. Then we sat at the table. Both detectives had a stiff, formal posture. After they got settled, Hargitay looked to my lawyer.

"You mind if we record the conversation?"

"By all means," she said. "If you're curious, we're recording as well. There are cameras in the ceiling and microphones throughout the office."

Hargitay grunted and pulled out his cell phone, setting it on the table between us.

"Okay," he said. "I'm Detective Jim Hargitay. With me is my partner, Detective Roger Vega. We're here to talk to Detective Joe Court about the murder of George Delgado. Sitting beside Detective Court is her attorney, Alexa Swaine. Is that correct?"

Alexa looked to me, so I leaned forward.

"Yep."

The two detectives focused on me. Neither blinked.

"Did you kill George Delgado?" asked Vega.

I shook my head.

"No."

The two detectives paused. I waited and said nothing.

"Can you elaborate?" asked Hargitay.

"No," I said. "You want elaboration, ask better questions."

Detective Vega rolled his eyes and leaned forward, but before he could say anything, Hargitay put a hand on his shoulder. Vega leaned back and crossed his arms.

"You're a detective," he said. "A good one, if your record means anything."

I smiled.

"Thanks. I try my best."

"You knew Detective Delgado, you know St. Augustine, and, presumably, you know the kind of trouble he could get into in St. Augustine. How would you approach his murder investigation?"

I waited for more information, but Hargitay said nothing.

"Is that a serious question?" I asked eventually. He nodded, so I shrugged. "After identifying the body and learning that it belonged to a detective from a neighboring jurisdiction, I'd send someone to his department to talk to his colleagues, friends, and family. I'd also investigate the scene where he was found and the body itself for forensic evidence. Using information from both the body and the statements of those who knew the victim, I'd put together a timeline of events prior to his death and a preliminary list of potential suspects."

"That's what we did," said Hargitay. His face was impassive. "Guess whose name kept coming up."

"Considering I'm here, I don't think I have to guess," I said. "Did you look into his old cases, by chance?"

Detective Vega pursed his lips and shook his head.

"Let's focus on you for the moment," he said. "You didn't like George Delgado, did you?"

"No."

"Is it fair to say you hated him?" asked Hargitay.

I considered him and then drew in a breath.

"Hate's a strong word."

"Did you hate him?" asked Vega.

I looked at him and shook my head.

"No."

"Even after he forced you out of your department?"

I crossed my arms and felt my skin grow warmer. At one time, George Delgado had been the St. Augustine County sheriff, a position to which the County Council had appointed him after the previous sheriff retired. A little over a year ago, he accused me of murdering a woman named Sasha Ingram. She had been crazy and dangerous, and I had tried to take her into custody. Before I could, she pointed a pistol at me, and I shot her. No one witnessed the shooting, and the forensic evidence supported multiple interpretations of the evidence. I quit to avoid a long, nasty investigation.

"I don't blame him for that," I said. "George was the sheriff, and he was told by the County Council that if he didn't get rid of me, the council would cut his funding.

He could fire me or lay off dozens of officers. He made the right choice."

Detective Vega straightened, while his partner cocked his head to the side and furrowed his brow.

"Can you prove that?" asked Hargitay.

I shook my head.

"No, but George told me that shortly before he died."

Hargitay said nothing, but Detective Vega leaned back and considered me before opening his mouth.

"And why would the County Council want to get rid of you that badly?"

"To be fair, I don't think it was the entire County Council. Mostly it was Darren Rogers. You've probably heard from him by now. I'm guessing he's tried to insert himself into your investigation already and point the finger at me."

Detective Vega blinked. Hargitay's body went still, but it only lasted a moment before he focused on the notepad in front of him.

"We'll circle back to that," said Vega. "Someone shot Delgado with a .40-caliber pistol. You have a .40-caliber pistol."

"Many people have .40-caliber pistols," I said. "You took that pistol a week ago, which means you've had ample time to test it. That I'm not under arrest means you know I didn't kill George."

"We know you didn't use that pistol," said Hargitay. "Do you have any other .40-caliber pistols?"

I shook my head.

"Nope."

"Why not?" asked Hargitay. "I carry a .40-caliber weapon. I like it. It's light, it feels good, and it shoots well. I'm surprised that you, as a woman who owns multiple firearms, wouldn't have more."

I glanced at him.

"I own firearms for work and self-defense. I don't collect them," I said. Hargitay opened his mouth and looked as if he planned to ask something else about my firearms. I spoke before he could. "Besides, I prefer the magazine capacity of a good nine millimeter and the stopping power of a .45. The .40-caliber is a compromise on both counts, and I don't like compromising. The department issued mine to me. Otherwise, I wouldn't own one. I'm glad they work for you, though." I paused. "You should ask me about Darren Rogers now."

"Okay," said Vega. "Tell us about Darren Rogers."

"Before he died, George was investigating Rogers for financial crimes. Rogers bought a lot of commercial property around St. Augustine. He then tried to use his position as county executive to force through projects that would benefit his property. People who stood up to him or threatened his plans in other ways died."

"What people?" asked Vega.

"To start with, Vic Conroy. He was a pimp who owned a strip club and hotel. He brought an unsavory element to St. Augustine, which prevented Darren from being able to book several big conventions. He was murdered. Arthur Murdoch owned a lot of commercial property Darren Rogers wanted, and he was murdered as well. Zach Brugler killed Darren Rogers's daughter in a car accident, and he died, too. Richard Clarke ran a racist church and protested at every major event in town. Like Vic Conroy, he was an embarrassment and prevented Darren from bringing in the big concerts and conventions he wanted. He also died."

The two detectives shifted in their seats.

"Do you have any evidence tying Darren Rogers to George Delgado's death?" asked Hargitay, narrowing his eyes.

"Not yet, but his death fits the pattern," I said. "If you investigate Darren Rogers or threaten his interests, you die. George investigated Rogers and threatened his interests, and somebody murdered him."

Neither detective spoke for a moment.

"Do you think Darren Rogers killed George Delgado?" asked Vega. "Because I've got to be honest. We met Mr. Rogers. He's an old man."

I shook my head.

"He hired somebody. He might have even used the county's slush fund to pay for it. George thought the county had so much dirty money on its books that no one would have even noticed."

Hargitay pushed back from the table. Vega stood.

"If this is all you've got to share, I think we're done here," said Hargitay. "Thank you for your time."

"When did Mr. Delgado die?" asked Alexa. "My

client is a busy woman. It's possible she was engaged at the time of his death."

The detectives looked to one another. Vega raised his eyes, and Hargitay shrugged. Then Vega turned to my lawyer.

"We don't know," he said. "We found him in the Mississippi River. Our coroner gave us a forty-eight-hour window. We've read reports Detective Court filed, so we know she was alone for a significant portion of that time. She had ample opportunity to murder Mr. Delgado and dump his body."

"In that case, it sounds like my client and I will be of no help to you," said Alexa, smiling and standing. "If you need to speak to Detective Court again, call my office. Otherwise, hang a left in the hallway. My assistant will see you out."

They said they would. Then they left. I looked to my lawyer. She considered me before speaking.

"That stuff about Darren Rogers is interesting, but it won't keep you from prison."

"What will?" I asked.

"Better proof than you have."

I stood up.

"I'll find it, then. Thank you, Alexa. I appreciate your help."

She followed me to the hallway. Her assistant's desk was empty, so we waited a moment for him to return. He started to lead me away a moment later, but Alexa stopped us both.

"Before you go, Detective," she said, "a word of advice. Keep this Darren Rogers information quiet."

"I've worked with most of my colleagues for years," I said. "I trust them."

"So did George," she said. "I can't defend you from a gunshot in the dark."

It was good advice, so I nodded and thanked her before leaving. As I walked back to my car, I thought about George Delgado and Darren Rogers and the current sheriff, Sheriff Dean Kalil. One way or another, I suspected this case would end my career in St. Augustine. I hoped and prayed that no one I loved would end up dead.

3

Mutton Chops lived in a valley between two hills about half a mile west of the town of St. Augustine. Luke parked his heavy SUV along the side of the road a block from the house and took three deep breaths. The sinewy remains of a long-harvested corn crop covered the field across the street, while deep woods lay behind the brick home. The nearest house was about two hundred yards to the north, but a thick stand of fir trees gave him the privacy he needed to do the task ahead. He couldn't even see a home to the south.

Luke's heart hammered against his rib cage. Kendra stirred in her infant seat in back. For a moment, he didn't remember where he was. That happened sometimes. He'd drive and zone out and then wake up hours later, having driven halfway across the state or having returned home to fold an entire week's worth of laundry. Earlier that summer, he had even gone grocery shopping, put Kendra down for a nap, and started planting zinnias in a raised flower bed in the backyard without even realizing it. All he could remember of that day was waking up, getting behind the wheel of his car, and then zoning out for the next four hours.

His lapses were unnerving, but he took heart in his muscles' ability to care for Kendra even when his mind went elsewhere. He loved her with his entire heart, and he'd care for her with every breath he had.

Now that the vehicle had stopped, the scent of gasoline began filling the car's interior. He couldn't allow his daughter to breathe the fumes, so he exited the car and then walked to the passenger's side for the gas can. Then he stopped. He wasn't a smoker, so he only carried matches or a lighter if he knew he'd have to use them.

"Shit," he said, pausing and looking up the long, hilly street. In the spring and summer, when wildflowers blossomed alongside the road, the street would be beautiful. Now, even the scrub brush in the ditch beside the asphalt seemed to have shrunk in the early winter chill.

"Fuck."

He wouldn't have sworn if Kendra had been awake. Even though she was still an infant, he watched his language around her. Irene just let the curses fly, but Kendra would grow up one day and have sensitive ears. She didn't need to hear that kind of hateful language. He wondered what Irene's mother had said to her when she was a baby. Had she watched her language? He doubted it.

Irene's mother believed her Ivy-League-educated daughter should have married a titan of industry or a fellow lawyer—someone who could take care of her precious baby. She didn't like that she had settled for her college boyfriend.

Irene hadn't settled, but she never told her mom that. As an undergraduate, Luke had been voted the most outstanding theater major of the past decade by his professors. The college even produced a play he had written as his senior thesis. It was a family drama, and it had a big ensemble cast. The actors and audience liked the play so much, the college agreed to run it again a year later.

Luke had never felt so proud of himself. Irene had been proud, too, although she was always quick to point out he hadn't earned a single cent on that play. She enjoyed pointing out his flaws and failures. Never once did he mention to her that she was a greedy, controlling shrew who had been resentful of him from the moment she found out he was just as smart and talented as she was.

He was ready to shut the passenger door, thinking this endeavor was a mistake, when he spotted the plastic bag on the front seat. He couldn't remember buying anything, but he reached down anyway and then smiled as he felt the familiar, boxy shape inside. Strike on Box Matches. Three hundred count. He must have gotten them when he picked up the gasoline.

He smiled and shut the front door before checking on Kendra. Her lips moved as if she were eating something, and she grunted, but she didn't open her eyes.

Luke didn't plan to be gone long, so he locked the SUV's doors and left his daughter there. He carried the gas can in the shallow ditch alongside the road. The brush and grasses had gone dormant for the season, and most of the area's birds had long since flown south. Occasionally, leaves crinkled around him as field mice or squirrels scurried about in the underbrush. Otherwise, he was alone. He enjoyed being alone.

No one passed, but if someone had, he would have told them he had run out of gas and planned to walk to the nearest station. His fingers tingled, and he felt an almost electric charge over his skin. If he hadn't been carrying five gallons of gas, he might have run.

He felt strong, strangely. Had Irene been there, she would have reminded him he hadn't done anything worthwhile yet and that he had abandoned their daughter on the side of the road while he went on his adventure. But he hadn't abandoned Kendra and never would. As soon as he finished this, he'd return to the car, and they'd go home. He'd feed her, and then they'd play with toys, and then he'd read to her before putting her in her play gym so he could contain her as he cleaned the bathrooms.

Luke didn't live the life he had wanted in college, but he liked the one he had. He even appreciated Irene to a degree. Her indifference and money allowed him to spend plenty of time with their daughter. That was the best gift anyone could give him.

Luke's footsteps slowed as he reached the corner of Mutton Chops's property. The home had a detached garage, minimal landscaping, and, maybe, a half acre of lawn surrounded by a thin layer of trees underplanted with oak leaf hydrangeas and other hardy shade-loving perennials. Neat red brick clad the front of the home, while gray vinyl siding covered the rest. It was a popular design scheme in contemporary homes. The siding was cheaper than masonry construction, and it likely lowered the property taxes as well. Irene wouldn't have stood for it, but Luke saw the utility of the design. Mutton Chops had parked in the driveway.

He crouched amongst the plants and hoped he blended in. The home had two windows on the side nearest him. Blinds covered both, giving Mutton Chops some privacy but also limiting his ability to see what happened outside his home. It was as good a spot to start his fire as anywhere. Then, he spotted a woodpile and fire pit on a concrete patio beside the detached garage. That was perfect.

He followed the tree line to the rear of the house, grabbed two big armfuls of dry wood, and carried them back toward his gas tank. Luke had never been a camper or hunter, but he had lit enough charcoal barbecue grills to understand the basics of combustion. He piled the wood against the side of the home before dousing it, the home's siding, and the surrounding ground with gasoline. Finally, he used the remaining few ounces of gas in his can to create a trail across the lawn.

Roughly four minutes had passed since he reached the home. The wood pile was small and covered in shadow. He wouldn't even be able to see it from the road. Unless Mutton Chops walked around to this side of the house, he may not see it for weeks. Luke could leave the pile there and drive away. No one would catch him.

Do it. Burn him.

The voice was right. Luke should burn him. Instead

of arguing with him after he asked him to turn down his music, Mutton Chops had gone after someone vulnerable, someone precious. He had tried to hurt an innocent child. Given the chance, Luke suspected, he would hurt other vulnerable people, too. Mutton Chops was a bully. One day, Kendra would learn how to protect herself from bullies, but for now, he was her shield. Luke lived with a bully. He knew how to handle them.

People like Mutton Chops—people like his wife— were weeds amongst humanity. You couldn't just chop a weed down and move on. To get rid of a weed, you had to pull it out by the roots and destroy it so that nothing remained.

He reached into his pocket for his box of matches. The reptilian voice giggled.

Do it. Burn him alive.

"I will," said Luke, his voice low as he struck a match on the side of the box. The odor of burning sulfur filled the air. Then, he knelt and tossed the match onto the grass. The gasoline blazed into life and sped toward the home. Within seconds, flames engulfed the wood and traveled up the side of the home, melting the vinyl siding and sending a plume of black smoke into the sky.

"Burn, motherfucker, burn," said Luke. For a moment, the flames transfixed his gaze. Then, all at once, the strength seemed to leave him, and he realized what he had done. His heart pounded as he picked up the empty gas can. He ran through the woods, this time not caring about crouching and remaining hidden. His SUV was about a half mile away, so he made it in about four minutes. By then, Kendra was awake and wailing. His heart ached whenever he heard her cry, but he couldn't do anything about it yet.

As he drove away, he looked in the rearview mirror at his daughter's bright red face. Her screams began growing less and less frantic, but she was still upset. He wanted to reach back and give her a pacifier, but he couldn't reach one without taking his hands off the wheel. In the meantime, he sang her a soft lullaby that she liked. Even if the fire didn't kill Mutton Chops, it would ruin his day. For now, that was good enough.

He looked in the rearview mirror at his daughter and smiled. Her eyes locked on his, and she stopped crying. She wasn't happy, but she seemed to appreciate having him there. Kendra may have been the only person in the world who loved him, and he was okay with that. He'd be her protector as long as he lived. Nobody would hurt his daughter, not Mutton Chops, not Irene, nobody.

"I'll get you a bottle as soon as we get home, sweetheart," he whispered. "Now, you just relax. Daddy will take care of you."

4

I left Alexa's office and walked about a block to a coffee shop near the St. Louis County police headquarters building on Forsyth Boulevard, where I bought a muffin and a cup of coffee. A steady stream of cops and civilians came in and out, but I paid them little mind.

Before she retired, my adoptive mother had been a captain in the St. Louis County Police Department, and she and I had gotten coffee in that shop together often. Mom and I had disagreed on things over the years, but she, my dad, and my brothers and sister were among the few steady presences in my life. I pulled out my phone to call her and tell her where I was, but then I got a text message from Ian, my half brother.

Need help. Come to the house.

I started to dial his number when my phone beeped again with another text.

Just come. Don't call. Emergency.

I texted him and asked what this was about, but he only reiterated that this was an emergency and that he needed my help ASAP. I groaned, grabbed my coffee and muffin, and texted him to let him know I was on my way.

Ian and his adoptive parents lived in St. Charles, a good-sized suburb northwest of St. Louis. Though he was my biological half sibling, Ian and I hadn't grown up together. I met him when he showed up on my doorstep and announced he was my brother. I would have told him

31

to leave, but one look at that fifteen-year-old, and I knew he wasn't lying. He had our mom's eyes.

We'd had disagreements and fights since then, but we were family. I cared about him and wanted what was best for him. Unfortunately, his adoptive parents had decided that his life was better without me in it. They were good parents, and they loved their son. They thought I was a danger to him, and they weren't wrong. Because of me, a crazy woman had gone to his school with a gun and murdered his vice principal. She hadn't found Ian, but if she had, he'd be dead now.

Something must have been wrong at the Staley household for this text message. Ian's parents were in their early seventies, and his father had cancer. I hoped he hadn't died.

With traffic, it took about half an hour to reach Ian's home in St. Charles. He lived in a new neighborhood, but the homes had historic designs so they blended into St. Charles's historic architecture. I parked on the street in front of his cheery two-story home and hurried up the walkway to the front door. It swung open before I could knock, and Miriam Staley, Ian's mom, cocked her head at me as she stepped out. She shut the door behind her and crossed her arms.

"Joe," she said. "I didn't realize you were coming."

"Ian texted me and said there was an emergency. Everything okay?"

She considered me and then shook her head. Her torso was stiff, and her breath was controlled and even.

She wore dark jeans and a black sweater. Her wavy, white hair blew in the slight breeze. Her throat bobbed as she swallowed, and her eyes never stopped moving. I was standing not ten feet in front of her, and she couldn't stop looking up and down the street.

"We're fine," she said. She adjusted her feet so they were shoulder-width apart. "I don't know why he'd say we had an emergency."

I shook my head. Miriam wasn't admitting it, but something had spooked her.

"I'd like to see Ian. I'd also like to see your husband."

She barked a laugh and shook her head.

"I'm afraid that's not possible. Thank you for coming out here, but if my son sent you a text message, I will deal with him. We have no emergency. You can go home."

I pulled back my blazer so she could see my badge.

"I'm not here as Ian's sister," I said, forcing a smile to my lips. "I'm here as a police officer responding to a potential emergency. Please get Ian and your husband out here, or I'll call the local police department and have them search your home. I don't want to be antagonistic, but you're scared about something. Ian wouldn't have texted me without reason. What's going on? If you can't tell me aloud, blink three times so I know there's a threat."

She shut her eyes and looked away.

"This is ridiculous," she said. "We are perfectly—"

Her front door opened before she could finish. Ian stepped out. He was still years away from being able to grow a beard, but that didn't stop him from trying. The collar of his baby blue polo shirt was open, and his brown leather shoes looked polished. He looked less like a boy and more like a young man every time I saw him. Our mom would have been proud of him.

He stepped past his mother and waved me forward.

"Come on in," he said. I didn't move. Mrs. Staley looked down.

"Joe says you texted her and said we have an emergency," she said.

He looked over his shoulder at his mom.

"We do. Now go back inside."

It wasn't my place to step into a family fight, but my mouth dropped open, and I raised my eyebrows, anyway.

"Dude, Miriam is your mom," I said. "Don't talk to her like that."

"Stay out of this, Joe," he said. "It's not your business."

I put my hands on my hips.

"You texted me, Ian," I said. "You made it my business. What's going on? And where's your dad?"

"Inside," said Ian. "He's trying to talk to his bank or something. I don't know."

I paused, hoping he'd continue and explain the situation better, but he kept his mouth shut.

"Why aren't you in school?"

Ian rolled his eyes.

"Because it's a waste of time," he said. "And my teachers are morons."

"Ian, that's not nice," said Miriam, lowering her voice. "We've talked about this before. They're trying their best."

"Their best sucks because they're idiots," he said, crossing his arms. I looked to Miriam, and she sighed.

"The school won't let him use college course credit to fulfill all his high school graduation requirements. He has to take gym and two laboratory science courses."

Ian rolled his eyes.

"I'm taking physics, and the teacher doesn't even have a physics degree. It's a waste of my time. I've already taken advanced classical mechanics at St. Louis University. When I tried to explain that to the teacher, he sent me to the principal's office for being insubordinate."

Knowing my brother, the teacher had been right to send him to the office. I cocked my head to the side.

"I'm sorry school isn't what you want it to be," I said. "We can talk about that later. For now, what emergency did you contact me about?"

Ian opened his mouth to say something, but Miriam sighed and covered her face before he could.

"God damn it," she said. I hadn't heard Miriam curse before, so my eyes popped open. I followed her gaze and looked over my shoulder to see a silver Mercedes stop in front of the house. The driver stepped out. He was about forty and wore a black suit, a white and gray striped shirt, and a red tie. His expression was smug and self-satisfied, and as he walked in front of the Mercedes, I saw a pistol in a vertical shoulder holster on the left side of his chest.

I twisted my torso so my left hip faced him and my right hip—the one with my pistol—was as far from him as possible. His eyes traveled up and down me before focusing on Ian.

"How you doing, sport?" he asked, smiling.

"Fuck off," said Ian. The guy smiled and laughed, then looked to Miriam.

"Where's your husband?"

At that moment, the front door opened, and Ian's father—Martin—stepped out. He was in his early to mid-seventies and had a weathered face, gray and white hair, and sunken cheeks. His sweater hung off him like a raincoat, and his slacks hung low on his thin hips. He put a hand on Miriam's shoulder before walking in front of his son. The mid-morning sunlight made his skin look grayish.

"Let's go inside," said Miriam, pulling Ian back. She looked at me. "You can come, too. We'll have coffee and talk."

"You two go inside," I said, shaking my head but not taking my eyes from the man in front of me. "I'll stay out here with Martin."

"If she's staying, I am, too," said Ian. The newcomer smiled.

"Sure. We can make this a family affair," he said. "Assuming blondie is family."

"She is," said Ian. "Now fuck off."

"Believe me, kid," he said, "I don't want to be here, either. I'll leave as soon as your dad gives me my money."

"What money?" I asked.

He smiled at me but then looked to Martin.

"You got my money, old man?"

Martin's shoulders trembled. I brought my hand down to my pistol.

"I've got ten thousand. That's all I've got, though. I can't get more than that. I'm retired."

The newcomer put his hands on his hips and pulled his jacket back, exposing the firearm against his chest.

"Do better."

That was all I needed to hear. I pulled my firearm from its holster and pointed it at his chest.

"Put your hands on your head and lower yourself to your knees," I said. "I'm placing you under arrest for harassment. By showing us your firearm, you've communicated a threat to assault us. Since Ian is seventeen, and you're over twenty-one, you've just committed a felony. Congratulations."

He looked me up and down.

"This pussy's got claws," he said. "Let me see your badge."

"Put your hands on your head," I said. I glanced to Miriam. "Call the police. Tell them there's an armed officer on site already and that I have a suspect in custody."

Miriam closed her eyes but didn't move.

"Miriam, do as I ask," I said, trying to keep my voice calm. "This is an armed man, and he has threatened your family in my presence."

The man with the gun narrowed his eyes at me and then focused on Martin.

"This is for real?" he asked, lowering his chin. "You called the cops on me?"

"She's my son's friend," said Martin, his voice weak. "I didn't call her. He did. She won't bother you. Just get in your car and go. I'll get your money."

The thug smiled at Ian and gave him the thumbs up.

"Good for you, kid. I would have thought she's out of your league."

"She's my sister."

"That makes sense now," he said, smiling before looking at me. "Put the gun away, honey. We'll all talk."

I shook my head.

"Put your hands on your head and then get on your knees. You're under arrest."

He considered and then shook his head before looking to Martin.

"I'll be back later," he said. "I advise you to be alone next time."

He got in his car and left. Without additional help, there was little I could do to stop him, so I holstered my firearm, took out my phone, and snapped pictures of his car and license plate. As he drove away, he waved. I clenched my jaw tight and felt heat come over me as I looked to Miriam, Ian, and Martin.

"Okay, folks," I said. "Talk. What the hell just happened, who is that guy, and why do you owe him money?"

Martin looked down. His shoulders sagged. I almost thought he'd fall. Miriam locked her eyes on mine and shook her head.

"This is a family matter, Detective," she said. "I regret that my son brought you into it. We'll handle it on our own. You can go now."

"That right, Ian?" I asked. He began to say something, but his mother clamped a hand over his mouth, stopping him.

"Ian is a minor in my custody," she said. "You may not talk to him."

"He's my brother, Miriam," I said, lowering my chin.

"And he's our son," she said. Her posture was rigid, and she looked as if she were on the edge of tears. I suspected that if I stayed, she'd break down. I didn't know whether that would help me learn what I needed to know.

"Do you feel safe here, Ian?" I asked, looking to him. He furrowed his brow and stepped back but said nothing. "A man with a gun just tried to extort money from your father on your front steps. Next time, he may not be content to visit and leave empty-handed. He may hurt somebody. How's that make you feel?"

Miriam closed her eyes.

"Please leave, Detective. We can handle this."

"I don't think you can," I said. "I don't know what's going on, but it's clear you're involved in something over your head."

Nobody spoke for almost thirty seconds. Then

Martin cleared his throat.

"My wife asked you to leave. If you don't get back in your car, I'll call the police."

I clenched my jaw but then forced myself to smile as I looked to my brother.

"Ian?" I asked. "What do you want me to do?"

He looked down but said nothing. This was an impossible situation for him, so I stepped back before he said anything.

"I'll leave," I said. "Ian, if you see that guy again, call 911. You can call me, too, but call them first. Tell them you're seventeen, and there's a man with a gun threatening your family. I'll be too far away to protect you."

I looked to Miriam and then Martin.

"And once you two come to your senses, call the police, too."

They turned and led their son into the house without saying a word. I sighed and walked back to my Volvo. If I had driven one of our cruisers, I would have had a laptop with access to our department's databases on which I could search for the Mercedes. That'd just have to wait, though. Hopefully Miriam and Martin would take my advice to heart and call the locals to tell them what was going on. If they didn't, somebody would get hurt.

5

I drove back to St. Augustine, expecting to go to my office and look up the Mercedes's license plate, but before I even reached the outskirts of town, my cell rang. I didn't like talking and driving, but the call came from my dispatcher, so I answered on the second ring and put it on speaker.

"Yeah," I said. "This is Joe Court. That you, Trisha?"

"Yeah. We've got a suspicious house fire in the county."

She gave me the address. The home wasn't on a major road, but I knew the area all the same.

"Okay. I know the street, and I'll be there in about half an hour."

"I'll tell the fire department to expect you."

I thanked her and then hung up. Nothing she said should have bothered me, but her tone was sharp. I had met Trisha on my first day of work in St. Augustine many years ago, and I thought we had been friends ever since. Since George Delgado had died, though, things had changed. She and George had never been close, but they had been colleagues for almost twenty-five years, and she thought I had killed him. It hurt knowing she thought I'd do that, but I couldn't change the situation.

I tossed my phone to the seat beside me and drove. The homeowner lived in a ranch-style home with brick and vinyl siding two or three miles west of downtown St.

Augustine. Nestled between two rolling hills and bordered by fields and deep thickets of woods, it was a pretty site. I parked along the grass out front behind a red and white SUV from the fire department. Officer Dave Skelton sat on the hood of a marked cruiser in the driveway. He stood when he saw me walking toward him.

"Morning, Dave," I said. "What have we got?"

"Hey, Joe," he said, reaching to his utility belt and pulling out a notepad. "Paul Cluney with the fire department's around the side of the house. His team put out the fire, but he stuck around to talk to us."

"Anybody injured?"

"Nah," said Dave. "House didn't burn, but Mr. Cluney says it looks like arson, so he brought us in."

I had worked with Cluney before, but I didn't know him well. He seemed competent, though.

"Stick around for now, but I'll send you on your way soon."

Dave sat on his cruiser again and wished me luck. I thanked him and walked toward the side of the house. Cluney was in his early to mid-fifties, and he wore black slacks and a white shirt with a fire and rescue badge on the breast. His bald head reflected the morning light like a mirror, and the radio on his shoulder spit static at periodic intervals.

"Morning, Mr. Cluney," I said, holding out my hand. "I'm Detective Joe Court with the St. Augustine County Police Department. How are you doing today?"

"Got a belly full of bacon and thermos full of coffee

in my car," he said. "I can't complain."

I smiled and looked toward the home. Someone had stacked firewood at the base of the home and lit it ablaze. The fire, then, had climbed up the side of the house, melting the vinyl but not catching the home's internals on fire. It'd take a contractor a weekend to fix the damage, but the home looked livable.

"So what have we got?"

"Attempted arson," he said, putting on some blue gloves and kneeling next to the home to sift through the debris on the ground. I knelt beside him and caught a whiff of gasoline. "It looks like our arsonist stacked firewood against the house like a teepee, then poured gasoline over top of it. He might have put some firewood on the ground, too, but I don't know. He then poured gas on the grass around the wood to create a trail. Then he lit it up.

"Fortunately, gasoline burns so quickly it didn't have time to heat the home's construction timbers to their ignition point. We hosed it down, but it mostly fizzled out on its own."

I stepped back and snapped pictures with my cell phone.

"And you think the accelerant was gasoline?"

"Yep," he said. "We'll run some tests, but you can still smell it."

"Did you find a gas can?"

"Yep," he repeated. "In the garage. It was empty, but it still had fumes inside. Your officer has it near his car."

"We'll dust it for prints and see what we can find," I said. "Is the homeowner inside?"

"Last I checked," said Cluney. "His name is Jason Kaufman, and he's cantankerous. Maybe he'll be nicer to you than he was to me, though."

I looked toward the house.

"Okay. I'll talk to him and forward my findings to your office."

"And I'll do the same, Detective," he said. "Good luck."

I thanked him and walked toward the front of the home. The roof overhung the patio in front, providing shade on sunny afternoons and protection from the rain on rainy days. Today, it just made the area gloomy. I knocked on the door and waved over Dave Skelton. He joined me on the porch just as Mr. Kaufman opened the door. He was in his late twenties to early thirties and had an earring and enormous sideburns. If I had to guess, I'd say he spent a lot of time in a tanning booth. The moment he saw me, his eyes flicked down to my chest.

"Hey," I said. "Thanks for coming out. My eyes are just below my forehead, by the way."

His gaze snapped up, and he smiled.

"Sorry," he said. "Just enjoying the view."

Skelton snickered but then stopped when I gave him a look. He straightened and mouthed that he was sorry.

"I'm Detective Mary Joe Court. With me is Officer Dave Skelton. Can I get your name and phone number?"

He laughed.

"I like a woman who isn't afraid to ask for my digits."

"Terrific," I said. "What's your phone number and full name?"

He said he was Jason Kaufman. Instead of telling me his phone number, he handed me a business card that said he was president of Kaufman International. It had two phone numbers and an email address on it.

"Ask me what I do for a living," he said, once I slipped his business card into my pocket.

"No, thanks," I said. "Tell me about the fire. When'd you notice it, what were you doing, and why do you have an empty gas tank in your garage?"

"I'll take your last question first. The gas tank is for my lawn mower. For your first question, I noticed the fire about forty-five minutes ago when my smoke alarm went off. I was doing some research in my office."

I jotted down a few notes in my notepad before looking toward the lawn.

"When'd you last mow the grass?"

He shrugged.

"I don't know. Two months ago. It's dormant now."

I considered him.

"Paul Cluney—the fireman who was out here earlier —said the tank was empty but still had gasoline fumes in it. If you mowed your lawn months ago and emptied the tank, why would it still have gasoline fumes in it?"

He smirked.

"I didn't empty the tank when I mowed the lawn months ago. I emptied it this morning when my car ran out of gas."

"How much gas did the tank have?"

He shrugged.

"Three or four gallons. Why?"

"Just curious," I said. "So what else did you do this morning?"

"If you want to know whether I've got a girlfriend, you can just ask."

I didn't bother looking up from my notepad.

"I don't care about your relationship status unless you believe your significant other would try to burn your house down. Is that possible?"

He shrugged and drew in a breath as he lifted his arms and put his hands behind his head.

"I have been known to drive the ladies crazy."

"Sure," I said, my lips flat. "Did you leave any pissed off enough to burn your house down lately?"

He lowered his arms.

"Not lately."

"Can you think of anyone else who might want to burn your house down?"

He frowned and shook his head.

"No. To know me is to love me."

"I'm sure that's true," I said, drawing in a breath before looking at him and squinting. "Do you have homeowner's insurance, Mr. Kaufman?"

He smiled and winked.

"Do you sell insurance on the side, Detective Court?"

"No," I said. "I'm wondering whether you had an incentive to burn your own house down."

The smile left his face.

"I'm insured, but no. I didn't try to burn my house down."

"Somebody did," I said. "If everybody loves you, why did somebody douse the side of your home with gasoline and light it on fire?"

"You got me," he said, shrugging. Then he paused and held up a finger. "There was one guy this morning. I went to the gas station to get some smokes and fill up the car, and some dude with a baby started yelling at me before I could get my gas."

"Why would a man with a baby yell at you?" asked Skelton, his voice incredulous. Kaufman said nothing.

"Answer the question," I said. "Why did someone yell at you?"

"I don't know," he said. "You'd have to ask him. Okay? Meanwhile, I've got business to attend to."

"What gas station did you go to?" I asked.

"The BP station in town," he said.

I thanked him, and he walked inside. Skelton gave me a sheepish look as we walked toward our cars.

"I didn't mean to intrude on your interview," he said. "It seemed like a good question."

"It was," I said. "Why don't you get back to your regular duties? I'll drive to the gas station and see about the fight."

He wished me luck and left at the same time I did. I

drove to the gas station and spoke to the manager who showed me that morning's surveillance footage. Sure enough, Mr. Kaufman got into a brief altercation with a guy filling up his gas tank. I couldn't hear anything, but it looked as if Kaufman was the instigating party. The altercation lasted just a few seconds. Then Kaufman knocked on the man's window and left. I doubted there was anything there, but I wrote down the man's license plate, anyway. I'd talk to him tomorrow.

After the gas station, I went to my station, wrote a report, and then headed home for a late lunch. Roy barked from the backyard the moment I opened my Volvo's door, but I ignored him and walked to the front door. Someone had taped an orange paper to the side of my house. The paper had the county seal on top and the words *LEGAL NOTICE* printed beneath it.

Pursuant to violations of statutes of the state of Missouri and the county of St. Augustine, the structures specified below have been condemned…

I stopped reading when I saw that it had been signed by Darren Rogers and that it ordered me to vacate the premises within forty-eight hours. My heart pounded, and waves of rage washed over me.

"What the hell is this?"

6

Any thought I had of seeing my dog and grabbing a sandwich left my mind. I ripped the notice from my door and drove back to town, fuming. Darren Rogers owned a dozen or more businesses around town, but he worked out of an enormous office in the county government center near St. John's Hospital. It was a three-story building with a limestone facade on the first floor and brick on the second and third. The windows had a bluish tint. I parked in a visitor's spot out front and slammed my door shut before crossing the lot and walking into the building.

The first floor had a day care for the children of county workers and offices for social workers and for the parks department. The second floor held offices for the various accountants who worked for the county, and the third floor held offices for elected officials. It was a modern, clean building that the county had erected twelve years ago for eight million dollars. As far as I could tell, it was money well spent.

I took the elevator to the third floor and walked to the end of the hall to the county executive's suite of offices. Rogers shared a receptionist with the office of general counsel and the public administration office. The receptionist smiled from behind her big wooden desk when she saw me.

"Can I help you?"

"Is Darren Rogers in?" I asked.

She cocked her head to the side and raised her eyebrows.

"Do you have an appointment?"

"No," I said, walking past the desk and to the hallway behind her. She stood.

"You can't go back there without an appointment, Miss," she said. "This is an office."

"He was just at my house," I said. "I'm expected."

She picked up her phone and dialed somebody, but she didn't stop me. Hopefully she wasn't calling the sheriff. This was a private matter. He didn't need to become involved. I passed four offices before coming to a T-shaped intersection. The left-hand hallway had a window that overlooked the parking lot. The hallway on the right overlooked the Mississippi River. Darren Rogers would have wanted the best office, so I hung a right.

Before I could reach his door, Darren Rogers stepped into the hallway, smiling.

"My door is always open for the county's finest, but you owe Monique an apology."

"I'll give it on my way out," I said. "Let's talk about the condemnation notice you tacked up on my door."

Darren smiled, stepped back, and swept his arm inside his office.

"I thought you'd be by," he said. "Come on in. We'll talk."

I stepped past him and into the room. Rogers had a big office with windows on two sides, four dark-stained bookcases, and a massive wooden desk. A round turkish rug covered the gray berber carpet in the center of the room. Two couches faced one another with a coffee table between them on the rug, forming a cozy seating area. Rogers gestured toward the couches.

"Have a seat," he said. "I'll call Monique and ask her to bring in some coffee. It'll be a good opportunity for you to apologize for pushing past her."

"No coffee," I said. "I got your condemnation order. If you want my house, I'll fight you in court."

He gave me a tight-lipped smile.

"You should have a seat, hon."

I crossed my arms and continued standing.

"Don't talk like that. I'm here to give notice that I intend to fight your order. It's bullshit."

Rogers ran a hand along the side of his head. If he'd had hair, he would have smoothed it back.

"That's a problem, Ms. Court. You're too late to fight back. You own a beautiful piece of property, but your lengthy absence and lack of proper management allowed it to become blighted. It became a detriment to the health, safety, and morals of the people of St. Augustine, so the county began condemnation proceedings. We sent a whole boatload of letters."

My position felt weaker than it had a moment earlier. A tremble passed through my back and into my legs as I uncrossed my arms and sat down.

"I didn't get any letters."

"You just stay seated," said Rogers, standing and

walking toward his desk. The tremble that had taken over my legs passed into my arms and hands. "Let me call up the file."

Rogers sat behind his desk, typed, and looked at me before typing again.

"Just so you know, the government doesn't take private property lightly. I've always believed that the power to take something from someone is akin to the power to destroy that person. It's one of the most vulgar uses of government power, and we don't use it unless we have no choice. There are procedures written in law."

He paused and seemed to read.

"In accordance with Missouri statute, we are required to send a notice via certified mail to a property owner at least sixty days before a condemnation hearing. We sent a letter about your property to the owner of record—that's you—on July 7. That letter included a listing of your rights and a description of the property."

I shook my head and closed my eyes.

"No one was living in the house on July 7, so no one would have signed for the certified letter."

Rogers looked at his computer and clicked several times.

"My files show the very first letter was sent one hundred and twenty-eight days ago and was signed for by Mr. Johnny Knockers. The second notice was sent ninety-three days ago and was signed for by Ms. Cherries Jubilee. We also posted a notice in the paper once per week for six weeks."

Heat began flooding my face, and I balled my hands into fists.

"What the hell is going on? No one should have been in my house, let alone Johnny Knockers and Cherries Jubilee. I wasn't there."

Rogers gave me a pitying look, then sighed and tilted his head to the side.

"I'm sorry, Detective, but people were there. The tenants you rented your home to while you were away allowed the yard and landscaping to become overgrown. And that was okay. You live out in the country. If the weeds grow up to your knees, that just means you're doing something right with the soil."

I closed my eyes and held my hands in front of me.

"The realtor was supposed to hire somebody to mow the lawn."

"I can't speak to that," said Rogers. "The tenants you rented to were problematic. They grew at least fifteen marijuana plants in your backyard and staged a small music festival during which illegal drugs were consumed in the woods behind your home. The county tried to contact you, but you hid your tracks pretty well. We hated to begin proceedings against a long-term resident, but your property became a den of iniquity."

I'd hidden my tracks because I hadn't wanted anyone to find me. I hadn't even told my mom where I'd gone. At the time, I'd thought I needed that space, that I wasn't strong enough to stay and fight. Maybe that was true. Life —and Darren Rogers—had shown me I couldn't run from my problems, though.

"The house should have been empty. I didn't lease it to anyone."

"Johnny Knockers and Cherries Jubilee say otherwise," said Rogers.

"No," I said, shaking my head. "Even you aren't obtuse enough to believe Johnny Knockers and Cherries Jubilee are actual names. They sound like strippers."

Rogers closed his eyes and tilted his head to the side.

"Hon, as the county executive, I follow the law, and the law is clear. Your home became a detriment to the health and well-being of St. Augustine County and was, therefore, blighted. The county's attempts to rectify the situation went unanswered. Our hands were tied. We didn't know whether you were coming back, so we began condemnation proceedings. You're free to go to the condemnation hearing—and even bring a lawyer—but it's a done deal. We did our job, and we followed the rules."

I clenched my jaw tight.

"This is my house. You understand that, right? You're talking about taking my house from me."

"Believe me," he said, "this isn't what we wanted."

Muscles all over my body felt tight, and I couldn't sit anymore, so I stood and started pacing behind the sofa.

"Why do you want my property?"

Rogers smiled.

"The county's had a project in the planning stages for years. I needn't tell you how beautiful our county is. You've lived here long enough to see it for yourself. Our parks, shops, and special events draw in hundreds of thousands of visitors every year. Some are what we term luxury vacationers. They can drop five hundred dollars a night on a hotel room without a second thought. Others, though, are less affluent. They're looking for cheaper accommodation. We've got public campgrounds, but we don't have a public RV park. Thanks to your property, though, we will."

My fingers balled into fists as my stomach tightened. I felt sick.

"You're going to tear down my house and turn it into a parking lot for RVs."

He tilted his head to the side and considered me.

"There will be some asphalt, but we'll keep the woods intact where possible. Your home will become the welcome center. It'll have restrooms and showers and offices. Maybe we can even give you a plaque there to commemorate your sacrifice. We can put your name over the toilets. Whenever a guest takes a dump, they'll think of you."

I clenched my jaw and drew in a long breath through my nose before speaking.

"You're a piece of garbage, and you're going to die in prison."

His smile broadened as he shook his head.

"I understand that you're upset, but calling me names won't help your situation. Remember, my side played by the rules here. We tried contacting you about a project in the county for your property, but you didn't answer that letter. We determined that your property was the best in the county for our project because of its location, its accessibility, and the blighted nature of the development.

"After extensive consideration, we hired a state-licensed appraiser to determine the value of the property. Then we passed a county ordinance authorizing the eminent domain taking of the property for our project. We then sent you multiple notices and ran an advertisement in the newspaper. Thirty days ago, we sent a written offer for your property. That written offer included a determination of the property's value.

"After we exhausted all other avenues, we sued. We couldn't serve you the papers personally because we didn't know where you were. You didn't tell your friends in the police station where you moved. At every opportunity, we acted in good faith."

I crossed my arms.

"That's bullshit, and we both know it."

Rogers locked eyes on mine.

"You're free to argue that in your hearing. You've got forty-eight hours to vacate your home. If you stay beyond that, you'll be trespassing," he said before standing and walking toward his desk. Once he stood behind it, he looked at me and then flicked his eyes to the door. "Now, if you can see yourself out, I believe I've given you more than enough of my time."

I swallowed hard.

"I'll fight this."

"If you do, you'll lose," he said. "It's like I told you

when we last met. You own a house in St. Augustine, but you're not one of us. Like lukewarm water, we will spit you out. You're not welcome in my county or my office. Get out."

"See you at the hearing," I said.

"Looking forward to it," he said, smiling. I wanted to knock that smug look off his face, but nothing I did would help my situation now. Once more, I needed a lawyer, but this time, I doubted he or she could do much to help.

7

I was so pissed off as I left Rogers's office that I couldn't think straight. Instead of going to my car, I walked around the city government building and felt the cold early winter air sap the heat of my anger. Green space surrounded the building. It was too small to be a proper park, but it had a few picnic tables, a dozen pin oak trees, and a concrete path that meandered past a little pond.

After ten minutes of walking, I lost my desire to punch anything that moved. Unfortunately, that allowed the situation to sink in. My shoulders fell, and my stomach contorted. If Rogers was right, I would lose my home.

As I walked to my car, I took deep breaths to force my nausea down. Rogers may have followed the letter of the law, but this shouldn't have happened. He'd had help. I put my car in gear and drove to my realtor's office in downtown St. Augustine. He worked out of the first floor of a historic, three-story brick building. He shared one interior wall with a candy shop and another with an insurance agent.

I parked out front and walked inside. The young woman behind the desk smiled when she saw me. Then her eyes narrowed with recognition. The smile left her face.

"Miss Court," she said. "It's been a while since we've seen you."

"It has been," I said. "Where's the boss? I need to talk to him."

She pushed back from her desk.

"Not here," she said. "He's showing a house to a couple from Kansas City. Afterwards, he'll take them out to lunch. Randall likes to do that with clients who live out of town. I'll tell him you came by, though."

I allowed my smile to slip away.

"What house?"

The receptionist tilted her head to the side.

"Is there something I can help you with?" she asked.

"Not unless you know Cherries Jubilee and Johnny Knockers."

She furrowed her brow.

"I don't follow."

"Somebody rented my house to them while I was away, and they grew marijuana in the backyard. I'd like to talk to your boss about that."

She considered me and then reached to her desk and flipped through her calendar.

"I can put you on the schedule tomorrow morning at eight," she said. "That's his next free appointment."

"Don't worry about it. I'll track him down," I said. "If he's showing a house to clients from Kansas City and plans to take them out to lunch, they must have a decent-sized budget. He won't be showing them starter homes. He's not showing them any homes that need big renovations, either, or he'd be out there with a contractor. That eliminates all but five or six houses in the county. I'll send a uniformed officer to each of them and have him picked up."

She drew in a sharp breath and opened her eyes wide.

"Don't do that," she said. "He'd lose the sale. We need it."

"Where is he?" I asked. "I'm not in the mood to argue."

She looked at her computer and typed before looking to me again. She gave me an address in a wealthy part of town, and I headed out once more. About fifteen minutes after leaving the realtor's office, I found his SUV in front of a two-story brick home. A pair of Japanese maples anchored the front door, while boxwoods shaped into spheres hid the home's foundation. It had lines reminiscent of a classic French Tudor home, but everything was too clean. The home had style but little soul. I liked old things. Maybe I was just a snob, though.

I parked and waited beside my Volvo for about ten minutes before Randall and two men a few years older than me emerged from the home. Those two might have been roommates, but I doubted it. They stood close together and shared one another's space. Both of them smiled and seemed to have liked the house, but they weren't my concern. I focused on Randall. He excused himself from the couple and walked to me with his hand extended in front of him as if he wanted to shake. I ignored it.

"Who the fuck are Cherries Jubilee and Johnny

Knockers?"

His smile faltered.

"Excuse me?"

"You leased my house to them when I was out of town," I said. "Who were they? They grew marijuana in my backyard and hosted a music festival in my woods."

He looked back over his shoulder to the couple. They stood in front of the home and smiled and waved. Randall smiled.

"Can we talk about this in my office?" he asked. "I need to talk to my clients. They're interested in putting in an offer for the house."

I scowled and looked past him.

"Randall's busy for the next few minutes," I said. "Check out the backyard again. Sit down and imagine throwing a barbecue with friends."

They seemed confused, but they walked to the backyard. I looked at Randall again and crossed my arms.

"Johnny Knockers and Cherries Jubilee," I said. "They sound like strippers."

He smiled and chuckled.

"They do."

I almost hit him. He must have recognized that because he shut up.

"Who were they, and where did you get off renting my house to them?"

He shook his head and stepped back and held up a finger.

"First, I never leased your house to anyone, and I

never violated our agreement."

I clenched my jaw before speaking.

"What did you do?"

He closed his eyes.

"Our contract allowed me to show prospective buyers the property. Furthermore, I was allowed to let in persons unnamed for promotional or sales purposes. Ms. Jubilee and Mr. Knockers were prospective buyers."

I almost laughed.

"Bullshit."

"It's true," he said. "Yours was a unique property, and it required me to use unique sales methods. The grounds were gorgeous, but the house was unfinished. Furthermore, the county building inspector had already been through the house and had a laundry list of needed improvements. It was a teardown."

"Fine," I said, throwing up my hands. "My house was a dump. Sure. Let's say that. You were supposed to sell it. Instead, you let two jackasses squat in it and grow drugs in the backyard."

"To be fair," he said, raising his eyebrows, "I thought they were performance artists. I didn't know they intended to use the property to grow marijuana or throw a music festival."

Again, I nearly hit him and restrained myself only by putting my hands in my pockets.

"How long did they stay?"

"A couple of months off and on," he said.

I closed my eyes and drew in deep breaths, trying to

calm myself down.

"You son of a bitch," I said, through clenched teeth. I took a couple more breaths and then planted my feet shoulder-width apart. "Because of those two, I'm losing my house. The county began condemnation proceedings against the property. They claim I allowed it to become blighted."

He tilted his head to the side.

"If your tenants grew drugs in the backyard and used the home to host a music festival at which people consumed drugs, you kind of did."

I lowered my chin and opened my eyes wide.

"Are you making a joke?"

"Apparently it's not funny."

"No, it's not," I said.

He sighed and looked toward the home. His clients must have been taking me up on my suggestion because they were still in the backyard.

"If it's the house you're worried about, I'd be happy to sell you a new one."

"Fuck you."

He straightened.

"Look, Joe, I know you want to blame me for this, but it's not my fault. This is on you. You had every opportunity to fix up your house. And I had nothing to do with the letters. You should have updated your address with the county assessor's office."

I held my breath. The fine hairs on the back of my neck stood on end.

"I didn't mention anything about letters," I said, my voice low.

He took a step back and then crossed his arms as he closed his eyes.

"Well, I..." he said before pausing. "You said the county began condemnation proceedings. There's a process for that, and it starts with sending a certified letter to the owner of the property. I can only speak in generalities."

I stepped forward. He stepped back.

"When did you allow these two squatters into my house?"

"They were there periodically," he said. "They never stayed more than a weekend."

"Just long enough to sign for the certified letters when the postman came by," I said.

He forced a smile to his lips and stepped back again.

"Bad luck, huh?"

"Yeah, it was," I said, my voice low. "When I spoke to Darren Rogers, he said a certified appraiser had already assigned a value to the house. You know anything about that?"

Randall shook his head.

"You can't blame a man for making a living," he said. "Our contract was void the moment you moved back into your home."

I forced myself to smile so I wouldn't curse at him.

"What'd you tell Rogers it was worth?"

"Twenty-five grand."

It felt as if he had just pushed me down an elevator shaft. I closed my eyes and shook my head.

"We had the property listed for a hundred and fifty."

"And after seeing how little interest there was at that price, I had to adjust my estimate," he said. "Property valuation is a tricky business."

I drew in two breaths before opening my eyes again. I looked him up and down before turning to my car.

"Are we okay, Joe?"

I guffawed and shook my head.

"No, we're not okay," I said. "How much did Darren Rogers pay you to screw me?"

He straightened.

"Mr. Rogers and his companies are valuable clients. I don't discuss my clients' private business."

I opened my door.

"Get a lawyer, jackass."

"I was just doing my job," he said.

I ignored him and drove off, feeling sick to my stomach. When I was in first or second grade, a little boy on the playground used to pick on me every day. My foster mother told me he must have had a big crush on me. I punched him in the face and told him to keep it in his pants. I had no idea what that meant, but I had heard my biological mother say it to someone.

Darren Rogers's fascination with me had nothing to do with affection, but the remedy to his interest was the same as it was to that little boy's: somebody needed to punch him in the face and teach him a lesson he wouldn't forget. Hopefully I could do that before another piece of

Chris Culver

my life imploded.

8

Aside from the attempted arson, I didn't have any major cases at the moment, but since I had taken the morning off, I still needed to put in a few hours at work. So I drove back to my station and started reading through a stack of cold-case files. After reading a file, I'd check our databases to see whether we had new information pertinent to the case, and I'd call the witnesses to see whether they had remembered something new or whether they had learned anything new about the case.

If we got lucky and found that a gun used in St. Augustine had been used in a recent murder in St. Louis, or that a suspect in a robbery here had been arrested in Chicago, I'd set the file aside to be reworked. If a case had no fresh developments, I'd reshelve it.

I spent three hours working my way through three files—one murder, one rape, and one assault. None of our databases and none of the phone calls I made gave me anything new on the rape or assault, but we had a strong suspect in the murder case, and he was currently serving a three-year sentence for trafficking after police in St. Louis found him with forty grams of heroin. We hadn't been able to find him before, so this was a big deal. Since he was sitting in prison—and would continue to do so for the foreseeable future—we didn't need to hurry. Marcus and I could rebuild the case and make sure he never set foot outside again.

I wrote Detective Marcus Washington an email to let him know what I had found and then pushed back from my desk, my stomach growling. It was a little after seven in the evening, and I hadn't eaten anything since breakfast, so I stopped by Able's Diner and picked up a meatball sandwich and a side salad before going home. Roy seemed happy to see me. Or at least he seemed happy to have someone feed him.

He wolfed his dinner down and then sat at my feet while I ate my sandwich and looked around my kitchen, wondering how many more times I'd see it. Nearly every nook and cranny in the house had a story. I had assembled and installed the kitchen cabinets myself after purchasing them in kit form online, I had refinished all the hardwood floors, and I had retiled the bathroom. The original baseboards and crown molding had been removed before I moved in, so I had replaced them with stuff I purchased on clearance at a millwork in St. Louis. I'd saved a lot of money on the materials, but none of it had been straight, and it had taken weeks to install everything so that it looked halfway decent.

My shoulders felt heavy as I set the second half of my sandwich in the fridge, my appetite having waned. I didn't want to stay in the kitchen, so Roy and I went for a walk after dinner, but it was dark and cold, and neither of us wanted to be outside. Afterwards, we watched something on Netflix and went to bed.

I slept well that night and woke up early the next morning to a gray, drizzly day. It fit my mood. After eating my breakfast—toast with peanut butter and jelly— I lingered over coffee. The kitchen sink dripped intermittently.

If Darren Rogers was right, I didn't need to worry about fixing that. I didn't need to think about whether I should install new wooden windows or fiberglass ones, either. The thought made my heart feel heavy. I had bought this house so I could think about and research those kinds of things. Maybe I was just naïve, but I used to even think about having kids and raising them in this house. Now I had lost all that, and it hurt.

I'd be late for work, but I poured myself another cup of coffee. I deserved a little time to myself.

At ten to eight, my phone beeped. Roy lifted his head. Morning roll call didn't start until eight, so my boss wouldn't know I planned to come in late yet. It shouldn't have been him. I ran my finger across the phone and groaned when I saw the message from my younger brother.

Need you. Please call.

I dialed his number and spoke as soon as he answered.

"What's going on, dude?" I asked.

"We need your help."

I thought he'd say that, but I still sighed anyway.

"The last time I was there, your father threatened to call the police on me," I said. "That's it for me. I tried to help, but I can't help people who don't want it."

Ian said nothing.

"You there?"

"They hurt him this morning," he said. "Dad."

"I'm sorry," I said, sinking into my seat. "What happened?"

"I don't know, but he's alive. He and Mom are at the urgent care center now."

I said nothing for a moment, hoping he'd continue. He didn't.

"Have they gone to the police yet?"

"No," he said. "And they won't. They're too stupid. Please come and talk to them. I don't want my dad to die."

I didn't know how much it would help, but Ian was my brother, and Martin and Miriam were his parents. They were all family...of a sort.

"Okay," I said. "I'll be there as soon as I can."

"Hurry."

"I will," I said. I told him to stay put and to call the police if anyone else showed up to the house. Then I dressed, downed my coffee, and got in my car. As much as I wanted to head to his place right away, I needed to do some research first. I got to the office during a shift change, so we had a lot of people in the building, many of whom I hadn't seen in a while. I said hello to several people but didn't let anyone stop me before reaching my office. There, I flipped through the pictures on my phone until I found the pictures of the Mercedes that had parked in front of Ian's house.

The pictures weren't great, but one had a clear shot of the license plate, which allowed me to look it up. The car was registered to Frank Ross of Des Peres, Missouri. I looked him up next to see whether he had a criminal record.

The police in southern Illinois had arrested him twice for speeding, and officers in Ladue, Missouri, had stopped him six months ago for driving under the influence but then let him go after their breathalyzer found no alcohol in his system. The guy sounded like a bad driver, but nothing made me think he was a gangster.

To be sure I had the right guy, I looked up Frank Ross's driver's license. His picture matched the guy I'd seen at Ian's house. Then I leaned back from my desk and stretched before calling the St. Louis County police's liaison officer. He patched me through to a lieutenant in the county's criminal intelligence unit.

"Hey, my name is Mary Joe Court, and I'm a detective with the St. Augustine County Sheriff's Department. You know the name Frank Ross?"

"Can't say I do, Detective," said the lieutenant, "but give me a second. Let me look him up."

I paused and listened as the lieutenant typed. When he spoke again, his voice was lighter than before.

"We've got a file on him. We've never arrested him, but his name's come up as a peripheral player in several Medicare fraud cases. He's also a person of interest in the murder of Dr. Wayland Michaels. He was a pediatrician accused of billing Medicare for procedures he never performed and for seeing patients he never saw. The doctor died before we could bring charges against him."

"And you suspect Ross was your triggerman—or was he a witness?" I asked.

"We heard a rumor he was involved," said the lieutenant. "Beyond that rumor, we couldn't find anything. He's dirty, but he's not stupid."

"Okay, thank you," I said. "His name's come up on a case I'm working. Looks like I'll be doing more work than I thought."

"If you find anything, keep us informed."

"Will do," I said. "Thank you."

I hung up a moment later and then stood, my gut tightening. Martin Staley had been an accountant, and he was being extorted by a man who committed financial crimes. I tried not to think ill of people, but I doubted the Staley family was as innocent as they professed.

Before leaving, I grabbed a cup of coffee in a paper cup from the break room. It wasn't good, but it would keep me awake. The drive to St. Charles was easy, and I reached Ian's house in an hour and a half. He met me on the front porch. Before I could ask what had happened, though, his parents came out the front door. Miriam rolled her eyes. Her husband just stared at me. A cast covered his left hand.

"Last time you were here, we asked you to leave," said Miriam. "I'll only say this once: get out, or we'll call the police."

I locked my eyes on her.

"Good. Call the police. That'll save me a phone call," I said. Then I looked at my brother. "Pack a bag. You're going with me."

Ian furrowed his brow and stepped back. Miriam narrowed her eyes at me.

"Excuse me?" she asked, putting a hand on Ian's shoulder. "This is my son. You have no right to order him around, badge or no badge."

"Normally, you'd be right," I said, "but circumstances have changed. Yesterday, I came here and witnessed Frank Ross trying to extort money from Martin. This morning, Ian contacted me and said somebody hurt his father. I don't believe Ian is safe in your custody, so I'm taking him with me. Is that clear?"

"You're not taking my son," said Miriam.

"Maybe she should," said Martin.

Miriam looked to her husband and shook her head.

"He's our son. We can handle this."

"No, you can't," I said. "Frank Ross, the guy who's extorting you, is a person of interest in an open homicide. You can pretend that everything's fine and that you've got everything under control, but we all know that's bullshit. What happened to Martin's hand?"

Neither Miriam nor Martin said anything.

"That guy with the Mercedes slammed it in a car door," said Ian. "Then he said he'd do the same to my mom tomorrow."

"It was an accident," said Miriam. "Ian doesn't know what he's talking about."

I crossed my arms and counted to five before answering so I wouldn't call her an idiot.

"I witnessed an extortion attempt yesterday. Today, Martin's been hurt, and I'm pretty sure Ian's not the confused one on this porch. If you two don't get help, somebody will die. Frank Ross might only ask for ten grand today, but next month, he'll ask for twenty. If you pay that, he'll ask for more. That's how these guys operate.

"And next time, if you don't pay, he won't slam your hand in a car door. Instead, he'll shoot you in the head. Call a lawyer, or call the police. I don't care who you talk to. Just pull your heads out of your asses and get help."

Miriam closed her eyes and held up a hand.

"You've said enough," she said. "Now it's time for you to leave."

I stepped back.

"If Ian has to call me again, I'll return with a court order to have him removed from the home."

Miriam lowered her chin.

"Excuse me?"

"You heard me, Miriam. You're endangering your son."

Her eyes became daggers.

"Get back in your car and leave."

"Remember what I said: you need help. Frank Ross is dangerous. The men and women he works with are likely even worse. This will escalate. If you don't want to get help, pack up your belongings and get out of town. It's your choice, but the road you're on is unsustainable. If you love Ian—and I know you do—do what's right for him."

"Get away from my family," said Miriam, her voice a snarl.

I balled my hands into fists before looking to Ian.

"If that guy shows up again, call the police. And consider sleeping at a friend's house until your parents wise up."

Ian started to say something, but his mom glared at him and stopped him cold. I left before Miriam could turn that glare toward me. If she and her husband had a death wish, that was their choice. I didn't know what they had gotten into, but it wasn't my responsibility to stop them from self-destructing. I just hoped they didn't take their son with them.

9

When I got back to my station, I found Officer Trisha Marshall sitting behind the front desk. She looked up and gave me a tight smile.

"Detective," she said before reaching to a button on her computer and speaking into her headset and directing a uniformed officer to a fender bender near the high school. When she finished that, she glanced up again and then turned to her computer. "The boss is looking for you."

"Do you know why?"

"I'm not his—or your—secretary."

She was right, but I didn't want to say that aloud. I swallowed, giving myself a moment before I spoke.

"Is everything okay?"

She looked up from her computer.

"I'm kind of busy," she said.

My shoulders fell just a little.

"Okay, then," I said. "Have a good one."

My old friend may have responded, but I didn't hear it. I walked toward the steps to the second floor. My throat felt tight, but I had work to do, and I needed to focus on that. I went by Marcus Washington's office, hoping to talk to him about the cold case I had emailed him about yesterday, but he wasn't in. Sheriff Kalil, however, found me in the hallway and sighed when he saw me. The sheriff was in his early fifties and had light brown skin, black hair, and brown eyes. My mom thought he was handsome, and outwardly, she was right. The more I learned about him, though, the less I liked him.

"Sheriff," I said. "Trisha said you were looking for me."

"I was. My office. Now."

He turned without saying anything else and walked down the hall. I grimaced and followed a few steps back. The sheriff had a massive office with a big picture window overlooking downtown St. Augustine. Prior to the station's recent top-to-bottom renovation, wind and rain had blown through that window so easily it might as well have been made of paper, but now, it was one of the nicest offices I had ever seen.

The sheriff sat behind his desk, and I sat in front. He crossed his arms and leaned back but said nothing. I waited a moment and then raised my eyebrows.

"Can I do something for you, boss?" I asked.

"You missed the roll call meeting this morning."

I leaned back.

"Yeah, sorry. I was in my office researching something."

"I saw," he said. "Frank Ross. He lives in St. Louis. Is he related to your arson case?"

I could have lied to him and said yes, but I chose the truth. That was a mistake.

"I received a tip about a potential extortion attempt."

"In St. Augustine?"

I paused.

"In St. Louis County."

The sheriff considered.

"Did it involve a St. Augustine resident?"

"Tangentially," I said, tilting my head to the side. "It involved me. Sort of."

The sheriff's nostrils flared as he breathed in.

"You're a detective in St. Augustine County. That means you restrict your law enforcement activities to St. Augustine County except where authorized. Is that clear?"

"Yes, sir."

"Since you were working a personal errand this morning, I'll be deducting half a day's pay from your next paycheck. Dismissed."

I stood but didn't leave. The sheriff was already annoyed at me. I figured I might as well go for broke and ask for a favor.

"I got some unfortunate personal news yesterday," I said. "The county is condemning my house so it can build a campground."

The sheriff blinked and then reached for a cup of coffee on his desk.

"Sorry to hear that."

"I'd like the afternoon off," I said. "I need to find a lawyer to represent me at the hearing."

The sheriff didn't even pause.

"Denied."

I sucked in a breath.

"It's an emergency. I don't have any pressing cases, so if I stay, I'll just be going through cold-case files."

He looked up at me.

"If you had asked me this morning, I would have said yes and wished you luck. Instead, you skipped our roll call meeting and worked a case in another county without telling me. You're lucky I'm not writing a letter of reprimand."

"You're right. I screwed up this morning, and I'm sorry. I need the afternoon off, though."

"Again, denied," said Kalil. "By the end of the day, I want to see some progress on your arson case. Now please leave. I've got some phone calls to make."

He turned to his computer before I could argue with him. I felt like an idiot, but I deserved that. When I got back to my desk, I checked my email and messages. Marcus had called about the cold case and said he'd start looking into it, so at least that was done. My arson investigation, though, didn't have a lot going on.

Yesterday, Dave Skelton had brought the gas can found at Jason Kaufman's house by the crime lab, and Kevius Reed, one of our evidence technicians, had searched it for prints. He found three sets. One set matched Officer Skelton, a second set matched Paul Cluney with the fire department, and the third set matched Jason Kaufman. So that got us nowhere. More and more, it looked like Kaufman had tried to burn his own house down. Whether I could prove that was another story.

I read through my notes and stopped when I came across the name Luke Glasman. He'd had an altercation with Mr. Kaufman at the BP station an hour before the fire. On video, Glasman had seemed angry, but he hadn't thrown a punch or become violent. There was a big step between arguing with a guy and lighting his house on fire, but my boss wanted to see progress on the case. This was the only lead I had.

I got Glasman's address from the license bureau database and headed out. He had a pretty house with a basketball hoop at the end of the driveway and an expansive front yard with tasteful landscaping. I parked on the street out front and stepped across the concrete pavers to the front door. A hand-printed sign on the door requested I knock softly to avoid waking the baby, but the moment I raised my hand to do so, the door popped open.

A man a few years older than me smiled and held a finger to his lips before stepping out and shutting the door behind him. I stepped back to give him some space.

"Luke Glasman?" I asked. He crossed his arms. Glasman's license said he weighed two hundred pounds and stood five feet ten inches tall. Most people lied about their height and weight, but he was probably honest. He was a little pudgy, but he had some muscles. I pulled my jacket back to show him my badge. "I'm Detective Mary Joe Court with the St. Augustine County Sheriff's Department. Can we talk for a few minutes?"

"Sure, I guess," he said. "Kendra's asleep."

"And Kendra's your daughter?" I asked.

"My pride and joy," he said. Then he looked down and sighed. "What can I do for you?"

I took my notepad from my purse and flipped to a blank page.

"I'm here to ask you about an altercation you had at the BP gas station yesterday morning."

For a second his shoulders seemed to tense, and his upper lip twitched.

"That was nothing," he said. "A misunderstanding."

"Can you tell me what happened?"

He straightened and cocked his head to the side.

"Can I ask you to keep your voice down?"

"Oh, sure, of course," I said, lowering my voice. "I didn't wake the baby, did I?"

He looked at the house.

"I'm more worried about my wife," he said, chuckling.

"Okay," I said, nodding but not smiling. "Sure. Tell me about this altercation at the gas station."

"It wasn't a big deal," he said. "I asked some guy in a Pontiac to turn his music down, and he refused."

The surveillance video didn't have sound, but that comported with what I had seen.

"He knocked on your window," I said.

"Yeah," said Glasman, shutting his eyes. "I think he was trying to say hi to Kendra."

"You seemed upset."

"I wasn't upset," he said, shaking his head. Before he could say anything else, the front door opened to reveal a woman in red silk pajamas. She was my age, more or less, and had brunette hair, pale skin, and bright blue eyes. She was pretty, but the mean look on her face ruined the image.

"I'm tired, and I can hear you talking in the bedroom."

"Sorry. If you want, there's a box fan in the closet," said Glasman. "Put it on, and it'll drown out a lot of noise."

"Am I the maid now?" she asked, shaking her head. "If you can't keep quiet, you put it up."

Glasman looked as if he wanted to snap at her, but then his shoulders fell and he seemed to shrink before drawing in a breath.

"Okay. I'll do it."

He walked away, and I smiled to the woman.

"Sorry if we woke you up. I'm Detective Mary Joe Court with the county police department. Are you Mrs. Glasman?"

She didn't return my smile.

"I'm Irene. Why are you here?"

"Your husband argued with a man at the BP station yesterday. I'm following up."

She lowered her chin.

"My husband had an argument that brought the police?" she asked. I nodded, and she sighed. "He didn't say anything."

I forced myself to smile.

"Has he talked to you about yesterday at all?"

She closed her eyes and gave me a pinched, annoyed look.

"I'm an attorney at a major law firm. My husband is the least of my concerns right now."

"I see," I said.

The pinched expression stayed on her face even as she gave me a tight, humorless smile.

"No, you don't see, but I don't care," she said. "People in my position don't have to care about people like you. That's why we go to college."

"I understand," I said again. She rolled her eyes and walked away but left the door open. Luke Glasman returned a moment later.

"Sorry for my wife," he said. "She's under a lot of stress."

"Stress is hard," I said. "It seems like you've got a lot going on here. After your altercation at the gas station, where'd you go?"

"Home," he said. "That guy with the mutton chops knocked on the window and woke Kendra up. I had to take care of her."

It was about what I had expected him to say. This guy didn't seem like an arsonist. Between his wife and his daughter, I doubted he had enough time.

"Thanks for talking to me," I said. "I don't imagine I'll be back. Sorry for waking up your wife."

He thanked me, and I walked back to my car. So that was a waste of time. If Mr. Glasman could put up with his spouse who ordered him around as if he were a servant, he could put up with an asshole at the gas station. Which meant I had nothing. The boss wouldn't like that.

10

I drove back to my station and typed up my interview notes for Sheriff Kalil's review. Then I spun around in my chair. My arson investigation was a loser of a case. Even if I made an arrest, it'd be for second-degree arson. That was a class-D felony, but the prosecutor would plea it down to third-degree arson, a misdemeanor. Nobody was hurt, the property damage was minimal, and, in all likelihood, the arsonist wouldn't do it again. This case was a waste of my time, which was probably why Sheriff Kalil insisted I do it.

I walked to the break room for a cup of coffee. George Delgado's favorite mug rested by the sink. Most of my colleagues used the paper cups our department supplied, but George had liked the feel of porcelain in his hand. I had seen him carrying that mug around more times than I could count, so it felt surreal to see it just sitting beside the sink, clean and ready for use.

The more you talk, the more I want to shoot myself.

The type was bold and black. George had been such an asshole. I poured my coffee into a disposable cup and walked back to my office, thinking of my old colleague. We rarely got along, but he didn't deserve to die the way he did.

The detectives from Cape Girardeau were probably good at their jobs, but their investigation was floundering even more than my arson investigation. They didn't even know where George died, only that he had floated down the Mississippi River to their area. I couldn't bring my colleague back, but at the very least, I could put his murderer in prison. With luck, I'd keep a knife out of my back at the same time.

So I stood and walked to Marcus Washington's office, expecting to leave a note on the cork board he had hung on his door. Instead, I found him sitting and talking on the phone. When he saw me, he smiled and held up a finger to let me know it'd be a minute. I waited in the hall to give him some privacy.

"Hey, Joe," he called a moment later. I walked inside. "What can I do for you?"

"You busy?" I asked, still standing near the door.

"Depends on what you need."

"I want to work George Delgado's murder."

Marcus drew in a breath before nodding toward his door. I shut it. For a moment, neither of us spoke, but then Marcus sighed.

"The sheriff told me I should contact him if you ask me about George's death."

"That sounds like something Kalil would do. Just so you know, I didn't kill George. We didn't like each other, but I wouldn't have hurt him. His retirement meant we were even."

Marcus smiled just a little.

"I know you didn't kill George."

The muscles along my spine relaxed, allowing my shoulders to fall and my chest to loosen. I pointed to a chair in front of his desk, and he nodded.

"I wish everybody saw it the same way," I said, sitting. Marcus leaned back.

"They'll come around," he said. "Now what can I do for you?"

I leaned forward.

"Like I said, I want to work George's murder. It'd be a lot easier if I had a partner."

Marcus crossed his arms.

"You're afraid Kalil will fire you or send you to prison, aren't you?"

"The thought had crossed my mind," I said, my lips turning into a tight smile.

"What do you think will happen to me if he finds out I'm working with you?"

I looked down.

"I don't know. If he catches me, I'll deny you have anything to do with my investigation."

"I appreciate that. What do you want to do?"

"You still got a key to George's house?"

Marcus paused.

"Yeah, but the detectives from Cape Girardeau already checked it out. They didn't find anything."

"They also think I'm their best suspect, and I didn't do it," I said. "Somebody may be feeding them bad information."

He considered that.

"You really don't like Sheriff Kalil, do you?"

"I'd say he's got some questions to answer, starting

with his relationship to Darren Rogers and how his election campaign raised a quarter million dollars for a guy who just moved to the county," I said. "That'd be a lot of money if he ran for state rep. It's an insane amount for the campaign of a guy running for sheriff of a rural county with fewer than fifteen thousand people."

Marcus furrowed his brow.

"He raised that much money?"

"That's what George Delgado told me," I said. "He may have been exaggerating, but Kalil's campaign still cost a lot of money, and it's fair to question where that money came from. George said he had billboards and even people knocking on doors, talking him up."

Marcus sighed and tilted his head to the side.

"He did. They were annoying. George had a couple of yard signs, but Kalil's face and people were everywhere."

"People who can funnel that kind of money to a small-town political candidate don't do it out of the goodness of their hearts. They were buying something. Makes me wonder what."

Marcus sighed again and then stood.

"All right," he said. "You haven't convinced me, but we'll walk through George's house and see what we can find."

Marcus signed out one of the station's SUVs, and we drove over. George had lived in a single-story brick home with a big yard and a pair of big black walnut trees in the front. The green and black husks of fallen walnuts littered the scraggly, dormant lawn like golf balls, and fallen leaves had begun piling against the home's foundation. Two rocking chairs and a coffee table decorated the covered front porch.

Marcus and I walked around the building to make sure it was still secure before using his key to open the front door. The home's interior smelled stale, but it looked clean. The entryway was open to the living room and kitchen. There was a dining room down a short hallway straight ahead. Green floral-print wallpaper covered the hallway and dining room, while the living room and kitchen had textured light blue wallpaper designed to look like linen cloth. It was prettier than I would have expected from a man who lived alone, making me wonder whether his ex-wife had put it up.

Marcus and I split up. He took the bedrooms and bathrooms, while I searched the kitchen and other common areas. Murderers who attacked victims at random were rare, so when I searched a typical victim's apartment, I looked for drugs, guns, or cash—things that could provide motive to kill.

I already had a good idea of why Delgado died, though: he knew too much and became a threat to someone. I also knew he didn't do drugs, that we'd find firearms, and that he had a stash of cash around, which he used to buy old furniture to restore on Facebook and Craigslist. His furniture-restoring hobby was one of the few personal facts I knew about him.

I spent twenty minutes in the kitchen and searched

through every drawer and cabinet, but I didn't go through his flour, sugar, or spice rack. He had an old stack of junk mail on a table beside the front door, but nothing looked pressing. The dining room was a complete bust.

After my search, I met Marcus in the entryway. He sighed.

"I got nothing," he said. "You?"

I shook my head.

"No blood, no signs of a struggle, no signs of forced entry…no signs that anything interesting has ever happened here. I can see why the detectives from Cape Girardeau weren't interested in it."

Marcus looked toward the house and then to me, his eyes narrow.

"What now?"

"We keep working. Do you know his ex-wife?"

"I do, and I've already spoken to her to make sure she's okay," he said. "She and George were friendly, but she doesn't know anything. Neither do his kids. They're heartbroken."

"We've got to find out who else he pissed off, then."

Marcus paused and drew in a breath.

"George was complicated," he said, finally. "At work, he was gruff and abrasive, but he wasn't corrupt. You were the only person he fought with, and he fought with you because he didn't think you spent enough time in uniform before becoming a detective."

I lowered my chin.

"I spent years in uniform."

Marcus shrugged.

"I'm not here to argue. You're a good detective, but you moved up quicker than anyone in our department's history. George thought that was too fast. That's all I'm saying. He thought you needed more time on the streets to learn the job. He thought you were naïve."

I wasn't naïve; he was just a jerk. Saying that aloud wouldn't have helped anything, though, so I wrinkled my nose.

"Sure, fine," I said. "Who else would George have talked to? Maybe Jasper Martin?"

Marcus tilted his head to the side as he thought.

"It's a good thought," he said. "He and Jasper worked together for years. He might know something."

"Can you call him?"

"I will. George thought you were naïve, but Jasper wasn't as charitable. He won't talk to you at all."

I scratched the back of my neck.

"Nice to know I was so loved."

"That's life," said Marcus. "Sometimes we don't get what we deserve."

He was right, so I nodded.

"Okay. Thanks for your help. I've got to hire a lawyer to help me save my house."

Marcus narrowed his eyes.

"What's wrong with your house?"

"It's a long story. I'll tell you some other time."

He wished me luck, and then we drove back to our station. It was nearing the end of the day, so I went to my office and checked my messages. Nobody had contacted me, so I started researching eminent domain attorneys around town. The first two I called didn't even answer their phones. The third guy at least picked up and asked me to tell him what had happened so far. I explained it as well as I could. He went silent for a moment.

"You still there?" I asked.

"I am, sorry," he said before pausing again. "This is tough. I'm not sure that I can help you. Your hearing is in fifteen hours, which isn't enough time to prepare. We can file for a continuance, but I doubt a judge will grant one this far along. The government will argue you had ample time to prepare."

"So I'm screwed," I said. The lawyer didn't respond for a few minutes.

"I'd say this is a challenging situation, and I'm not sure that you have many—if any—options. Sorry."

I swallowed a lump that threatened to grow in my throat.

"Me, too."

He wished me luck and then suggested I bring the paperwork by his office after my hearing to make sure everything was in order. I said I'd think about it before hanging up. Then I drove home, walked Roy for about a mile up and down the street, and then got drunk in my living room. It was a fitting end to a shitty day.

11

Luke Glasman had not enjoyed a pleasant evening. Kendra had been cranky and unwilling to go to sleep, so she had kept him up until at least eleven. Irene had been cranky, too, but she had kept to herself and didn't bother him. Luke hated his wife. He had known that for months, but now he felt an almost visceral reaction to her whenever she entered the room. He missed sex with her, but he might have choked her to death if given the chance, so it was for the best that they kept their distance.

Unfortunately, Kendra's crankiness continued through the night. She had woken at three in the morning, so he gave her a bottle and put her back to bed. Kendra's pediatrician said he could start weaning her off the bottles at night soon, but she had screamed whenever he tried. He finally got her down again at a quarter to four, and she had slept until six.

He thought Irene might have taken her then, but Irene said she was tired and refused to get out of bed. The reptilian voice said he should smother her with a pillow, but the rational part of him knew that was a terrible idea. Irene weighed around a hundred and twenty pounds. He could have carried her corpse, but he didn't know what to do with it. They had a chest freezer in the garage that could hold her, but what would he do with her body then? The neighbors would notice if he started digging a giant hole in his backyard. He couldn't burn her, either. She'd stink.

Until he could figure out how to dispose of her, Irene would continue drawing breath. One day he'd kill her, though, he promised himself. If she didn't give a shit about her only child or husband, she didn't deserve to live.

As Kendra played in her Pack 'n Play the next morning, Luke made coffee and buttered toast. When Irene walked in, she took the toast from his plate.

"Thanks," she said. "I was hungry."

In his mind's eye, he reached up and grabbed her by the neck and squeezed as hard as he could until she stopped chewing, but in reality, he just stood and put two fresh slices of bread in the toaster. She smiled.

"You make coffee?"

"It's still brewing."

"Get me some when it's done," she said, sitting at the breakfast table in their kitchen. The room was clean, and the air held just a hint of lemon oil. It was one of Irene's favorite smells. The odor reminded him of the cheap, imitation lemon lollipops he had eaten as a kid, but he didn't dare say that. It'd only set Irene off. It was easier to stay silent and brood than argue with her. She wasn't worth the aggravation.

Once the coffee maker beeped, he poured Irene a cup and got his toast. He sat kitty corner to her at their breakfast table. She looked out the window as she sipped.

"What'd you think about that detective yesterday?" she asked.

He shrugged and ate.

"She was fine."

"Bet it was fun to have a little excitement," she said, looking to their daughter, who cooed as she played about ten feet away. "She was pretty, too."

"She was," he said.

"Think she was prettier than me?"

He looked up and pretended to study his wife before looking to his toast.

"Yep. And it wasn't close."

Irene's face went red, and her eyes narrowed. Then she pushed back from the table and stood so she could lean over him.

"Don't get used to the attention," she whispered. "I can't imagine there will be too many attractive women in your future."

He sipped his coffee before flicking his eyes to her.

"Get ready for work," he said. "Make some money. It's one of the few things you're good at."

Again, she looked as if he had slapped her, and again, that made him smile. She stalked away from the table, and he sipped his coffee before putting it down and kneeling beside his daughter's Pack 'n Play. Kendra reached for him through the white mesh exterior, so he reached in and picked her up. She laughed and leaned forward to bite his nose, and he patted her back. Luke felt good and wanted to do something. It was cold, but maybe he and Kendra could bundle up and go hiking.

While Irene got ready for work, Luke packed a day

bag with two changes of clothes for Kendra as well as diapers, some ready-to-feed bottles of formula, wipes, pacifiers, and everything else he thought he'd need for a day on the town with his little girl. Then, shortly after Irene left, he fed Kendra another bottle and changed her into clean, warm clothes and got in the car.

He didn't have a destination in mind, so he and Kendra drove around town for about twenty minutes. Then they stopped at Rise and Grind, a little coffee shop downtown. Kendra sat beside him in her little car seat, but he kept the cover over her to keep the germs out. An elderly couple at the table next to him watched as he drank his coffee and enjoyed a pecan roll.

"How old is your little one?" asked the older woman, eventually. Luke smiled at her.

"Six months," he said.

"I bet she's lovely," said the woman. "May I see her?"

He hesitated.

"She has a heart defect," he said. "So I keep her pretty well covered whenever I'm out. I know I'm just paranoid, but she's my baby."

The older woman smiled.

"Good for you," she said. "You're a good daddy."

He thanked her and focused on his coffee once more. He watched people and read the *St. Louis Post-Dispatch*, while Kendra napped. It was a nice morning, but it didn't scratch the itch at the back of his mind. He kept thinking back to the cop and Mutton Chops, the man from the gas station. He wished he had killed him. That would have been supremely satisfying. Still, he wondered whether Mutton Chops's brush with death had changed him. Was he more thoughtful, slower to judge? Luke doubted it. People like Mutton Chops didn't change. They were rotten to the core. So was Irene.

Punish them all. They deserve to die.

Rather than acknowledge the reptilian voice, he listened to it and sipped his coffee. The voice didn't bother him as it once did. Normal people didn't hear voices, but they also slept more than him at night and didn't spend their days fielding abuse from a spouse so insecure in herself and her place in the world that she heaped vitriol on everyone she could. He was done with Irene now. He and Kendra both deserved better.

Luke finished his coffee. The voice was right. The asshole with mutton chops had gone out of his way at the gas station to hurt an innocent baby. Luke had punished him, but there were millions of other assholes out there. Someone needed to teach them a lesson. Luke couldn't kill them all, but he'd kill those he could. Then, eventually, he'd murder Irene. It'd be glorious.

But he was getting ahead of himself. First, he had other work. He carried Kendra to the car and removed the cover over her car seat. She smiled and reached for him. He hadn't washed his hands lately, so he just kissed her forehead. Then he got in the front seat and drove. The slow swaying of his SUV and the murmur of its tires on the pavement mesmerized and pacified the baby. She looked out the window as he drove home, content and quiet.

Luke had spent his life in the theater, but he was hardly a makeup artist. Still, he had some talent. He carried his daughter inside and put her in a playpen. Then he used his wife's makeup to contour his face and make his cheeks look fuller. Finally, he pulled on a padded suit he had last used in a show in college but that had long gathered dust in the back of his closet. The suit added what looked like fifty or sixty pounds to his body. As a last touch, he put on a wig with long, greasy brown hair. He looked unruly and older than he was. His friends would recognize him, but a stranger would never see the man beneath the costume.

After that, he put Kendra back in her car seat, grabbed his gas can, and got in the car and drove to the BP station at which he had met Mutton Chops. Instead of parking near the station, though, he parked a block away on top of a hill. It gave him a view of the fuel pumps and the station's customers. Kendra murmured and played with a rattle with a mirror on one side. Luke became a hunter, waiting for his prey.

Dozens of cars passed under his watch in the first hour, but the men and women inside those cars seemed courteous if not patient. After an hour and a half had passed, Luke sighed, wondering whether he was wasting his time. The world had assholes galore. He had found Mutton Chops at the gas station earlier, but that didn't mean he'd find another jerk just like him. Still, he didn't leave right away.

And then the universe rewarded his patience.

A white pickup truck pulled into the lot. Its owner had installed a thick metal guard over the grille and lights, giving the truck a menacing look. Even from a block away, he could hear the heavy diesel engine and its modified exhaust. The car was designed to draw attention, but Luke wouldn't have given it a second look had a little girl not darted from a minivan nearby. She must not have seen it because she ran right in front of it. Luke held his breath as the heavy truck slammed on its brakes. Then the driver honked.

The little girl stopped and held up her hands, and an older man—probably in his fifties—opened the truck's door. He wore a straw cowboy hat and a white button-down shirt that was open at the collar. The little girl had light brown skin and dark hair down to her waist, and the cowboy shouted the sort of racially charged names one would expect to hear at a Klan rally rather than at a busy gas station. Even from a distance, Luke could hear. It must have terrified the kid.

The little girl's mom ushered her back to the car while the cowboy glared. Luke smiled. He had his mark.

Do it. Hurt him.

The reptilian voice sounded gleeful. Luke felt strong and confident. More than that, he felt righteous. The cowboy had hurt a child. He shouldn't have done that. Luke checked himself in the rearview mirror to make sure his makeup hadn't run. Then he grabbed the gas tank from the front well of his vehicle and checked Kendra.

She had fallen asleep. This would all be fine.

He walked to the gas station, unsure what he was about to do but knowing he needed to be close to the cowboy to do anything. As he walked, he bent and picked up a rock from a flower bed outside a dentist's office. It was a white river stone about the size of a tennis ball. His fingers trembled, and he felt strength course through him.

As he reached the gas station, though, he knew bashing in a man's skull with a rock wouldn't do, so he walked to an open pump near the cowboy's truck. The older man caught Luke's gaze and narrowed his eyes.

"You need something, Chief?"

Luke shook his head, set his gas can on the ground, and reached into his pocket for a pair of latex gloves.

"No," he said. "Just admiring your truck. What is that, an F250?"

"Piss off."

Once he had his gloves on, Luke reached for the nozzle and stuck it into his gas can. Then he looked toward the station and waved. A moment later, the clerk turned on his pump. As he felt the gasoline stream through the hose, he knew what he needed to do. The cowboy was five or six feet from him.

Luke released the handle and pulled the nozzle from his can, then held it at his side as he looked to the cowboy. The older man spit tobacco juice on the ground at Luke's feet but said nothing. Luke considered the mess before looking to the cowboy again.

"The little girl you almost killed says hi."

He lifted the nozzle and pulled the handle. The scent of gasoline filled the air as the liquid shot from the pump and onto the cowboy. The older man staggered back and rubbed his face. Luke had only held the stream on him for a moment, but a modern gas pump could push ten gallons of gas out a minute. The cowboy was dripping in seconds. Luke reached to his pocket and pulled out the box of matches he knew would be there. The reptile inside him giggled.

Do it. Torch him. Burn him.

Luke flicked a match across the strike plate and smelled the burning chemicals. Once he was sure the match was lit, he tossed it. The cowboy screamed as flames exploded all over his body. The smell was awful, but the sound was exquisite. Unfortunately, Luke couldn't stay long. He grabbed his gas can and ran back to his car, feeling exhilarated. The suit started to slip off his shoulder, and two old men stepped out of a barbershop nearby, but no one tried to stop him. They were probably too terrified.

The moment he reached his car, Kendra woke with a whine that turned into a scream. He looked in the rearview mirror and started singing a lullaby as he turned the heavy SUV on. As he pulled away from the curb, he sang to his daughter until the giggles overtook him.

"One asshole down. A couple million to go."

This would be fun.

12

My hearing started at ten, but I didn't have the day off, so I skipped my morning run and went into work early to put in a few hours. The building was quiet. Jason Zuckerburg, our night shift dispatcher, was working the front desk. On most occasions, he was a jovial, outgoing man, but today, he just yawned and waved when I told him hello. That was better than Trisha's reaction when I'd last seen her, so I appreciated it.

In my office, I checked my messages and email and then sat down with a stack of cold-case files from the early sixties. I found nothing new, but I put in the hours. That mattered to my boss, so that's what I did.

At a little before ten, I left the building and walked to the county's historic courthouse. Four men wearing fishing waders and plaid jackets stood outside with signs protesting...something. They seemed peaceful and happy, so I smiled to them and walked into the building. My hearing was in the main audience chamber, so I climbed the steps to the second floor and walked inside. A dozen people sat on chairs in the gallery. Four lawyers stood near the judge's bench.

I walked to the bailiff, who recognized me and smiled and pointed out the clerk of court when I asked. She had white hair that hung just below her ears, and she wore tasteful makeup and a gray skirt and black sweater. A gold broach in the shape of a cat decorated her chest.

When she saw me approaching, she held up a finger before reading through a document in front of her. I waited until she smiled at me.

"Can I help you, Miss?"

"Hopefully," I said. "I'm Mary Joe Court. I'd like to talk to you about a continuance."

She blinked and straightened. When I first saw her, I thought she had looked like a grandmother. Now, she looked more like a stern schoolteacher. She drew in a breath through clenched teeth.

"If you had come a week ago, I could have helped you," she said, sliding the sleeve of her sweater back to expose the watch on her wrist. "But your hearing is in fifteen minutes. You're too late."

I forced myself to smile.

"I heard about the hearing two days ago and haven't had time to prepare. Can you talk to the judge, please?"

She crossed her arms and raised her eyebrows.

"This is a busy courtroom," she said. "We have a schedule."

I kept the smile on my lips, but it was hard.

"You also have a job to do," I said. "Please tell the judge I'd like to file for a continuance. If he's uninterested in talking to me, that's fine, but it's his choice."

She scowled, turned around, and walked to her boss, Judge Jim Kessler, near the front of the room. He had signed warrants for me in the past, so we had a cordial relationship. He looked at me, and then he spoke to his clerk. Then he left the room. His clerk walked to me.

"Judge Kessler says you should have a seat in the gallery. He'll be with you as soon as he can."

So I sighed and waited in that wood-paneled courtroom. Darren Rogers and a cohort of attorneys came about five minutes later. They looked smug and confident. At ten, the court's bailiff walked toward me and told me the judge wanted to see me in his chambers. Darren Rogers and one of the suited men with him followed me in.

Judge Kessler sat behind his desk and glanced at Rogers.

"I didn't ask you to come in."

"All the same," said Rogers, "I thought it'd be important for St. Augustine County to have a representative present for any discussions involving Ms. Court's home or this hearing."

The judge considered him.

"I'll give you a chance to speak, but if you or your attorney interrupts me or Ms. Court, I'll ask you to leave."

"That's fair," said Rogers.

"I'm glad you approve. Everybody sit down," said the judge. I sat in a high-backed leather chair in front of the judge's desk. Darren sat beside me. His attorney, who didn't have a chair, continued to stand. The judge's chambers had wood-paneled walls and a hardwood floor. Water stains marred the plaster ceiling, and the radiator behind the judge's desk clicked every few moments. The courthouse was a beautiful building, but its mechanical systems were showing their age. I wondered where in the line it stood for a renovation and whether its standing depended on the rulings made by its judges.

The judge looked at me and furrowed his brow.

"You told my clerk you just received notice of this hearing," he said. "That shouldn't be."

I agreed with him and described coming home and finding the notice on my door. Then I told him about my visit to Darren Rogers's office, during which he explained that my property was a blight on the community and that St. Augustine intended to take it for a public purpose.

"And the notice you found on your door was the first notice you received?" asked the judge.

"Yes," I said.

The judge looked to Darren Rogers.

"Your turn," he said. "What's going on?"

Rogers smiled.

"I appreciate Ms. Court's predicament, but she's leaving out a few important facts," he said. "As I intended to say at the hearing, we tried to contact her dozens of times over the past six months regarding her property. She never once responded. Furthermore, the county has a genuine need for the property because we plan to build a public RV park on it. Ms. Court's neighbor has already sold us thirty acres of prime real estate, but we need Ms. Court's acreage, too. A creek runs through her property, and that creek is vital to the success of the park."

I scoffed and shook my head.

"That creek is nothing but a mosquito breeding ground," I said. "Half the year, it's stagnant. The other half of the year, it's dry. If that's vital to your project, you need to reevaluate your project."

Darren Rogers started to retort, but the judge held up a hand, silencing him.

"I'll ask the questions. Let's keep the commentary to a minimum, please."

"Ms. Court's property is a blight to the community," said the county's attorney. "Her tenants grew illegal drugs in the backyard and threw a music festival during which dozens of teenagers took and sold hallucinogenic substances. Her property is a danger. As a police officer, she, of all people, should understand the danger of illegal drugs."

I squeezed my jaw shut.

"I was out of town for an extended period, and I didn't rent my home to anyone. My realtor allowed people to live in the home without my permission. I'm still trying to figure out what happened there."

The judge looked to Darren Rogers and his attorney.

"We've got some issues to discuss," he said. "Did you know the tenants in Ms. Court's home were there without permission or that she was out of the area?"

"I don't believe that's pertinent," said Rogers. The judge lowered his chin and opened his eyes wide, but before he could speak, Rogers's attorney cleared his throat.

"The law requires us to send our notices to the property owner's registered address. We did that. It's not the government's responsibility to track her down."

My face grew hot.

"They wouldn't have had to track me down," I said. "Mr. Rogers knew where I was. He sent a letter about my character to an attorney in Cloverdale, North Carolina, where I was staying. That letter was then introduced in court in a custody proceeding."

The judge crossed his arms and gave Rogers a hard look.

"Is that true, Mr. Rogers?"

Rogers gave his attorney a smug look.

"Ms. Court is ill-informed about that letter," said the lawyer. "Ms. Court left the St. Augustine County Sheriff's Department under a cloud of suspicion. Ten months after she quit, the department received a phone call from an attorney in private practice in Cloverdale, North Carolina, requesting a character reference. Not knowing Ms. Court, the sheriff forwarded that request to Mr. Rogers's office."

"And you wrote a letter?" asked the judge, looking to Rogers.

"I did, sir," he said. "I explained the suspicious circumstances of Ms. Court's departure and my opinion of her work performance. At no time, though, was I told Ms. Court lived in North Carolina. For all I knew, she had applied for a job at this gentleman's business while living in Timbuktu.

"Ms. Court did not update her address with St. Augustine County, the state of Missouri, or any agents thereof. We had no idea where she was. We only had her tax records to go on, and they said her primary place of residence was her house in St. Augustine County. My office followed the law step-by-step. We upheld our responsibilities and duties."

The judge shuffled through the papers on his desk and read for a moment before leaning back and looking at Darren Rogers.

"According to the paperwork your office filed, Ms. Court didn't sign for a single notice."

"As required by Missouri statute, we sent the notices via certified mail," said the attorney. "We did everything right and stand by our actions."

Judge Kessler drew in a deep breath and then lowered his chin.

"You may have followed the letter of the law, but you didn't follow its spirit. I think you know that."

"And yet we are a nation governed by law," said Rogers. "It'd be unfair for you to step outside the law today. Ms. Court has had ample opportunity to take part in these proceedings. Instead, she waited until the last minute to respond. The county has already invested hundreds of thousands of dollars in this process. It would be unfair to allow her to object at this point."

The judge looked toward his desk. I leaned forward. Muscles all over my body felt tight, and knots began twisting in my belly.

"Please," I said, my voice a whisper. "This is my house. I love that house."

The judge blinked and then exhaled as he thought.

For a few beats of my heart, he said nothing. Then he sighed.

"I'm not sure what we would gain if I granted Ms. Court's request for a continuance," he said. I shut my eyes and felt my stomach plunge into my shoes. My cheeks felt tight, and I balled my hands into fists. "That said, what the government has done to Ms. Court is unfair. Mr. Rogers, you had every reason to believe Ms. Court hadn't received the notices you had sent about her property. You knew she couldn't fight this, and yet you proceeded anyway. That's shameful."

Rogers shrugged. I wanted to hit him.

"Let's end this today," said the judge. "You said the county's already invested a significant amount of money in the project. Save the county some money and make Ms. Court a fair offer on her property."

Rogers looked to his attorney. The attorney looked to me.

"We've had an appraiser out to the property," he said. "We're happy to offer you the full appraised amount. Twenty-five thousand dollars."

I closed my eyes and shook my head.

"That's a bullshit number, and Darren knows it."

The judge cleared his throat and gave me a tight smile.

"I understand this is a difficult situation, but please refrain from using foul language in my courtroom," he said. "If the appraiser gave your property a value of twenty-five thousand dollars, that's a fair offer."

I clenched my jaw tight before speaking.

"The appraiser—my real estate agent—rented my house to Johnny Knockers and his girlfriend Cherries Jubilee without my permission. He's as much a player in the fraud as Darren Rogers."

Judge Kessler looked to Darren Rogers.

"The appraiser is licensed by the state of Missouri," said Rogers. "I can't speak to his other business interests."

It took everything I had not to stand up and scream at him. Instead, I focused on the judge. He gave me a sympathetic look.

"Ms. Court, I'm sorry for what's happened, but based on what I've heard and the documents they've already filed, the government has proved that they've followed the letter of the law. Given the status of this action, I don't believe allowing a continuance would change the situation. So I'm denying your request."

The strength left my gut at once. My shoulders fell, and I leaned back in my seat. I felt as if somebody had slapped me.

"What now?" I asked. "That's my house. What do I do?"

"You work with the county's right-of-way agent to settle on a price. If you can't come to a deal, we'll hold a commissioners' hearing. During that meeting, the commission will report the fair market value of the property. At that point, you can file an exception to the commissioners' awards and ask for a jury trial to determine your property's value."

I clenched my jaw.

"But by then, I'll already have lost it."

"You already have lost it," said Rogers. "We're just haggling on price now."

I closed my eyes.

"I hate you."

"Sorry to hear that," said Rogers.

"If that's everything, we've got a hearing ahead of us," said the judge.

"Thank you, Your Honor," said Rogers. His attorney echoed the statement. Then I heard footsteps across the floor. I didn't look up until I felt a soft hand on my shoulder. It was the judge.

"I'm on my way out," I said. "I just need a moment."

"Take your time," he said. I counted to ten before I straightened. The judge gave me a genuine smile. "Can I give you some advice, Ms. Court?"

"Sure," I said, shrugging, unsure what he could tell me at this point.

"Get a lawyer next time you deal with Darren Rogers. He's one mean son of a bitch."

I couldn't have agreed more.

13

After that meeting in Judge Kessler's office, I knew I couldn't change anything, so I didn't bother sitting through my hearing. It wasn't even ten-thirty, so the bars were still closed, but I still wanted to get drunk. The money didn't bother me. Between the trust fund my biological mother had left me and property I had inherited from my friend Susanne, I had more than enough money to spend the rest of my life in comfort.

I loved that house, though. It was the first major purchase I had ever made, and I had poured myself into every nook and cranny. I had sanded and restored the old hardwood floors myself; I had painted the entire exterior; and I had rebuilt the deck. Roger, my old dog and one of the truest friends I would ever have, was buried in the backyard. That home held my memories. Some were good and some were bad, but they were all mine.

My throat felt tight. I didn't want to go to work, so I took a walk. Unfortunately, my phone rang before I could go more than a quarter mile. It was Trisha from my station. She hadn't been very conversational since George Delgado died, so I doubted this was a personal call.

"Hey," I said. "It's Joe Court."

"Detective," she said. "Where are you? You're supposed to be at work."

I clenched my jaw tight so I wouldn't snap at her.

"I was in a judge's chambers," I said, allowing the full

measure of my anger into my voice. "Is that a problem, Officer Marshall?"

"Yeah, well, the sheriff needs you on another case," she said. "There's been an incident at the BP station in town. A man died."

I slowed and looked down.

"What kind of incident?"

"Find out yourself," she said. "I'm just the dispatcher."

"Thank you," I said. "Tell the sheriff I'm on my way to the station."

Trisha hung up. I wanted to call her back and snap at her, but I didn't have time. A dead guy at a gas station needed my attention.

Five minutes after Trisha's call, I reached my Volvo and then drove to the BP station. There, pools of white foam covered the ground. Someone had strung yellow police tape around the station, shutting it off to all but law enforcement. Four uniformed officers already stood outside. A fire truck had parked near the hydrant on the edge of the station's asphalt, but no firemen hustled around.

I parked a block away on the street and walked up the cracked, pitted sidewalk to the edge of the station's asphalt lot. Katie Martelle, one of our uniformed officers, lifted the crime scene tape when she saw me approaching. I thanked her and ducked under. We were standing about twenty feet from the nearest fuel pump, and even though we were outside, the stink of spilled gasoline and burned skin was strong enough to make me gag.

"The body's beneath the foam," said Katie. "Once the guy in the store saw him burning, he hit a button to turn off the pumps and release the fire retardant to keep anything else from going up."

That likely saved his station, but it cost us evidence. I looked toward the fuel islands. People had abandoned the cars they had been filling, so half a dozen cars sat beneath the station's covered awning. White fire-retardant foam dripped from them.

"Was it an accident?" I asked.

"No. This was a murder. Sergeant Reitz interviewed a witness who said that a heavyset man walked to the station and started filling a red five-gallon gas can. Then he pointed the nozzle at a guy in a cowboy hat and sprayed him with gasoline. He then lit a match and tossed it at him."

"Jeez," I said. "That's an awful way to go."

Katie nodded. Her face looked ashen. As the breeze dissipated, the smell of burning hair became stronger. I took my wallet from my purse and gave her all the cash I had.

"Go down to the hardware store and pick up some respirators with organic vapor filters. Someone in the paint department can help you out. I don't know what this foam is, but I don't want to breathe it in. Buy as many as you can. The department'll reimburse you if I didn't give you enough."

"Yes, ma'am," she said before walking toward her

cruiser.

"Hey, Katie," I said. She turned and raised her eyebrows. "Please don't call me ma'am. I'm twenty-nine."

She smiled.

"Sure thing, Detective."

That was better than ma'am, so I thanked her before turning toward the gas station once more and looking for Sergeant Bob Reitz. I found him standing near the front entrance to the convenience store at the north end of the parking lot. The morning sunlight glinted off his scalp and the polished brass badge attached to the front of his crisp uniform. He nodded as a middle-aged man in jeans and a maroon sweater beside him spoke.

I walked around the edge of the asphalt so I wouldn't step in the foam beneath the awning. Bob gave me a tight smile before looking to the man beside him.

"Mr. Wolff, this is Detective Mary Joe Court with my department. Can you excuse us for a minute? I'm sure she'll be back to talk to you."

Wolff stepped back. Bob and I walked about twenty feet away. He looked toward the foam.

"Body's beneath the awning. He's the round shape beside the white pickup. It's pretty gruesome."

"Katie said you spoke to a witness who said it was intentional," I said.

"I did," said Bob. "He's sitting in my car now, but he's pretty shaken up. Mr. Wolff manages the station and said they've got surveillance cameras on either end of the convenience store, so they should have the attack on

115

video. I've had the other witnesses taken to our station so we can interview them there."

He did well, so I thanked him and looked over the station and surrounding streets. The BP station lay in the bottom of a valley between two long, sloping hills. Homes and other businesses dotted the surrounding landscape. Potentially, there were hundreds of witnesses but also hundreds of places our killer could hide.

I looked toward the white pickup and the shape that lay beside it. Every murder was horrific in its own way, but burnings seemed especially cruel. A victim shot in the heart or the head had the comparative blessing of a fast, painless death, but a victim who was burned died in agony.

It was almost worse if you survived. You'd spend weeks or months in a hospital in pain so severe you'd wish they'd put you in a medically-induced coma, and then you'd spend the rest of your life disfigured. It took a lot of hate to spray gasoline over somebody and light him on fire, and I shuddered to think of the person who was capable of doing it.

"We need a strategy to deal with the media," I said. "Once the nature of the crime gets out, they'll swarm. Let's push back everybody half a block. If anybody complains, tell them there's a risk the gas tanks beneath the station have ruptured."

"I don't know if the reporters will believe it," said Bob, "but we can do that."

"You think they're as cynical as we are?" I asked.

The sergeant's lips didn't so much as curl.

"I don't know how they could be."

I smiled and looked toward the manager.

"You said his name was Mr. Wolff?"

Bob pulled a notepad from his utility belt and flipped through his notes.

"Adrian Wolff," he said. "I've got his address and other contact info if you want it."

I said I did and wrote down the information. Then I walked to Mr. Wolff and introduced myself. He shook my hand and then told me a story very similar to the one Katie Martelle had told me earlier. A heavyset guy walked to the station, filled a gas can, and then hosed down a man in a cowboy hat. Then he lit him on fire. The interaction was two minutes or less from start to finish.

"Did you recognize either person?" I asked.

"I didn't know the fat guy, but I know the cowboy. He's a racist, but we're not allowed to refuse him service. The owner won't let us."

I narrowed my eyes.

"You think this was racially motivated?"

Wolff shrugged.

"I don't know. Maybe. He almost killed a little girl who darted in front of his truck, and then he yelled at the little girl's mom when she grabbed her. He said he was going to call INS."

"Let me see this video."

He agreed and led me through the store and to the office in back. A big desk crowded the tight space. A white board that listed which employees were on duty when hung on the wall. While Mr. Wolff spooled up the video, I snapped a picture of the white board with my cell phone in case I needed to talk to the other employees. Then he and I watched a video that showed what he had described.

The cowboy pulled into the gas station and nearly hit a little girl who had darted away from her mother. Then, after her mother grabbed her, the cowboy yelled at them both. A moment after that, a heavyset man with shaggy hair walked into the frame and began filling up a red gas can. He and the cowboy spoke, and then the heavyset man doused him with gasoline, lit him on fire, and ran.

I had Mr. Wolff play the video three times. The attacker moved like a dancer, and he had a lean face. If I didn't miss my mark, he was wearing a padded suit. That would mean he had hidden his identity, which meant he had planned the attack.

I reached into my purse for a business card, which I then handed to the gas station's manager.

"Please forward this video to me," I said. "My email address is on the card."

He said he would and then rewound the video again at my request so I could see the cowboy's license plate number. I wrote it down, thanked Mr. Wolff for his time and cooperation, and then left the convenience store. Bob Reitz was talking to some civilians just beyond the yellow crime scene tape, but he excused himself when he saw me coming toward him.

"Mr. Wolff is forwarding the video to me," I said.

"In the meantime, I'd like you to check every business on the street and see if they've got additional surveillance video of our attacker fleeing. I'd also like some uniformed officers to talk to the residents who live nearby and see if they've seen our attacker around here or if they know who he is."

Reitz jotted down my instructions.

"Dr. McEvoy is on her way to process the scene," he said, glancing toward the pumps. "The foam will make her job difficult. It also looks like our attacker wore gloves."

Which, again, indicated he had planned this.

"Tell her to do her best," I said. "I'll see if I can ID the victim. Is your cruiser open? I'll use your laptop."

He pointed toward his car before giving Katie Martelle and our other uniformed officers instructions. I walked to the sergeant's cruiser and sat in the front seat. The surveillance video had given me the victim's license plate number, so it took about thirty seconds with our department's databases to ID him: Laughton Kenrick.

Laughton had been fifty-three years old, had weighed two hundred pounds, and had been six feet all. When I got to his address, I swore under my breath, having recognized it. Laughton had lived at the Church of the White Steeple, a several-hundred-acre racist stronghold once owned by a man named Richard Clarke. Clarke was dead now. I suspected he had been murdered, but we had never found his body. He had used the church to further his personal fortune and to spread a racist ideology

119

throughout Missouri. He had even run for a congressional seat on a pro-segregation platform.

I doubted Kenrick's racist buddies would appreciate my investigation into their friend's death. My lousy day had just become a lot worse.

14

I called Sheriff Kalil's cell phone. He answered after three rings.

"Hey, boss," I said. "I'm at the BP station, and I've identified our victim as Laughton Kenrick. He lives on the grounds of the Church of the White Steeple. How should we approach this?"

The sheriff grunted.

"I hate those people."

"To be fair, I doubt they're your biggest fans, either," I said.

He paused.

"You've got to handle this," he said. "If I go there and tell them one of their own's dead, they'll riot. Take Dave Skelton and Bob Reitz with you. They can take care of themselves if the shit hits the fan. Treat the case like any other murder."

I doubted they'd avoid rioting on my account, but I nodded anyway.

"You need a media strategy," I said. "I saw the surveillance video. It'll go viral once it hits the internet."

I could practically hear him grinding his teeth.

"And why do you think it'll hit the internet?"

"Because this is a horrific crime, and we can't keep the media out of it," I said. "The surveillance video's going to leak. We can't stop that."

The sheriff, once more, grunted.

"Maybe *you* can't."

Unless his powers of persuasion were well beyond those of anyone who had ever lived, he wouldn't be able to, either, but that didn't matter. He could live in a fantasy world if he wanted.

"I'm just calling to let you know we ID'd the victim. I'm not interested in arguing."

"Good. Because you'd lose the argument."

I forced myself to smile.

"Sure," I said. "I'll contact Sergeant Reitz and Officer Skelton and have them meet me at the church."

"You do that," said Kalil. "And make sure you leave somebody competent in charge of the crime scene at the gas station. I'll hold you responsible for any screwups there."

"Fine. Anything else?"

The sheriff grunted and hung up without saying another word. I called Dave Skelton and told him what was up. He told me he was twenty-five minutes from the Church of the White Steeple. I thanked him and then sat on the hood of my Volvo to wait for Bob Reitz to finish his sweep of the neighborhood's businesses. When he returned, he flipped through his notepad.

"The dentist's office up the road has a video camera pointed out front that should have some usable footage for us. Dr. Kinsella, the chiropractor on the same street, has a similar setup. I haven't seen video from either place, but they said they'd email the footage to me."

"Great," I said. "I've got a new assignment. We're

going to the Church of the White Steeple."

Bob grimaced and put his hands on his hips.

"Do we have to?"

If I had thought that was a serious question, I would have admonished him, but Sergeant Reitz was a good cop. He knew what the job required of him and did it without complaint. I smiled.

"Yep," I said. "Victim's name is Laughton Kenrick, and he lived on the grounds. Dave Skelton's already on his way. He'll meet us at the gates."

Bob tilted his head to the side to speak into his radio. Before keying his microphone, though, he focused on me.

"I'll be there soon. I'll call for Sergeant Patricia to take charge of the scene here."

My lips curled into a smile.

"When did Doug make sergeant?"

"Couple months back while you were away," said Reitz. "We needed another sergeant, and the sheriff found money in the budget. It was about time. Doug does good work."

"He does. I'm glad to hear it," I said. "Call him in and meet us at the church."

Bob said he would and then stepped away from my car.

I drove for about fifteen minutes before reaching the main gate. The Church of the White Steeple occupied a beautiful piece of rural St. Augustine County. Unfortunately, the property was surrounded by a rusted scrap-metal fence topped with razor wire, making it look like some kind of post-apocalyptic outpost. The fence was about five feet high, and the razor wire on top rose an additional three feet. In case somebody didn't pick up on their desire for privacy, a church member had sprayed *STAY THE FUCK OUT* in neon green paint on the gate's exterior.

I parked alongside the road and stepped out of my Volvo but didn't try to get anyone's attention inside. Dave Skelton arrived about five minutes later in a marked cruiser, so I walked him through the case and my investigation so far. He asked a few questions, but mostly he listened.

"How likely do you think it is that our killer's inside?" he asked.

I hemmed and hawed before shaking my head.

"Not very," I said. "If somebody at the church wanted Kenrick gone, they would have just killed him out here. We wouldn't have even known he was dead."

Skelton agreed. For the next ten minutes, we sat on the hood of his cruiser to wait. He told me about his kids, and I told him a little about my brothers and sister. It was an enjoyable conversation.

When Bob came, I had him honk his horn three times to announce us. A few moments after that, a young woman with brunette hair masked by a crappy blond dye job came bouncing on the back of a four-wheeler. I told her we needed to talk to Michael Clarke—the church's current leader—about one of his congregants. The woman didn't seem to trust us, but she pulled out a two-way radio and contacted somebody else. A few minutes later, a minivan pulled to the gate, and Michael Clarke stepped out.

Clarke was in his late forties or early fifties. Cigarette smoking had turned his skin leathery and stained his teeth a dull yellow. He smiled when he saw me, but that smile faded as his eyes traveled to Sergeant Reitz and Officer Skelton.

"It's always nice to see you, Detective Court," he said. "But I'm afraid this is a bad time. My congregants and I are fixing the roof over our church. We're kind of busy."

"I won't waste your time, then," I said. "One of your congregants, Laughton Kenrick, was murdered this afternoon at the BP station in town. I'd like to talk to you about him."

For a moment, Clarke didn't react. Then he blinked and his chin lowered. His breath became shallow.

"Laughton's dead?" he asked. I nodded, and he brought a hand to his mouth. "He was a good man."

He was a racist who very nearly ran over a child with his enormous truck and then called her mother vile names, but if I said that aloud, it'd only endear him to Clarke even more.

"I'm sure he was," I said. "Can we talk to your residents?"

At first, Clarke seemed not to register what I had asked, but then he shook his head.

"No, you may not," he said. "This is a church. It's

Chris Culver

sacred ground."

"We're here to work a murder. The more we learn about Mr. Kenrick and the life he led, the more likely we'll find his killer. Does he have any enemies?"

Clarke's eyes traveled up and down me. Then he narrowed his eyes.

"Of course he's got enemies. We're in the middle of the greatest war of civilization the world has ever seen. Our church is one of the world's last bastions of humanity."

Dave or Bob snickered behind me, but I kept my face as neutral as possible.

"I understand your views," I said. "Did anyone in particular dislike Mr. Kenrick?"

"Everyone loved him."

Somehow I doubted that, but giving voice to my disbelief wouldn't help anybody.

"He was murdered by a heavyset man with unkempt brown hair in his thirties or early forties. Does that sound familiar?"

Clarke shook his head.

"You're saying a white man murdered him?"

"I am," I said. "We have it on video."

"That's hard to believe."

"It's still true," I said, keeping my lips flat. Neither of us spoke for a moment. Then the minivan's rear sliding door opened, and a pregnant woman stepped out. She had blond hair, and she wore a tight sweater and black yoga pants. One hand rested on top of her swollen belly.

"I can take her around," she said. "Just her, though. I don't trust these other guys."

Clarke considered her and then looked to me.

"Is that agreeable?"

I didn't want to go in there alone, but as long as I had officers waiting for me outside, Clarke and his buddies wouldn't hurt me. This church was their refuge from the world, the one place they could express themselves without scorn. If they hurt me, though, officers from law enforcement agencies across the state would roll through their property and seize everything they could. Rational self-interest would keep me safe, but I'd look out for trouble, anyway.

"Sounds great," I said.

Clarke opened the gate wide enough for me to step through and then introduced me to Sophie Marie Hitler. Somehow, I doubted that was her real name. Clarke drove the minivan away, and Sophie and I walked. Laughton, she said, had hung around the church for years, but he had only moved onto the property in the past six months. She didn't know him well, but she said he was always respectful toward her and the other women around the property. The men liked him, too, because he was good with his hands and worked hard.

Sophie didn't think anyone at that church could do wrong, and she didn't know anyone at the church who fit my description of Laughton's killer. Talking to her about Kenrick was a waste of time, but he wasn't the only dead man on my mind.

"What can you tell me about Richard Clarke?" I asked.

We stood about thirty feet from the barracks in which Laughton Kenrick and seven other men had lived. Sophie cocked her head at me and narrowed her eyes as if the question surprised her.

"Richard's dead," she said. "What do you want to know?"

"I hear he was murdered," I said. "Nobody found the body, though."

She shrugged.

"You cops came, and then you left without doing anything."

I reached into my purse for a notepad.

"I'm here now," I said. "Tell me about him. Did you know Mr. Clarke?"

"Yeah," she said, swaying and smiling just a little. "He was real important around here. Would you like to see where he died?"

My eyes popped open, and I lowered my chin.

"You know where he died?"

"We think so," she said, already walking down a footpath that led between the barracks and an administrative building. "Come on. I'll show you. It's a bit of a walk. Richard walked every day. He liked the tranquility."

I followed but said nothing. We meandered down a footpath beaten into the earth past the barracks building, through a field of prairie grass, and to the edge of a thick wood. Sophie didn't slow down before plunging in. I checked my phone to see whether I had any reception out here. A single bar flickered. Bob and Dave would worry about me if I stayed out here too much longer, but I needed to see this. George Delgado had tried to investigate Richard Clarke's murder, but the church hadn't cooperated. I couldn't squander this opportunity. Plus, I was pretty sure I could outrun a young woman who was at least six months pregnant if she tried anything.

I followed her down a narrow path. The trees here were taller and had thicker trunks than those in my backyard, but deer trails and small creeks crisscrossed the woods, just as they did behind my home. It was peaceful. I could see why Richard Clarke had liked to walk here. Sophie walked a couple hundred yards and stopped beside a big pin oak tree with flowers strewn about its base.

"Richard loved tulips," she said. "We try to bring some by when we can."

Aside from the flowers against its trunk, nothing about the tree or surrounding ground stood out.

"So you think he died here?"

"This is where we found his blood. The day he disappeared, we heard a gunshot but didn't think anything of it until he didn't come home at his usual time. Since he liked to walk here, we came out to find him. Instead, we found a puddle of blood on the ground and drag marks through the woods."

I looked at the ground, but those drag marks had

disappeared months ago.

"What'd Detective Delgado say?"

Her eyes lost their focus for a moment, and she looked down.

"He didn't come out here. I don't think they wanted to find him."

Delgado very much had wanted to find him, but nothing I had to say would convince her of that. He probably hadn't come out to the woods because he hadn't felt safe.

"I'm sorry for your loss."

"Me, too," she said. She paused. "I loved him, but I'm the lucky one. He gave me his final gift for the world."

She patted her stomach. I tried not to shudder. Sophie was probably twenty-five. Clarke could have been her grandfather. People could love whomever they wanted, but that was gross. I tried to disguise my gut reaction by looking around me. Hundreds if not thousands of people had had a motive to shoot Richard Clarke, but few could have taken him out on his own property in the middle of nowhere and then hidden his body before any of his followers could find him.

Clarke was one of six men who had died in the past few months in St. Augustine County, and all six men had thwarted Darren Rogers. Clarke and his racist buddies had protested at the St. Augustine County Spring Fair and other major events around the county, embarrassing us all and scaring away potential advertisers, sponsors, and tourists. Arthur Murdoch had been a property owner who refused to sell Darren Rogers property. Dr. Nico Hines had sold opioids to addicts across the county. Zach Brugler had killed Darren Rogers's daughter in a car accident. Vic Conroy had pimped out dozens of young men and women in his truck stop, hotel, and strip club. George Delgado had investigated Darren Rogers for financial crimes.

Rogers was an old man. He hadn't killed these men himself, but he had blood on his hands. I wished I could prove it.

15

Hanging out in the woods with Sophie wasn't getting me anywhere, so I asked her to take me back to Michael Clarke's office. She complied with my request and led me to a little brick house with a big front window and evergreen hollies planted along the foundation. Clarke sat in the front room behind a desk, but he stood when he saw us.

"Sophie show you what you needed to see?"

"She did. She's great," I said, smiling to her. She beamed back at me and held her arms around her belly. I turned toward Clarke. "The members of your church express controversial opinions often. Do people contact you about that?"

Clarke winked.

"You asking whether we get hate mail?"

"I was trying to be diplomatic, but yes."

He stood and led me down a carpeted hallway to a bedroom. The church had furnished it with metal storage shelves that held dozens of white cardboard boxes. My shoulders fell at the sight.

"This is your hate mail?"

"Yep. My dad liked to read at night. He said it kept his edge up. I had planned to clean it out after he died, but I've been so busy taking care of his estate and church that I haven't had time. These letters go back two decades. It's like the history of our mission. Walking in here, it feels like I'm stepping into a museum."

I swore under my breath. The room held dozens and dozens of boxes, each of which could hold hundreds of letters. This would take months to read and process.

"It's possible Mr. Kenrick died because of his involvement with the church. Are your files organized in any way?"

"By their time of arrival," said Clarke. "I had planned to throw everything out, so take what you want."

I asked him for any correspondence received in the past six months, and he directed me to a shelf with three heavy boxes on it. Then he had two of his congregants carry them to his minivan so he could drive me and the boxes to the front gate. Sophie came with us in the van. Before leaving, she gave me a hug.

"You come back here when the race war starts," she whispered into my ear. "We'll keep you safe. We could even find you a husband."

I paused before extricating myself from the embrace.

"Thanks, Sophie," I said, unsure what else to say to that. She winked and turned toward the van. Michael grabbed two of the cardboard boxes, and I got the third. We carried them to my Volvo while Dave Skelton and Bob Reitz watched with quizzical looks on their faces. Finally, I thanked Michael for his help and the tour of the property.

"I hope you get the son of a bitch who murdered Laughton."

"We'll do everything we can," I said.

He thanked me, closed the property's gate, and drove back toward his compound. Bob looked toward my car.

"You must have made an impression if they gave you souvenirs."

"A young lady carrying Richard Clarke's child also offered to find me a man."

Dave Skelton narrowed his eyes and cocked his head to the side.

"Wasn't Richard Clarke in his seventies?"

"He was," I said.

"When you say a young lady was carrying his child, do you mean that blonde girl who gave you a hug?"

"Yep," I said, smiling. "You thinking about joining the church now?"

He shook his head.

"No, but I suddenly understand the appeal of a religious life."

"I'll tell your wife that," said Bob, before looking to me. "You have what you need?"

"I'm good," I said. "You guys go back to work. I've got hate mail to read."

They both wished me luck. I drove back to my station as the sun set and carried the boxes to my office, where I started going through the contents. The first letter writer used the word *fuck* forty-three times in the first page of an eight-page handwritten screed. This would be a long evening.

In college, when Luke and Irene were dating, life had been sweet. Irene was from the East Coast, but he had met her while they were undergraduates at a university in St. Louis. Luke had grown up in the area, so he showed Irene the sights. Afterwards, they could stay up all night talking. They couldn't get enough of one another. In everything she said, he found subtle shades of meaning, and she laughed at his jokes and smiled when he talked about his professors or classmates.

They married three months after graduation, and that had been wonderful, too. Afterwards, she went to Yale Law School, and he went to the Yale School of Drama to study playwriting and set design. They had both been so busy that their late-night conversations grew further and further between. But they had still loved each other.

After Irene graduated, they returned to St. Louis, where she got her first job. The pay was astronomical compared to his salary as a teaching fellow, but her hours were long and hard. Luke had planned to finish a PhD, but Irene became so absorbed in her career that it never happened. He had thought about moving to Chicago on his own, but he had doubted their marriage would survive the strain. Now he wished he had gone. At least then he'd have those happy memories to reflect upon.

Since then, Irene had sucked the fun out of life. He

wanted to leave her, but if he did, he'd never see Kendra again. He couldn't admit it aloud, but Kendra was his daughter in name only. He didn't know who her biological father was. Irene might have a good idea, but he doubted she could be certain either. The day she told him she was pregnant, he had decided to leave her once and for all, but his lawyer had advised him to wait and get his affairs in order. Besides, if he could prove the baby wasn't his, he'd have leverage over his wife in their divorce proceedings.

But then Irene went into labor six weeks early, and his daughter was born. He didn't even get to hold her before doctors put her in an incubator, but he fell in love with her the moment he saw her face. She was perfect and helpless and vulnerable. He couldn't leave her with his wife. That beautiful little girl had bound him to a monster tighter than any cord or cable ever could. He couldn't leave Irene because she was his only tie to his daughter.

And that was why they had a TV in the dining room. Irene hated eating alone and insisted that he join her in the dining room whenever she was home. Without the TV, she'd spend their time together berating him. With the TV, they never spoke a word. It was glorious.

Luke had already eaten a turkey sandwich and was now feeding Kendra pureed peas, most of which she spit out. Irene watched and rolled her eyes.

"She doesn't even eat the peas," she said. "She just spits them out. It's gross."

"She eats some," he said. "She poops green, too, for

your information."

Irene closed her eyes and put her fork down.

"You're disgusting."

"You married me," he said, smiling.

She opened her eyes and looked at him, then smiled as sweetly as she could.

"I wish I hadn't."

"Me, too," he said.

Irene's mouth fell open with surprise, but she said nothing. Now and then, though, he caught her giving him sidelong, curious looks out of the corner of her eye. That made him feel good about himself.

After a commercial break, the newscaster came back with, in her words, "a chilling story from a sleepy vacation town to the south." Luke glanced at the TV and found himself looking at Fourth Street in St. Augustine. He hadn't seen the surveillance cameras, but the gas station must have had some. His heart started beating faster as he saw himself walk onto the screen.

"Look at this," he said. "It's at the BP station in town."

Irene stopped looking at her pork chop and focused on the screen. Even though Luke knew what would happen next, he held his breath. His heart pounded, and adrenaline poured through him so that muscles all over his body quivered. As Luke watched, the man on the screen, his avatar, began filling up a gas can. Then he turned the hose on the cowboy and lit him on fire. Luke laughed as the newscaster came back on the screen.

"That's not funny," said Irene. "That's awful."

He looked to her.

"Don't you get gas there?"

She shook her head, stood, and picked up her plate. "I'm going back to work. I don't want to stay here with you tonight. If you can laugh while a man burns to death, you're fucked in the head."

Luke picked up Kendra's spoon again and smiled at her.

"Right before he died, the victim almost ran a little Hispanic girl down with his truck and then threatened her family. He deserved to die."

Irene closed her eyes and stopped moving.

"You don't know that."

"I was there," he said. "Look at the video again. See if anybody looks familiar."

She put her plate back on the table and took the remote from Luke's outstretched hand. Their DVR always recorded the last few minutes of television they had watched, allowing her to rewind and watch the video again. Then she did it again and again. Finally, she slowly put the remote down and looked at him. He smiled.

"I'm stronger than you think," he said. "The cowboy's not the first guy I killed, either. I met another guy at the gas station, and he came after Kendra. I burned his house down around him. Kendra and I are better off without you. Get out of my house, but be sure to tell whoever you're fucking at work hello for me."

She backed away, and he kept feeding his daughter. A

few moments later, he heard the door to the garage slam shut. Luke didn't really know whether he killed anybody else, but that didn't matter.

Telling her was a bad idea.

"It's okay," said Luke. "She won't tell the police, but even if she did, no one would believe her."

I hope you're right.

"I am."

Luke hadn't spoken to the reptilian voice directly before, but it didn't talk back to him or belittle him or try to talk over him. That was refreshing.

He got Kendra to bed at about eight, and she slept until four in the morning. Then, he fed her a bottle, changed her diaper, and put her back to bed, where she slept until seven. It was an easy night. Unfortunately, his doorbell rang at twenty after eight, interrupting his morning. The sun was up, but he wasn't even dressed yet, and Kendra was in the middle of eating. They were sitting around the kitchen table. He leaned close to her. She reached for his nose and giggled.

"Sorry, sweetheart," he whispered. "I've got to get the door."

He unbuckled her from the seat and carried her to her room, where he put her in a playpen with some toys. Then he went to the front door and found the strikingly attractive police detective he had spoken to earlier standing on his porch. She smiled at him.

"Mr. Glasman, good morning. I'm Detective Joe Court. We spoke earlier. How are you doing today?"

Luke smiled, but his insides trembled. Surely Irene wouldn't have gone to the police. Even if she had, the police wouldn't have believed her. She was a lying, manipulative shrew. No one should believe her.

"I'm fine," he said. His hands trembled. "Did we have an appointment this morning?"

The smile never wavered from her face. It seemed genuine, too. Women smiled at him often, but mostly because they enjoyed seeing a man with a baby. He wondered whether Detective Court smiled at every man she ran into, or whether he was special in some other way. If she thought he had killed the cowboy at the gas station, she would have come with backup. This was fine. She was here to chat.

Send her away. She's dangerous.

He had listened to that reptilian voice before, but he knew it was just his subconscious. It was overreacting. Detective Court wasn't dangerous. She was just a cop. Luke wondered whether he was trying to convince himself of that or whether he actually believed it.

"No, we don't have an appointment, but I had hoped to talk to you, anyway. Is your wife around?"

His back stiffened, and he swallowed hard.

"No. She's gone for the day."

"Good," said the detective. "May I come in?"

"I'm not dressed, and my daughter's a little fussy."

"I'll only be a minute," she said, already stepping forward. He stepped back to give her some space, and she took that as her invitation to come inside. Not knowing what else to do, he shut the door and considered her. She was pushy. He kind of liked that.

"Can I get you some coffee or something?" he asked.

"Yes, please," she said.

"Come on in," he said, gesturing toward the kitchen. The detective walked in front of him, giving him a very pleasant view from behind.

Don't let her distract you. She's a deceiver.

Maybe his subconscious was right. Aside from his admission to Irene, she wouldn't have had anything against him. Latex gloves had kept him from leaving fingerprints at the gas station, and his makeup, wig, and body-shaping outfit had changed his appearance. She couldn't have been here for the case. Maybe she liked him. Stranger things had happened.

When they reached the kitchen, he poured the detective a fresh cup of coffee. She sat at the breakfast table without waiting for his invitation, so he refilled his own cup and joined her.

"So," he said, drawing the syllable out. "What can I do for you?"

She sipped her drink and then tipped her cup to him.

"Thank you for the coffee," she said. "It's good. Where's your daughter?"

He smiled even though the fine hairs on the back of his neck were standing on edge and his innards contorted into knots.

"In her room playing. She has a heart defect, so I try to keep her away from too many people. Germs can make her very sick."

The detective sipped again before putting her coffee on the table and sorting through her purse for a notepad.

"I'm sorry to hear about your daughter's illness, but I'm here because an officer who works with me reviewed surveillance footage from a dentist's office near the BP station on Fourth Street. He found a big red SUV shooting up the street within minutes of the Flamethrower's attack yesterday."

Luke almost spit out his coffee and covered it up by coughing. The detective stood, walked to the counter near him, and got a paper towel from the rack beside his stove.

"Thank you," he said, taking it from her and wiping off his mouth. "I choked a little. Who's the Flamethrower?"

"There was an attack at the gas station yesterday," she said. "A heavyset man doused another man with gasoline and set him on fire. The media's taken to calling him the Flamethrower."

Luke's knees started bouncing under the table, and he ran his thumb across the inside of his palms nervously. When she looked down to his hands, he brought them below the table.

"Irene and I saw that on the news," he said. "It's awful."

"Did you see anything at the station?"

He picked up his coffee, but his free hand trembled. He balled it into a fist. The detective didn't seem to notice.

Get it under control. Breathe.

It was good advice. He drew in a breath and brought his hands under the table, where he squeezed his fists tight.

"I don't think it was me," he said.

"It looked like your car," she said. His throat felt tight, but he shrugged.

"Maybe it could have been," he said. "Kendra and I drive a lot. It calms her when she's upset."

"I see," said the detective. She smiled. "I've seen the entire video. Mr. Kenrick, the man who died, almost ran over a little girl. Then witness statements say he called her and her mother names and threatened to call INS on them. If anybody deserved to be lit on fire, he did."

Don't listen to her.

He didn't need the reptilian voice to know she was baiting him. He blinked and picked up his coffee. She straightened and cocked her head at him, making him wonder for a moment whether she had heard the same voice he did. That was crazy, though. The voice wasn't real.

"Nobody deserves to be murdered," he said after taking a sip. The hot liquid gave him something to focus on. His fingers stopped trembling.

"Of course," said the detective, smiling. "You ever written a letter to the Church of the White Steeple?"

His hands trembled so that he nearly spilled his coffee. As he put it down, he rubbed his wrist.

"Carpal tunnel," he said. "It acts up when it gets

cold."

"I understand," said the detective. "You ever written a letter to the church?"

"Yeah. Someone from the church called a friend of mine a vile nickname because he wore a yarmulke. I wrote their reverend a letter asking him to have more respect for other faiths."

"Their reverend is dead now," said the detective. "The man from the gas station yesterday was a church member."

He shrugged.

"Then he was an asshole," said Luke. He closed his eyes. "Why are you here, Detective? Do you think I'm this Flamethrower guy?"

"Nah," she said, shaking her head and standing. "I just thought I saw your car on surveillance footage and wanted to make sure."

"Maybe it was me," he said. "Like I said, Kendra and I drive a lot. And now that the big truck stop near the interstate is closed, we get gas at the BP station. It's the closest station to the house. Are you questioning everyone who gets gas there now?"

"Only those near the station at the time of a murder," she said.

This was bad, but she had nothing tying him to the crime. The guy on the video looked nothing like him, he hadn't left fingerprints, and he hadn't used his credit card to purchase gas. He was clear.

"My wife's a lawyer, and she's got a temper," he said.

"If she finds out I spoke to the police without having an attorney present, she'll skin us both alive."

"We wouldn't want that," said the detective. "I'll see myself out. Thanks for the coffee, Mr. Glasman."

"Sure," he said. The detective walked to the front door. As her Volvo left, he pressed his back against the wall and allowed gravity to pull him down. Then he covered his face with his hands and swore. Then he thought for a few moments and realized the importance of that visit.

She hadn't arrested him.

She hadn't even accused him of a crime. If she could prove he had done anything, she would have come with an arrest warrant. She was fishing, which meant she had nothing. She was desperate. The strength came back to Luke's legs, and he pushed himself to his feet. Kendra reached toward him when he entered her room. He smiled and picked her up.

"We did it, baby," he whispered. "We got away with it."

She giggled at him. This was just what he needed. He felt happy and powerful. The world made sense. He tickled Kendra's cheek again. She giggled once more and grabbed his hand.

"Who do you want to kill today? Mommy? You want to kill Mommy?"

Kendra threw her head back and laughed. Luke couldn't help but smile. Even Kendra wanted Irene dead. He had to do it now. It was fate, and he wasn't one to argue with fate.

16

As I drove away from Luke Glasman's house, I shuddered. Something about him was just...off. Mostly, he had looked like a caring, dutiful father, but when he mentioned his wife, his eyes had grown black, and his entire expression changed. It sent icy shivers down my back.

Over the years, I had interviewed and interrogated murders, rapists, arsonists, burglars...you name the crime, and I'd talked to somebody who'd done it. I had even sat across the table from a serial murderer who had persuaded a young woman outside his prison to murder people and bury their heads in my backyard. I had seen cold, black eyes before, but I hadn't seen them juxtaposed against the caring, friendly demeanor of a father. Glasman didn't fit the typical profile of a vigilante killer, but he was hiding something. We needed to watch him.

I drove back to my station and headed to my office to write an after-action report. Since I had already been in that morning, I didn't bother going by the sheriff's office to inform him of my comings and goings. If he needed me, or if he wanted to know what I was up to, he could read my reports.

About twenty minutes after I sat down to work, Marcus Washington knocked on my door. I saved my document and pushed back from my desk.

"Morning," I said. "Come on in. What's up?"

Chris Culver

He sat in a chair in front of my desk and leaned back.

"Last we spoke, you said you were going to lose your house. You doing okay?"

I crossed my arms.

"The county has passed an ordinance mandating the creation of a public RV park that takes my entire property, and the realtor I hired to watch my house while I lived in North Carolina instead conspired with Darren Rogers to steal it from me. By the time I figured out what happened, it was too late to fight. I have to be out by midnight or I'm trespassing in my own home. So no. I'm not okay."

The more I spoke, the more real my predicament felt. Before it had been abstract and formless. It was an idea, but now that I had spoken it and shared my predicament with someone else, my loss felt concrete somehow. My lip threatened to quiver, and my throat felt tight, so I swallowed and looked away. Marcus said nothing for a moment.

"Stay in your house. Nobody in this department will bother you," he said. "I'll make sure of that."

I looked at him and smiled, but I couldn't put much feeling behind it.

"That's kind, but the sheriff'll fire you if you interfere. This is my fight, and I lost before I even realized what was happening."

He exhaled and then raised his eyebrows.

"I'm sorry."

"Me, too," I said, forcing myself to lean back and try to appear nonchalant. "I'll stay at my parents' house until I find a new place. It'll be fine. That's not why you're here, though. What can I do for you?"

He remained silent for a moment before crossing his arms.

"When we were at George's house, you suggested I contact Jasper Martin and ask whether he might have known where George was before he died."

"Yeah," I said. "What'd he have to say?"

"Nothing. They haven't spoken since Jasper was fired. George cut him off when he found out Jasper had leaked your personal information to the press in St. Louis."

I lowered my chin and narrowed my eyes.

"Really?"

"Really," said Marcus. "Like I said, George was complicated. He was prickly, abrasive, and judgmental, but he had a personal code, and he believed in the work we did."

I considered Marcus and my answer before speaking. George may have been complicated, but he was also vindictive and mean. Marcus had said George's problems with me began because he thought I was promoted too quickly. If that were the case, though, he could have talked to me. He could have tried to mentor me. Instead, he tried to tear me down at every opportunity. He tried to humiliate me, he gave me menial assignments, and then he forced me out of the department at the first opportunity. I was glad Marcus hadn't seen that side of our old colleague, but it was real.

"That's unfortunate about Jasper," I said. "What else do you have?"

He looked at my desk and then leaned forward. "The police in Perryville found George's truck."

I crossed my arms.

"I didn't realize it was missing."

"He's got two trucks," said Marcus. "One's at his house. It's registered and legal. The second truck is the one he used to go hunting. It's a piece of junk, but it's got mud tires on it, and George didn't care if he hit something with it."

"What do the guys from Cape Girardeau say about it?"

"Nothing," said Marcus. "They don't know about it. The truck's not registered, but I put some feelers out for it on the sly and got a hit. A uniformed officer found the truck in a spot where hunters park. He didn't write a report until he came back a week later and found it still there. Then he found the license plate on the back expired fourteen years ago and called it in. His CO called me."

"That's good work," I said. "You want to drive or should I?"

"I'm driving," he said. "Dr. McEvoy's already in the car out front. I was just supposed to get you."

Before moving, I considered him.

"Does the sheriff know what we're doing?"

"Nope. Does that change anything?"

"Nope," I said, standing and starting toward the door. "Let's go."

Marcus had already signed out one of the department's big SUVs, and Darlene McEvoy sat in the back with two fishing tackle boxes full of gloves, bags, and other gear she needed to catalog and store small pieces of evidence. We sat in the front and headed out.

Perryville was a little town with about eight thousand residents. Though it was only thirty-five miles southeast of St. Augustine, its flat landscape and wide-open fields made it feel like a different world. Before doing anything else, we stopped by the police station, a single-story brick building with an extruded metal roof.

Marcus had gone to high school with their assistant chief and introduced us. Within five minutes of our arrival, the four of us headed toward Delgado's truck in two separate vehicles. We drove for almost twenty minutes on US-61 until we reached an area with rolling hills and deep woods. A thick layer of desiccated brown leaves covered the ground. Given time, wind and the surrounding terrain would grind those leaves into a rich mulch, but until then, they stayed where they had fallen.

We pulled off on the side of the road near a bald area beside the woods. Someone—George, presumably— had left an old Chevy truck with rusted wheel wells and a cracked rear window nearby. The surrounding ground was so beaten down that little vegetation grew, and the miniscule amount that did grow had gone dormant and brown with the season.

The four of us got out of our cars and walked toward the truck. Darlene put her tackle boxes on the ground and pulled out gloves for all of us. She'd process the evidence, but gloves would guarantee we wouldn't accidentally leave prints on surfaces we touched. Before anyone did anything else, I took almost sixty pictures with my cell phone to document the scene. I thought I found blood on one of the rear quarter panels, but it was just rust. Hopefully Darlene would have better luck than me.

After taking my pictures, I stepped back, and Darlene got to work. She started dusting the truck's door handles for prints, and I looked to Marcus's friend, Assistant Chief Dempsey Blackburn. He was forty or forty-five and had a well-trimmed beard and a grizzled face. If I had seen him on the street, I would have pegged him for a contractor or somebody who worked hard in the sun. Marcus had said he was a good cop, and I hadn't seen anything to make me doubt that.

"How near are we to the Mississippi?" I asked.

He tilted his head to the side as if he were thinking.

"Ten to fifteen miles at least, and it's rough terrain," he said. "I wouldn't want to hike it."

So even if Delgado was murdered here, his killer must have had another car or truck to transport him. Unfortunately, the ground was so hard and beaten down that we didn't have tire prints. I looked to Blackburn.

"What's special about this place?" I asked. "Why would a recently retired police officer from St. Augustine come here?"

He looked toward the woods.

"My brother-in-law claims he pulled an eighteen-point buck from these woods, but I'll believe that when I see it, and he's never let me see it."

I wasn't a hunter, but I presumed that was a good thing.

"So the area's popular with hunters. Anyone else come out here?" I asked. "Hikers? Campers, anything like that?"

"I don't think so," said Blackburn. "It's private property, but the guy who owns it lets deer hunters on the land to keep the population low."

"We'll talk to him and see if he saw anyone with Delgado," said Marcus.

Blackburn shook his head.

"You could talk to him, but he lives in Marble Hill in Bollinger County. He owns and farms a couple thousand acres here, but he lives there. I doubt he saw anything, but I'll give you his number."

I tried not to grimace.

"Okay," I said, sighing. "Marcus, do you mind staying here while I go up the street? We passed a couple of gas stations along the way. Maybe they've got surveillance video of Delgado coming out here."

Marcus agreed, fished his keys from his pocket, and tossed them to me. I thanked him and then started the heavy SUV. The first station was about a mile away. It had two fuel islands in front and a small bait and tackle shop instead of a convenience store. They only had one surveillance camera, and it focused on the building's interior to catch shoplifters. So that was a bust.

The next two stations I visited were much more modern. Both had cameras that pointed toward the road out front, but only one had kept the footage from the time in which Delgado disappeared. I watched on a tiny monitor in a cramped, concrete office that smelled like cheese. It took twenty minutes, but then I saw Delgado's truck pass by. A moment after that, my breath caught in my throat when I saw a familiar SUV.

The station manager emailed me the video, and I drove back to Delgado's truck. Marcus and Blackburn were deep in the woods, looking for any signs that Delgado might have been killed there, while Darlene searched the old pickup. It was frustrating going because somebody had wiped it down. Marcus and Blackburn came back a few minutes later, and I showed them both the video.

Marcus swore under his breath.

"Something I missed?" asked Blackburn.

I considered what to tell him. Marcus answered before I could decide what to say.

"Joe and I have seen the SUV before. We think the driver is a professional who was hired to kill some prominent people in St. Augustine."

Blackburn took a step back and raised his eyebrows.

"Jeez," he said. "Why would somebody hire a hit man to kill a detective?"

"Because George found something he wasn't supposed to find," I said. "And, unfortunately, it means Marcus and I might be next. We need to catch this guy."

17

Marcus, Assistant Chief Blackburn, and I spent the next hour looking for shell casings or other signs that Delgado had been gunned down somewhere in those woods, but we might as well have been looking for black cats in a dark room. Even if we had brought metal detectors, it was unlikely that we would have found anything. We were wasting our time. Eventually, we left the woods, and our phones reacquired a weak signal. Marcus's phone beeped first, but mine beeped a second later. I checked out the screen and looked to him.

"Sheriff Kalil?" I asked. He nodded. "Paper, rock, scissors?"

He nodded again and slipped his phone in his pocket. I chose paper, and he chose scissors. My shoulders fell.

"Best two out of three?" I asked.

He smiled and shook his head.

"Nope. Good luck, Joe."

I grunted and dialed the sheriff's personal cell phone. He picked up on the second ring.

"Boss, hey," I said. "It's Joe Court. Marcus told me you called. My cell phone didn't ring."

"Butthead," said Marcus, his voice low. I smiled at him but focused on the call.

"Where are you, Detective?"

I walked to our SUV and pulled open the passenger

door so I could have somewhere to sit.

"Perry County. I'm working a case with Detective Washington and Dr. McEvoy."

"I appreciate your honesty," said the sheriff. "Just to settle my curiosity, what county pays your salary?"

I smiled, but I didn't feel like smiling.

"St. Augustine."

"Then why are you working a case in Perry County?"

"Because that's where our evidence led," I said. "We're just doing our jobs. You'll get my report, and it'll outline everything I've done and why."

He made a guttural noise.

"Tell me about your case."

I closed my eyes and brought my hand to my forehead.

"Sure," I said, sighing. "A uniformed officer from Perryville found George Delgado's truck near a popular hunting spot. They called us, and Marcus, Darlene, and I went to check it out."

The sheriff paused. Then I heard him draw in a breath.

"Jesus, Joe," he said. "You are the primary suspect in that murder."

"Which, with all due respect, is why our department should investigate it. I'm sure Detectives Hargitay and Vega are good guys, but they're in over their heads if I'm their primary suspect."

A red pickup drove past on the road. Darlene, Marcus, and Blackburn watched it but never turned to

me. They could hear me, but I appreciated that they
avoided watching me.

"George Delgado's death is not our case. I wish it
were, but it's not. He died outside our county."

"How sure are you of that?" I asked. The sheriff
paused.

"Are you accusing me of something?"

"I'm asking a question," I said. "George was a St.
Augustine officer. He lived and worked in town. How do
you know he didn't die in town?"

"Because we would have found the murder site by
now," he said. "George is dead, and that's an honest-to-
God tragedy, but it's not your tragedy to investigate. Your
case is the murder of Laughton Kenrick. To remind you,
he's the man doused with gasoline and set on fire in town.
What are you doing for that case?"

I closed my eyes and drew in a breath so I wouldn't
snap at him.

"I'm working it," I said. "I went by a potential
witness's home this morning, but he claims not to have
seen anything. Kendrick was a member of the Church of
the White Steeple and lived on the property. The minister
at the church gave me six months' worth of hate mail the
church has received. At least half the letters make threats,
but very few reference fire, and none mention dousing
members of the church with gasoline and lighting them
afire."

I let the sheriff process what I said. A moment later,
he cleared his throat.

"Continue."

"I've taken this case as far as it can go based on the evidence we've got," I said. "Hundreds of people had a motive to kill Kenrick. The man was a first-class asshole, and he was a member of a community that vilified everyone who looked even slightly different than them. My team and I have talked to dozens of potential witnesses, but nobody admits to having a good look at Kenrick's attacker or knowing who he was. The surveillance video is helpful, but we can't use it to identify the attacker yet.

"The news has already picked up the video, so people know what this guy looks like. Somebody will recognize him, and when we get the appropriate tip, we'll make an arrest."

The sheriff grunted.

"We've already gotten tips. Hundreds of them. The phone's been ringing nonstop since the video aired."

I scratched my forehead and sighed.

"Any of them promising?"

"I don't know," said the sheriff. "You should consider looking into them."

"I will," I said. "We're almost done here, and—"

"No, you're done now," said the sheriff. "If you, Dr. McEvoy, and Detective Washington aren't back in our station within the hour, I'll report your SUV stolen and have you dragged in wearing handcuffs."

I straightened and drew in a breath.

"Seems a little excessive."

"You forced my hand, Detective," he said. "Now do as I ask or experience the consequences."

He hung up. I squeezed my phone hard and then clenched my teeth before getting out of the car. My team looked at me.

"We need to get going," I said. "Sheriff's pissed and wants us back. Unless one of you wants to spend a night in jail for stealing an SUV, we've got to get back within the hour."

Marcus looked down at his watch and then raised his eyebrows before looking to Blackburn, his friend.

"We've got to go," he said. "Thanks for hosting us."

Blackburn nodded, and we all piled into our vehicles. Within moments, we were driving home, no closer to finding our murderer than we were when we left St. Augustine. With Delgado's killer still out there, we didn't have this kind of time to waste. Unless we moved, people would die. I wished I had some idea of how to find him.

Muscles all over Luke Glasman's body tingled. He and Kendra would kill Irene, but it had felt so good to kill Laughton Kendrick that he didn't want to stop. He thought about getting in his car, driving to the Church of the White Steeple, and mowing down everyone he came across, but he wouldn't survive long enough to do any real damage. From what he had seen of similar groups on

TV, those rednecks probably had enough heavy weaponry scattered around their property to take on a platoon of Marines.

He needed to think smaller. His attack on Laughton had worked because he hadn't seen Luke coming. He couldn't douse anyone else with gasoline. People would expect it. They'd be on their guards. No, Luke needed a new tactic, and he had come up with one watching the surveillance video of his attack.

Laughton Kendrick had driven a giant truck with a metal guard over the grille. The guard protected the vehicle from brush, but more than that, it would have made an excellent battering ram. The moment he realized that, Luke had driven to an auto parts store south of St. Louis, where he had purchased the biggest, heaviest grille guard he could find.

It cost fifteen hundred dollars and contained almost two hundred pounds of hardened steel. Bolting it on had been a chore, but he had managed it in his garage while Kendra played with a rattle. Now, his simple red people carrier felt menacing and right. Nobody would mess with him in that car. It'd shut Irene herself up. And if it didn't, she'd shut up the moment he rammed her with it at sixty miles an hour.

Once he got the grille guard on, he and Kendra had driven to Walmart's parking lot and watched as people went about their business. Busy parking lots, Luke had found, were great places to identify the rude and cruel. Surrounded by three thousand or more pounds of steel in their cars, drivers felt invulnerable and strong. Moreover, their often dark windows conveyed a sense of anonymity that allowed people to let their inner selves shine through. It made it easy to find potential targets.

For an hour, Luke had waited and watched. He had found a couple of good potential targets, but two of them had kids, which made them a hard pass. A third had an empty gun rack in the back of his truck. Luke didn't know anybody with a gun rack, but he suspected the people who had them were likely to also have concealed-carry permits. Luke's work was too important to take the risk of going after an armed man. Not only that, he refused to put his daughter in danger from stray bullets. He had to be careful.

After an hour, he lowered his binoculars and looked in the rearview mirror as Kendra started babbling. He smiled.

"Hey, baby girl," he whispered. "You doing—"

He never got the chance to finish his thought. Somebody rapped hard on his window. He fumbled with his binoculars. Once his fingers squeezed around them again, he looked to his left and groaned. The pretty, blonde detective stood outside, waving and smiling at him and motioning for him to lower his window. He hadn't even seen her walking up to him.

He held up a finger and put his field glasses on the passenger seat before hitting the button to roll down his window.

"Can I help you...Detective?" he asked.

"You sure can," she said, smiling. "I was just at my station following up on a few tips called in about the Flamethrower when a concerned citizen called my dispatcher and said a man in a red SUV was watching people in Walmart's parking lot. The caller thought he must have been some kind of pervert, scoping out potential targets. I happened to be in the area, so I came out. You're not a pervert, are you, Mr. Glasman?"

"No," he said, shaking his head. "I didn't realize watching a parking lot was a crime."

"It's not, but it's creepy," she said. "Can you tell me what you're doing?"

"I like people watching."

She smiled again. It sent a chill down his spine.

"When people go people watching, they usually do it in public parks and malls and restaurants. Why are you doing it here?"

He stammered one answer and then thought better of it and stopped. Then he shrugged and closed his eyes.

"I don't know," he said. "It seemed like a good place to people watch."

She considered him and then shook her head.

"I don't believe you."

He almost told her that was none of his concern, but then he took a different tack.

"Fine," he said. He closed his eyes and exhaled out of his mouth. "You got me. I was looking for the Flamethrower."

She raised her eyebrows and lowered her chin.

"At Walmart?"

"Yeah," he said. "He's not an idiot, so he won't go back to the gas station. You've probably got officers all over there. This is the next best place in town to find assholes, though."

She nodded as if that made sense. The knot in his gut untangled just a little. She believed him. On television, detectives had almost mythical abilities. They could spot a liar across a room, solve a crime with nothing but their wits, and fight their way out of even the most dangerous of situations. Detective Court wasn't on television, though. She was just a woman. He could lie to her and get away with it.

"Why does he interest you?" she asked.

He scoffed and shook his head.

"That one's easy, at least. My life sucks. I've got a daughter, and I love her all the way. She's my moon, my sun, and my stars, but I want more. When I get up in the morning, I change diapers, I warm up bottles, and then I do the dishes. That's my entire day. Women, at least, can take their babies to playgroups. There are classes and support groups for stay-at-home moms. Dads? We get screwed. The last time I took Kendra to a class, the moms looked at me like I was a goddamn child molester. I just wanted to sing songs and play with my daughter. Does that make me a bad person?"

Luke's face grew warm, and he squeezed the steering wheel. The detective shook her head.

"No, it doesn't."

"The whole fucking thing—parenting—screws dads who want to stay home with their kids. When people see me with Kendra, they assume I'm some kind of out-of-work bum who can't find a job. I'm not. I chose this life because I love my daughter."

The detective shifted so that her right hip, the one that held her pistol, was pointed away from him. She lowered her hand toward the pistol. She must have felt threatened, so he lowered his voice.

"Sorry. I get a little excited sometimes."

"That's okay," she said. He looked at her and sighed.

"I thought, maybe, I could help you," he said. "Okay? I know you think I did it, but I didn't. I thought if I could catch the guy, maybe I could get in the paper. Maybe people would realize I'm not just a jerk who can't get a real job."

He hadn't planned the outburst, but it felt good to let it out. It was honest. He wasn't just tired of his life...he was weary. Luke had never expected life to be perfect, but he hadn't wanted an unending shower of shit, either.

He looked toward the steering wheel.

"You're the first person who's listened to me in a long time," he said. "Thank you."

The detective drew in a slow breath.

"I appreciate your position, but you need to go home, Mr. Glasman," she said. "The man you're hunting is dangerous. We don't need an amateur detective getting in the way."

He squeezed the steering wheel tight. Thousands of

cold pins seemingly stabbed him in the side as rage built inside him.

Nobody talks to you like that. Teach her a lesson.

The reptilian voice was wrong, though. Someone did talk to him like that. Irene. Detective Court needed to learn how to treat people with respect. Like Irene, she now had to die.

"You're right," he said, forcing a smile to his lips. "I'll be leaving now."

The detective stepped back from his car.

"Take care, Mr. Glasman. And remember what I said: This is a dangerous world. Some risks aren't worth taking."

The voice whispered to him once more.

You're the danger. We'll show her soon enough.

He closed his window. As he looked in the rearview mirror, Kendra's lips moved, but no sound came out. He put the car in gear and gave her a disbelieving smile.

"Was that you talking?" he asked. "Are you in my head?"

I've always been here, Daddy. I love you.

Luke had dreamt of hearing her say that. He nearly melted into his seat.

"I love you, too, honey," he whispered. "Let's burn her. Let's burn them all."

18

Once Luke Glasman's car pulled away from the side of the road, I got back in my car and spent the next fifteen minutes writing up my recollections of our conversation. Though the news media had pounced on the BP station's surveillance video, we hadn't released a lot of information about the Flamethrower's attack on Laughton Kenrick yet. When Glasman and I had last spoken, I had told him Kenrick was a member of the Church of the White Steeple—an organization Glasman had specifically denounced in a letter—but I had said nothing about the Flamethrower's motivations. Glasman, though, had supplied one: he implied that the Flamethrower was hunting people he considered assholes.

Had Glasman said the Flamethrower was hunting racists, I wouldn't have batted an eye. Kenrick was a racist, so it'd be natural to assume the Flamethrower was targeting racists. Glasman, though, had said assholes, like he knew something.

I might have been looking too much into it, but it was an anomaly. I would have followed him to see where he went, but he would have recognized my car. So, I drove back to the station and went to the sheriff's office. He didn't seem happy to see me, but I walked him through my meeting with Glasman and my thoughts. He listened but balked when I requested we put a plainclothes officer in an unmarked vehicle outside

Glasman's house at all times.

"Let me get this straight," said the sheriff. "You have surveillance video of the murder at the BP station, and on that surveillance video, a heavyset man with unkempt dark hair lit Mr. Kenrick on fire?"

"That's right," I said.

"What does Mr. Glasman look like?"

"He's lean and has a trim haircut."

The sheriff leaned back and laced his fingers behind his head.

"That's what I thought," he said. "I deny your surveillance request. I'd also advise you to take him off your list of viable suspects. Mr. Glasman may be creepy, and he may act suspiciously, but if you've got evidence that clears him of the crime, common sense says he's not a good suspect."

I crossed my arms.

"What if he's working with a partner?"

The sheriff narrowed his eyes and considered.

"Do you have any evidence to suggest he's got a partner?"

"Not yet, but it's possible."

The sheriff drew in a breath and then shook his head.

"Until you get further evidence, consider Mr. Glasman cleared. If he's not on the video, he's not your murder. We will not violate Mr. Glasman's privacy or waste county resources because one of my detectives gets a little tingle in her uterus. I don't know what protocols you've followed in the past, but going forward, I want you to focus on evidence, the kind a prosecutor can use in court. Am I clear?"

I didn't know what a little tingle in my uterus would feel like or what he was trying to imply, but the comment was inappropriate. Since he was my boss, though, I straightened and forced myself to smile.

"Yes, sir."

"Good," he said, focusing on some papers on his desk again. "Now get out. I've got work to do."

I kept the smile on my face as I left the room. My head throbbed, and I felt hot despite a chill in the air. Maybe he was right to deny my surveillance request, but he shouldn't have dismissed it out of hand.

Instead of heading to my office, I went by the break room for a bottle of water. The cold liquid took the edge off my anger but did little to diminish the underlying feelings. My evidence against Glasman was circumstantial, but it was enough to warrant further investigation. If the sheriff didn't see that, he needed to get his eyes checked.

I walked back to my office and started looking up Glasman. Unfortunately, I didn't find a lot. St. Augustine County had never arrested him, investigated him for a crime, or even interviewed him about a crime prior to my interview about the fire at Jason Kaufman's house. As best I could tell, no other law enforcement agency had either.

Next, I checked him out on Facebook. He had hundreds of friends, but he rarely posted, and when he

169

did, he posted pictures of his daughter. He also had an account on Twitter, but I couldn't find any tweets. Finally, I searched for him on Google to see what popped up. Most of the results were several years old, but they showed that Mr. Glasman had been active in the theater when he was younger. He had designed sets for many productions and had even written at least one very well-regarded play.

I leaned back and then called up the surveillance video of Laughton Kenrick's murder at the BP station. When I'd first seen that video, I had thought the heavyset man moved a little too light on his feet for such a heavy man, but I hadn't given it much thought beyond that. Now that I saw it again, though, I was struck by how unevenly distributed the man's weight was. He had a big belly, but he didn't have the rounded cheeks or hips I would have expected of someone that size. Everybody carries their weight differently, but he didn't look natural.

The sheriff wouldn't believe me without more evidence than I could give at the moment, but the more I watched that video, the more convinced I became that our murderer was Luke Glasman in a padded suit and a lot of makeup. I went back to his Facebook page and searched for his most recent posts.

He always had a lot of people comment when he posted pictures of Kendra, but few went beyond short platitudes that said she was adorable. On each post, though, four or five people made longer comments that asked how he was doing. I wrote down their names. Once

I had more evidence against Glasman, I'd call them and see what they had to say about him.

At a little after five, I shut down my computer and drove home. Roy was in the dog run out back, and when he saw me, his tail wagged so hard I almost thought he would fall over. I smiled and let him out. He jumped around me and then ran a few laps around the yard to get some energy out. It was always good to see a happy dog.

Normally, I'd take him for a walk right away, but this was a special day. Unless some miracle happened, I'd lose my house at midnight. Knowing Darren Rogers, he'd have the sheriff knock on the door at 12:01 to see whether he could arrest me for trespassing.

It was cold, but I didn't want to go inside just yet. Instead, I walked to the front porch with Roy and sat down and watched the limbs of the oak tree out front sway ever so slightly in a gentle breeze. Then I sighed and called my mom on my cell phone. She answered quickly.

"Hey, hon," she said. "Can I call you in a little bit? Your dad and I are arguing about where to go for dinner tonight."

I smiled just a little.

"Just go to Dewey's. That way you both end up happy."

Dewey's was a small pizza chain with outlets in several cities in the Midwest, including Kirkwood, where my parents lived. Mom seemed to consider the request.

"That's a good idea," she said. "I think we'll do that."

"Now that I've prevented a fight, you mind if Roy

and I stay with you for the night? I'm kind of losing my house."

"Say that again."

I hadn't wanted to get into it on the phone, but I walked her through what had happened. When I finished, Mom went silent. Then she started swearing and didn't stop for a good minute or two. It made me feel better that she was angry on my behalf.

"I can't believe the court would just let him do this to you," she said. "Who does Darren Rogers think he is? That's your house. You bought and fixed up that house. The county can't just take it. That's wrong."

"Yeah, it is," I said. "And every time I think about it I get so angry I can't keep my thoughts straight. I can't change anything. My attorney says my best option is to get the best price I can for the property. That's what I'm focused on."

"You should be focused on Darren Rogers."

"This isn't about him," I said. "This is about finding a place to live until I can get a new house."

Mom didn't hesitate, but she softened her voice.

"Stay with us," she said. "Are you packed? Your dad and I are home, so we'll be down with the truck in an hour."

"You don't need to come," I said, shaking my head. "I'm leaving most everything. The furniture is all from secondhand stores, anyway. There's a women's shelter in town, and I'll ask if they want my stuff."

"Are you sure?" she asked. I said I was, so she wished

me luck and said she loved me. I asked her to take some pizza home for me and told her I'd be there in a few hours. After the phone call, I threw every item of clothing I owned into duffel bags or suitcases and piled them in the back of my Volvo. Then I grabbed Roy's big tufted bed and a bag of dog food and put them on the backseat. The car was so full I looked like a college kid coming home for the semester.

I loved my parents, but their house wasn't home anymore. My home was right in front of me, and the longer I stared at it, the more my throat tightened and the sicker and more helpless I felt. I didn't want to leave. I didn't want to lose this place. Some of the best—and worst—memories of my life had taken place in that yard and under that roof. I didn't want to cry, so I called to Roy and started walking up the road for what would likely be the last time.

After our walk, Roy and I drove north to my parents' house. Mom hugged me as soon as I got there, while Dad took Roy into the backyard. Then he helped me carry in my clothes and put them in my old bedroom.

It was a bad day, but I didn't cry or get drunk. I didn't need to. Darren Rogers may have taken my house, but I had a family that loved me, a dog, and a job. I had what I needed, and one day—hopefully a day very soon —I'd make sure he got what he deserved. And if I was right about even half the things I suspected he had done, he'd have the rest of his life in prison to regret pissing me off.

19

Luke was relaxing with a cup of chamomile tea in the living room when Irene came home. A mystery novel lay open on the leather couch cushion beside him, but he hadn't been reading it. Instead, he had been focusing on Detective Mary Joe Court. She was insidious but attractive and powerful. Her position and authority shouldn't have turned him on, but it did. Undeniably, she was beautiful, but he had also sensed a keen mind beyond her golden locks and trim, fit body.

He wondered how his life would have been different had he met a woman like her in college. She may have ordered him around, but she would have done it out of affection. Irene did it out of spite. Not anymore, though. That was over. Irene walked into the room and tossed her purse on the couch before allowing herself to fall onto the pillows.

"What'd you make for dinner?"

"Kendra had some cream of wheat and milk," he said. "I made a hash with potatoes, eggs, and leftover steak."

"Be a dear and go warm mine up," she said, slipping off her shoes. "I'm tired."

He picked up his book and pretended to read.

"You don't have any," he said. "Had you been home when I was cooking, I would have gladly made you some. Since you weren't—and since you didn't call—I didn't. I thought you'd eat at work."

She swore and shook her head.

"I don't ask for much from you. Clean the house and make me dinner. That's it. When you're not working, you can do whatever you want. That's our deal, and believe me, you get the better end of that bargain."

He kept the book open and glanced up, smiling.

"I wish you could hear yourself," he said. "You sound like a middle-aged harpy on a bad sitcom."

Irene's expression flattened.

"I'm not middle-aged."

He returned his gaze to his book.

"If you don't think you're middle-aged, I'd say you don't understand the term."

He could almost feel the room grow colder as her anger grew. It made him smile just a little.

"What's gotten into you?" she asked, standing. "I'll make my own dinner."

He pointed toward the hallway.

"Kitchen's to the right," he said. "In case you didn't know."

"Fuck you," she said before turning and stomping across the carpet to the hardwood that led to their kitchen.

"Hey, Irene," he said. She stopped and looked at him, her chin low. "I want a divorce."

For a second, her eyes popped open with surprise. Then a wicked smile lit her face. Luke reached into his pocket for his phone and opened an app to record the conversation in case she said something degrading or rude to him. Every little bit would help during their divorce proceedings.

"Who are you calling?" she asked.

"A divorce lawyer," he said.

"Put the phone down," she said, her voice ice. He obliged but only because he wanted her to keep talking. "Why do you want a divorce?"

"Because you're mean to me and the baby," he said. "I don't think you have a kind bone in your body. Maybe you did at one time, but it's gone now. I wish I knew where it went."

She crossed her arms.

"Fine," she said. "I'll give you a divorce, but you get nothing. The house is mine, the retirement accounts are mine, and I get to keep the baby. You get no alimony, child support, or contact with me or Kendra ever again. How's that sound?"

He shook his head.

"Not going to happen," he said. "Especially when the judge finds out that you're having an affair."

She laughed and then ran her hands through her hair as she considered him.

"You know what," she said, smiling malevolently, "I guess it's time I came clean. You're right. I am having an affair. He's my third boyfriend this year, and he's so much better than you. He's got money, a job, and a place of his own. You're just a loser who mooches off his spouse."

Luke snickered and returned his gaze to his book.

"We both know who's the talented one in this family."

Her eyes narrowed as she glared at him.

"We do. Me. I'm a lawyer, and one day, I'll make partner at my firm. Nobody will stop that."

"Yeah, partner at your firm, law degree," he said. "Those are big deals."

She crossed her arms.

"I know what you're doing. Shut your condescending mouth."

"How many partners does your firm have?" he asked. "A thousand nationwide? And how many people graduate from Yale Law School each year? A couple hundred?"

Irene's eyes were flinty, but she said nothing.

"Do you remember that theater reviewer from the *New York Times* who read one of my plays? He called me a generational talent. Anybody from a major newspaper ever called you that?"

She blinked, and when she spoke, her voice was husky but controlled.

"You were a good playwright," she said. "Sucks you couldn't make any money with it, though."

"Money's not everything," he said. "After our divorce, I'll start working again. I still get offers, and I've got a lot of friends who work in a lot of theaters. The pay'll suck at first, but I'll take home at least half your salary, too."

She scoffed.

"You're funny," she said. "Nobody will hire you after I'm done with you, and no court in the world will give you a thing after I tell them how you beat me at night when you get drunk."

He snorted.

"I've never hit you in my life," he said. "And I haven't been drunk since college."

"Oh, you sweet, stupid man," she said. "That doesn't matter. By the time we go to trial, I'll have half a dozen friends ready and willing to testify that I've called them late at night with stories of your wild, drunken rampages. I'll even have pictures. You're not the only one with a talent for stage makeup."

He said nothing, but inside he laughed. This was better than he had expected.

"I'd never get a job again."

"I know," she said. "Now shut up and go to your room. We'll put this talk of divorce behind us until Kendra's eighteen. Never forget that I can hurt you. The moment I start crying on the witness stand, there won't be a dry eye in the courtroom. The world will forever know Luke Glasman, the celebrated, sensitive playwright, as a man who beats his wife. You'll never see your daughter again, you'll never work...your friends will abandon you, too. I'll make sure of that. By the time I'm done with you, you'll be nothing. You'll be less than nothing. I will grind you into dust."

He reached to his phone to end the recording. Then he stood up.

"And I thought I was the dramatic one," he said.

"Well, if you plan to tell everybody I beat you anyway, I might as well do it for real."

She sighed and shook her head. Then she laughed.

"You don't get it, do you?" she asked. "I won. You're a loser. Marrying me was your greatest accomplishment. I don't even remember what I saw in you. I wish I did. Maybe I wouldn't find you so repulsive."

He looked to his phone and rewound the recording for thirty seconds. Then he hit the play button. Irene's face went red as she heard herself threatening him. Then she lunged at him. He held her back and put the phone in his pocket.

"Nobody will believe that," she said, her voice low. "Delete it."

"I don't think so," he said, shaking his head. "I'll hang on to this. As long as you do as I say, no one will ever hear it. If you come after me or my daughter, though, the world will know you for the conniving, evil witch you are."

She narrowed her eyes.

"Are you recording this, too?"

"Nope."

Then she smiled.

"Kendra's not yours. Her actual father is a lawyer from Kansas City. I met him at a bar in Clayton after a trial, took him to the Ritz Carlton, and let him do whatever he wanted to me."

"Good for you," he said. "Now why don't you go

give your boyfriend herpes? You're no longer welcome in my house."

"Fuck you," she said.

He smiled, and she swore a stream of invective so loud and long that Kendra awoke, crying. Then she walked to the couch, grabbed her purse, and left the house. Luke went to his daughter's room and picked her up. Her face was red, and she looked so sad and helpless. He held her and bounced with her on the carpet. She put her head on his chest and sucked on a pacifier.

"It's okay, sweetie," he whispered. "She won't bother us anymore. Daddy took care of her."

After being woken, Kendra didn't seem ready to go back to sleep, so he took her to a rocking chair and sat. Her little body relaxed as the chair rocked and creaked. Luke hadn't expected the night to progress as it had, so he didn't know what to do next. With one fight, his life had changed. He couldn't go back to being a mild-mannered stay-at-home dad.

With the recording, Irene wouldn't dare contest a divorce. She'd give him everything he wanted, including full custody of their daughter. He and Kendra could move to Chicago or New York. Both had active theater communities. If they wanted, they could even rent an RV and drive across the country. They'd have the time of their lives, and it'd all be on Irene's dime.

It sounded fun, but the more he thought, the more he realized it wouldn't work. Irene was mean, but she wasn't stupid. His recording would become the first battle in a protracted war, one he didn't have the resources to fight. She knew how much Kendra meant to him, so she'd use the baby as leverage. Unless he missed his mark, she'd admit to an affair, but only so Kendra's biological father would come forward and assert a custody claim. As much as Luke loved his daughter, he had no real claim on her if she wasn't his biological child.

To prevent that, he had only one option. He sighed and looked down to his daughter.

"Mommy made herself a target," he said in a soft, singsong voice. "Yes, she did. Yes, she did. Daddy will burn her alive. Oh, yes he will."

The baby looked up, spit out her pacifier, and giggled as she reached for his nose. He kissed her hand and knew he had made the right choice. Irene had to die. It was the only way to keep his daughter. Plus, they'd both enjoy hearing her scream. That's what life was about. Family and fun.

Once Kendra's eyes started closing, he carried her to her crib and tucked her in.

"Good night, sweet girl," he whispered. "May angels watch over you and carry us both beneath their wings."

He closed the door and walked to the kitchen table. He had a murder to plan.

20

Roy and I stayed in my old bedroom at the end of the hall on the second floor of my parents' home. It had been nearly fourteen years ago when I moved into this house. The first day, I installed a deadbolt and a chain lock to keep everyone out while I slept. The door still held my modifications, but I doubted anyone had used them in years. I appreciated that my parents had kept them, though. They reminded me of how far I had come.

Roy and I went to bed at eleven. I slept well, but as he had a tendency to do, the dog woke me up early in the morning by licking my face and shaking the bed. I took him downstairs so he could go outside, but I found my dad in the dining room, already drinking a cup of coffee and reading the newspaper on his iPad.

"Hey, buddy," he said, petting Roy's cheeks and paying me no attention at all. "It's so good to see you."

Roy bowed in front of him as if he wanted to play.

"I'm here too, you know," I said, pulling out a chair. Dad looked to me and then reached across the table to pinch my cheek.

"Hey, buddy," he said. "I'm glad to see you, too."

"Thanks, Dad," I said. He smiled and looked through a big open archway toward the kitchen. "There's coffee in the pot. I just made it, so help yourself. Does he need a w-a-l-k?"

I yawned and stretched and then shook my head.

"He's okay. I can put him in the yard."

"Can I take him for a walk?"

As soon as Roy heard my dad say the w-word, every muscle in his body went rigid. He lowered himself just a little as if he were ready to pounce.

"He'd like that," I said, yawning again. "I think I'll stick around and drink your coffee."

"We won't be long," said Dad, already standing. The two of them left a moment later, and I poured myself a cup of black coffee and enjoyed a few minutes of silence. When Mom walked into the kitchen a few minutes later, she smiled at me and then went to the coffeepot before joining me at the dining room table.

"Hey, hon," she said. "Do you have to work today?"

I grunted.

"Unfortunately," I said. "After work, I'll start looking for a temporary place closer to St. Augustine. We'll be out of your hair soon enough."

Mom smiled and covered my hands with her own.

"If it were up to your dad and me, you, Audrey, and Dylan would live with us forever," she said. "And Roy's welcome, too. Doug's been researching dog breeders for weeks because he wants one just like Roy. Plus, he thinks Roy will help him find out what happened to the Baum family."

I sipped my coffee.

"Who's the Baum family, what happened to them, and why does Dad think Roy can help him learn the truth?"

183

"They were the elderly couple who used to live next door. Your dad suspects the new neighbors murdered them to buy their house at auction from their children. He can't imagine they'd just move out without telling him."

I put my coffee down.

"Dad wasn't close with them, was he?"

"Nope," said Mom, blowing on her coffee.

"Why would the Baums tell him they were moving, then?"

Mom hesitated.

"It's a very long story that involves a hair dryer and a frozen turkey. Your dad thinks he saved their Thanksgiving one year. You can ask him about it when he and Roy get back."

I narrowed my eyes at her.

"Dad needs a hobby."

"Yep," said Mom.

After that, we had a quiet morning. She told me about a weekend trip she and Dad were planning, and I told her a little more about what had happened with my house. She cursed both Darren Rogers and the realtor who had let Johnny Knockers and his girlfriend Cherries Jubilee stay without paying rent or signing a contract. I tried not to dwell on it. Given the circumstances, I couldn't change things, and if I kept thinking about the house, I'd get an ulcer. Or I'd run Darren Rogers down with my car. Either was probable.

"Did you at least get everything out?"

"I got the stuff I wanted," I said. "I didn't have a lot of expensive stuff, but there's a picture of Erin in the living room. I forgot it."

"You can call her Mom," said my mom. "She gave birth to you. It doesn't hurt my feelings."

My relationship with Erin had been complicated. Even years after she died, I still didn't know everything about her or how I felt about her. Hopefully one day I'd forgive her for losing me to the foster care system, but I wasn't there yet, and I didn't want to talk about her. I did, however, want to talk to the woman in front of me, my real mom.

So we talked for about half an hour while Dad and Roy walked. Eventually, I went upstairs to shower and get dressed. Dad was okay spending the day with Roy, so I hugged my parents and drove to work at a little before seven. By the time I arrived, my colleagues were already assembling for the morning briefing. I took a spot in front so the sheriff could see me.

The meeting was short but pointless. Two drunks got into a fight at The Barking Spider last night, and one hit the other with a chair, splitting his skull open. The victim survived, but he could have brain damage. His attacker was sitting in a holding cell, awaiting an arraignment hearing. We had also picked up two individuals for driving while under the influence.

Then it was my turn to give an update about the Flamethrower. I stood and looked over my colleagues.

"We're working the case. At the moment, we have

limited forensic evidence. The victim, Laughton Kenrick, was an abrasive man who had a considerable number of enemies. He lived at the Church of the White Steeple, and the morning he died, he shouted racist names at a little girl and her mother. Our suspect pool is wide. We do have the attack on video, and the public has supplied us with several tips."

"Have any of those tips gone anywhere?" asked the sheriff.

"To the best of my knowledge, no," I said. "I haven't been by my desk this morning to check, though."

Marcus cleared his throat from the other side of the room.

"Your suspect pool may be large, but your attacker's method is specific. Have you found any other similar crimes?"

"Good question," I said. "Nothing's been reported like that in St. Augustine or Missouri, but I haven't checked the NCIC database yet. I'll do that this morning. Anybody else got questions?"

Nobody did, so I sat down. The sheriff ended the briefing, and I went to my office a few minutes later. The FBI's National Crime Information Center—NCIC—database was a massive repository of criminal records from all over the country and included information on everything from identity theft to gang intelligence files to a list of suspected terrorists.

I connected to it and searched for homicides involving fire. That gave me about a hundred results over the past year, most of which involved house fires that grew out of control and killed the home's inhabitants. The United States had somewhere between eight and eleven thousand murders a year involving handguns, so murders with fire as the murder weapon were rare. None of the reports I read mentioned a murderer that used gasoline the way the Flamethrower did, though.

After about an hour, I stood, stretched, and got a fresh cup of coffee in the break room. There, I found Marcus talking to Gary Faulk, one of our uniformed officers. I said hello to them both, but then Marcus excused himself from Gary and nodded to me.

"Can I talk to you for a minute?"

"Sure," I said, pouring my coffee. "What do you need?"

"Let's go to your office."

I agreed. When we reached my office, he sat in a chair in front of my desk, and I shut my door.

"What can I do for you?" I asked, crossing the room to my chair.

"First, sorry if I called you out in the briefing this morning. I should have asked you in private."

"Not a problem," I said. "I should have checked NCIC earlier. Incidentally, I didn't find anything on our guy. If he's killed people before, he's changed his method."

"It was worth a shot," said Marcus. He paused. "Can we talk about Perryville?"

I leaned back and crossed my arms.

"Is the boss giving you a hard time?"

"Nah," he said, shaking his head. A smile cracked his lips. "I just blamed you for everything. He believed it."

I sighed and loosened my arms across my chest.

"Glad to hear it worked out for you. What's going on with Perryville?"

Marcus leaned forward but kept his elbows on the chair's arms.

"So, Delgado's dead. We think the guy who killed him also killed Arthur Murdoch and Zach Brugler."

"Arthur Murdoch, Zach Brugler, Vic Conroy, Nico Hines. Quite a few people," I said. "They were all on Darren Rogers's shit list, and now they're all dead."

Marcus stared at something on my desk for a moment before glancing at me again.

"What do we do?" he asked.

I uncrossed my arms, rubbed my eyes, and sighed.

"I don't know. We don't know anything about this guy except that he kills people."

Marcus shook his head.

"We also know he's smart, and he's not murdering strangers out of the goodness of his heart. This guy was a pro. He rented a car under a fake name and made several of the deaths look either accidental or like a suicide. If he killed Richard Clarke, he made him disappear."

"I'm with you," I said.

"If he's that good at his job, he won't be cheap. Delgado said Rogers was in debt because of his real estate deals. How'd he pay for a hit man?"

I shrugged.

"I don't know that we can answer that without looking at his finances. He might have had money George didn't know about."

"That's possible," said Marcus, "but Rogers is elbow deep in the county's business, right? You think he could have used the county's money?"

I paused and considered.

"Before George died, he gave me a spreadsheet that listed every payment the county had made to vendors and contractors for the past couple of years. It had a lot of irregularities, but one account in particular had problems. It was called St. Augustine Express Pay. The county funneled millions to it, and it's not clear where that money went."

"It's time we learned about that account," said Marcus.

"I was going to let the FBI handle it eventually, but you're probably right," I said. "The spreadsheet doesn't give us any information but the name and the dollar amounts involved, but somebody's got to be authorizing the payments. That means the Department of Fiscal Management has the routing number and account numbers. Once we've got those, we can subpoena the bank for more information about who has access to the account and the transactions it processes."

Marcus turned toward my door.

"I think I might know somebody who could help.

Let me make a call."

Before he could open the door, I called out to him.

"Hey, Marcus, be careful," I said. "Delgado died after looking into this account. I don't want to bury another colleague."

21

After meeting with Marcus, I went by Sheriff Kalil's office. As had become common, he seemed put out by my mere presence, but at least he listened when he said I wasn't feeling well and needed to take a sick day. He grunted and said he planned to deduct a full day from my sick leave since it was still early in the morning.

Once I left the building, I sat in my car and thought for a moment before driving to the public library. I had two tasks: first, I needed to find a decent lawyer to handle my house situation, and second, I needed to find a new place to live. Once I got to the library, a helpful aide set me up on one of the public terminals so I could work.

The lawyer situation turned out to be easy. When I had looked for a lawyer prior to my hearing, I had kept my search local, figuring that so close to the hearing, it'd be easier to work with a St. Augustine attorney than to work with one who practiced elsewhere. Now I wasn't under the same time constraint, so I broadened my search to include attorneys in St. Louis. Once I had a good list, I carried it to a picnic table in the library's courtyard.

The first office I called couldn't help, but they referred me to a boutique law firm that specialized in real estate law. Within half an hour, I had an attorney on the phone. I told her about my situation, and she paused and drew in a breath.

"Okay, Ms. Court," she said. "I feel for your

situation. These proceedings are always difficult, but your situation—because it involves fraud—is tough. We can challenge whether your property is actually critical to the RV park project, we can fight the county's valuation of your property, and we can claim the county never negotiated in good faith with you.

"The unfortunate thing here is that it appears the county followed the letter of the law. If St. Augustine wants your property, they will get it. The question is a matter of cost. If we work together, my office can go full scorched earth and throw up every procedural roadblock we can. We will fight everything they throw at us and cause their court costs to balloon. This might get them to the negotiating table, or it might push them away from the table. It depends on the individuals involved."

I considered and smiled just a little.

"I like the idea of hitting their pocketbooks," I said. "That's what matters to them."

"Well, the flip side of that is that this strategy will cost six figures, and it will lose in the long run. There's something noble about putting up a good fight, but there's also something noble about knowing when to surrender."

I should have expected that answer, but part of me had hoped she might know some secret, arcane piece of law we could throw at them—some statute from prior to the Civil War about the government taking private property. My shoulders fell, my throat felt tight, and my arms and legs felt heavy.

"I'll think about that," I said.

"I'm sorry," she said again. "It's a tough situation. My staff and I would love to give you whatever help we can. If you're interested in working with us, feel free to call us back any time of day and ask to talk to our business manager. She'll walk you through your options and our fees."

I thanked her and then hung up, feeling almost sick to my stomach. I liked the thought of attacking Darren Rogers through the court system, but he wouldn't bear the brunt of any damage my attorneys caused. My bank account was fine. I could afford to spend money, but if my attorneys forced him to spend two or three hundred thousand dollars of the county's money on legal fees, he'd just shift money from other departments and shortchange social services. Satisfying my vendetta wasn't worth hurting innocent people.

I walked back inside the library with my chest and shoulders feeling heavy. Since I had lost the house, I needed a new place to live. Until his very recent murder, the biggest landlord in town had been Arthur Murdoch. He had owned a significant portion of the town's waterfront and many of its apartment buildings, but since he was dead now and his kids were fighting over his estate, renting an apartment from them would be a little difficult.

I browsed the internet, but I couldn't find much. Finally, I went to Airbnb and looked for a temporary rental so I could get out of my parents' house. I wanted to stay at least a month so I wouldn't feel rushed into buying or renting the wrong house, and I needed it immediately. That limited my options to four properties, all of which cost five to six thousand dollars a month despite how crappy they were. Beggars evidently couldn't be choosers.

I tried calling the owner of my favorite property, but his phone went to voicemail. The second property owner answered right away and said she was in town if I wanted to tour the place. I said I did. An hour later, I had a signed rental agreement for a furnished four-bedroom brick home for fifty-five hundred dollars a month. The home was bigger than I needed, but it had a fenced yard for Roy, and the owner didn't mind that I'd be bringing a dog. That made it just fine for now.

I thanked her, got the keys, and plopped down on the sofa. No sooner had my new landlord left than I got a call on my cell phone. I answered without looking at the screen.

"So I may have done something you're not going to like, Joe."

It was Marcus Washington. I sighed.

"Oh yeah?"

"How do you feel about going on a date with a really nice guy? He's in his early thirties, and he's a CPA. My wife says he's cute."

I opened my mouth to say something, but I realized I didn't have anything to say. Then I cleared my throat.

"I appreciate that you're looking out for me, but I've

got a lot going on at the moment. Dating isn't my priority."

"Andy works for the Department of Fiscal Management, and he's got information we need."

I closed my eyes and shook my head.

"And how do you propose I get this information?"

"However you can," he said. "He and I never talk about work. It's a rule on our softball team. If I ask him about the county's slush fund, he'll shut me down. If you ask him about it, maybe he'll talk. Think of it as going undercover."

I sighed.

"Fine. What time?"

"Eight this evening," he said before pausing. "And Andy really is a nice guy. You might even like him."

I shook my head without thinking.

"This is a job, not a date," I said. "Your buddy works in an office that oversees an illegal slush fund. He might be a nice guy, but there's a reasonable chance he's a felon."

Marcus said nothing for a moment.

"You're right. I'll call him back and cancel," he said. "I shouldn't have put you in this position."

I thought for a moment and then shook my head.

"No. This might be our best shot to get what we need without Darren Rogers finding out," I said. "I'm in, but please don't pimp me out again without asking first."

He promised he wouldn't, and then I hung up and called my sister. She answered quickly.

"Hey, Joe," she said. "I'm at work, so I can't talk long, but what's up?"

"I've kind of got a date tonight," I said. "You want to help me get ready at Mom and Dad's house?"

Audrey almost squealed in delight.

"I'll clear my afternoon."

It didn't take an entire afternoon to get dressed, but it was nice to see Audrey anyway. We talked and hung out, and she helped me pick out clothes and makeup. When we finished, I stepped back. I wore a black skirt and matching top that crisscrossed behind my back. It was pretty, and I had last worn it on a date with an old friend of mine. My makeup, however, made me sigh.

"I look like a prostitute."

Audrey squinted at me and made me tilt my head down.

"If you look like a prostitute, you're high end," she said. "I think that's what you want, isn't it?"

Sadly, it was, so I nodded.

"It was good to see you," I said, giving her a hug. "And thanks."

"I always like seeing you," she said. "I wish you lived closer."

"I lost my house, so maybe I will," I said. She asked what I meant, but I didn't have time to go through everything, so I told her to talk to Mom about it. She said she would.

"You look great, Joe," she said. "Remember to let your boobs do the talking. Men like that. And laugh at his jokes even if they're bad."

"I got this," I said.

She wished me luck, and I smoothed my skirt in the mirror. I hated getting dressed up like this and then lying to some guy I had never even met. Hopefully it'd be worth it.

22

Luke hadn't seen his wife in almost twenty-four hours, making this one of the best days of his married life. For twenty-fours, no one had said he looked stupid for dancing around the kitchen with his daughter, and no one had called him a loser or a failure. It had felt like a vacation.

Now, it was nearing eight in the evening, and Luke cradled his daughter in his arms on the sofa in the living room. She looked at him and then around the room as she enjoyed her bottle. Earlier, he had put her on the carpet on her belly, and she had pushed herself to all fours. For a moment, it had looked as if she'd crawl, but her arms weren't strong enough yet, and she had fallen to her belly. It wouldn't be long now before she was fully mobile. It had done his heart good to see that.

After Kendra finished her bottle, he changed her and got her ready to sleep. Her eyelids were already going heavy as he set her in her car seat and covered her with a thick, fuzzy blanket. Cradled safely and comfortably, she'd be fine for a few hours. That gave him time to work.

He sat at his computer and rocked Kendra's car seat with a foot as he opened the St. Augustine County assessor's website. Since property tax records were public information, the county put them all online and even allowed visitors to search by property owner. Realtors and other real estate professionals could use that information to develop sophisticated databases that contained the sales prices and tax history of large swathes of the county, but for people like him, they served a much simpler but still important purpose: to find people.

Detective Mary Joe Court had insulted him and dismissed him as if he were nothing. In her view, he was a useless amateur, someone too weak to even protect himself or his daughter. He planned to show her how wrong she was.

He searched the county's records and found one for a twenty-one-hundred-square-foot home and five-acre parcel of land outside the limits of the town of St. Augustine. She paid two thousand dollars a year in property taxes, which meant her home must have been a dump. He and Irene paid north of eight grand for a half-acre piece of property.

Since he didn't know the area, he looked her address up on Google Maps so he could determine the best way to approach and escape the area unseen. The detective lived in the middle of nowhere. The nearest neighbor was about a quarter mile away, and satellite imagery showed a thick pocket of woods between them. He could park alongside the road down the street from her house and no one would see him. With luck, he'd catch her at home and burn her alive, but at the very least, he'd take something important from her.

He looked to Kendra and smiled.

"We're going for a ride, honey," he whispered. She stirred and stretched but didn't open her eyes. He grabbed her seat and carried it to the car, where he strapped her in facing the rear. Then he got his gas can, a black mask he had last worn when he and Irene went skiing in Aspen, and a black leather jacket.

The drive to the detective's house was easy. The sun had set almost two hours ago, so it was dark outside, but the sky was clear, and the moon was big. Anyone who drove by would see him, but he couldn't help that. He drove past the home slowly, just to check the place out. No lights illuminated the interior or exterior. Importantly, no dogs barked at him, and no cars waited for him in the driveway. The detective wasn't home. That was unfortunate. He'd have to kill her some other time.

About two hundred yards past her house, he killed his headlights and crept along the side of the road until he found a place to park. This would be the second house he had tried to burn in the past week. When he had tried to burn the first one—the one owned by the asshole from the gas station—his hands had shaken, and he had been so nervous he'd felt almost sick. He was still nervous this time, but his excitement overwhelmed his nauseated feeling. Muscles all over his body twitched, and his stomach felt as if he had just eaten something rotten, but if he had let himself, he would have started laughing like a giddy idiot.

He closed his door and then opened the passenger door to get his gas can and other tools. Even though he had seen Kendra sleep her way through severe weather and shouting matches between her parents, he crept along and tried to remain silent so as not to wake her. She didn't even stir.

He hurried toward Detective Court's home and then scampered across the road and up her gravel driveway. Windows throughout the house were dark, but his heart still hammered against his chest. He knew she was likely at work, but he hoped she was inside. She deserved to burn. Her backyard had a fenced-in area around a big oak tree but little landscaping. Still, the woods in back and surrounding landscape would have made it pleasant on a fall or spring afternoon.

He put his gas tank down and began collecting firewood and leaves from the area around her home. Once he had a sizeable collection, he pushed it against her home beneath a window and doused the organic matter with gasoline. Then he spread the rest of his gas on the clapboard siding. Finally, he went to a wood pile beside her detached garage for larger logs. Those, too, he doused with gasoline and laid beside her home.

Within five minutes of arriving, he struck a match, tossed it toward the burn pile, and then stepped back as flames licked the side of the home. When he had burned the asshole's home, he had been so scared that he'd run off immediately after lighting it up. Here, he stayed and watched. The flames were beautiful as they flickered, danced, and grew. Then the flames changed so that he saw them for what they were: he had unleashed a monster, a kraken, a golem to do his bidding.

"Kill," he whispered. "Destroy."

The fire obeyed. The windows cracked as the flames rose higher and began covering the interior of the home and then the exterior of the second floor. He felt alive. He felt like dancing. Luke, once a cave dweller like everyone else, had seen the light and could never return to the darkness. Tears sprang to his eyes, and he nearly fell to his knees. Irene would die next. Then he and Kendra would be free.

But first he had to escape.

He took his gas can and ran to the road where he'd parked. When he reached his car, Kendra's eyes were open, and she looked around happily. He smiled at her as he turned the heavy SUV on.

"Did you wake up, sweetheart?" he asked, his voice singsong.

Did you kill her?

She used her reptilian voice, the one he loved hearing so much.

"She wasn't home," he said. "But I will. She'll burn before I'm done. So will your mom."

Good. You're all I need.

He pulled away from the side of the road and drove past the detective's home on his way back to town. Already, he could see the glow of the fire reflected on the woods around him. The home was beyond saving. As he drove, he looked in his rearview mirror at Kendra, but she had fallen asleep again.

"I love you, sweetheart," he whispered. "This is all for you. The world will burn for you."

23

I left my parents' house and drove south to St. Augustine. The Barking Spider, a bar one step above a dive, was so jammed I couldn't even find a parking spot in the lot. My "date," Andy Bernstein, sat on a bench outside the bar's front door. I parked in the grass overflow lot next door and walked toward him, smiling. He wore dark slacks and a dark button-down shirt. When he saw me, a smile lit his face so that even his lively green eyes seemed happy to see me.

"Joe?" he asked. I smiled and said hi, and he tilted his head to the side. "Marcus said you were pretty. He was right."

I felt myself blush just a little, wishing he had said something dickish instead. It would have made lying to him easier.

"Thank you," I said. "Marcus said you were nice. I'm glad to see he's right, too."

He smiled again and then looked toward the bar.

"It's kind of loud in there, and we'll have to share a table with strangers," he said. "On the plus side, at least the beer is flat and expensive."

I laughed a little and looked down.

"Let's go elsewhere," I said. "We're both dressed, and Café St. Clair has the best martinis in town."

He agreed, and we got in our separate cars and drove. Café St. Clair was an upscale French restaurant on the first floor of an old Victorian mansion by the river. I had never eaten there—mostly because I refused to spend more than a hundred bucks a person on dinner—but their chef had attended Le Cordon Bleu in Paris and then worked in a very nice French restaurant in Washington, DC, before moving here. Audrey and I had gone for drinks there twice when she was in town. She liked to pretend we were fancy.

I parked on the street a few blocks from the restaurant and enjoyed the walk. We got a table near the bar. The conversation was awkward at first, but I led the conversation to our jobs.

"I hear you're a CPA with the county," I said. "That must be interesting."

"No," he said, shaking his head. "It's just a job. You're the one with the interesting job. You're a detective."

I raised my eyebrows.

"It's more infuriating than interesting," I said. "But you're the town's accountant. You know where the bodies are buried. Financially speaking, at least. I bet you know some secrets."

His smile slipped. I finished the last sip of my martini and asked whether he'd like another.

"No, I think I'm okay with the one," he said. "You're beautiful."

I smiled.

"That's just the liquor talking."

He closed his eyes and shook his head, then looked

down at his hands.

"That's not what I mean," he said. "Marcus is a friend, but he's not the kind of friend who'd set me up with someone else. We play softball together."

"He said that," I said, feeling my stomach sink. "It seems like a fun group."

"You can stop," he said. "You're out of my league, and nobody's that interested in an accountant's job. What are you after?"

I considered him and then looked for our waitress. She came from the bar.

"Can I get you another martini?"

"No," I said. "I'd like a Manhattan on the rocks. Use a good rye if you've got one and three dashes of bitters. Half sweet vermouth and half dry."

The waitress nodded and looked to Andy.

"For you?"

"The same," he said, flicking his eyes to our server before looking at me again. Once our waitress left, he sighed. "That's quite a drink order."

I shrugged.

"Marcus must not have mentioned it," I said. "I'm a borderline alcoholic. When life's rough, I sometimes cross the border."

"How's life now?" he asked.

"Rough," I said. "I'm working the murder of one of my colleagues. George Delgado."

"And you think I can help?"

I considered him and then shrugged.

"It's possible," I said. "Have you heard of a payment processor called St. Augustine Express Pay?"

He said nothing. Our waitress must have been watching for a break in our conversation because she came by with our drinks and then set them in front of us before disappearing again. She was good at her job. Attentive but understanding that our tense conversation required a measure of privacy. She'd get a good tip.

"I've heard of it," he said, "but it's not a payment processor. It's just a high-interest checking account."

"I see," I said. "How much money is in it?"

"I have no idea," he said, furrowing his brow. "And what does it have to do with a murder?"

I ignored the question and leaned forward.

"If my records are right, that account should have at least fourteen million dollars in it. That's a lot of money."

Andy considered me and then crossed his arms.

"What records do you have?"

"Just a spreadsheet. It's nothing special."

Andy sipped his drink and then seemed to watch as condensation formed on the outside of the glass.

"The account is a rainy-day fund. When the County Council allocates funding, we put it into that account until it has to go to a vendor. We also store excess sales tax revenue in that account. There's nothing illegal about it. When the county has extra money, we put it in there so we can have a reserve for emergencies. I don't understand why you're interested in it."

"So you've audited this account?"

He hesitated before shaking his head.

"No, but we've never had a problem with it. St. Augustine is a tourist town," he said. "When the national economy is strong and people are taking trips, we do great. During recessions, we do poorly. We save in boom years and spend in bust years. If you have a problem with that, you've got a problem with good governance."

Until that moment, I had kind of liked him. .

"To clarify, the county puts tax dollars into this fund?"

"Yeah," he said. "This year, the county ran a small deficit, so we covered that with money from the fund. Three years ago, we had good weather during the Spring Fair, so we had a lot more people than usual. With the sales tax receipts, we ran a two-million-dollar surplus that year. You should be happy. Without that fund, we would have had to cut everybody's budget, including the police."

"Have you heard of any department or county agency overpaying for goods and funneling the money through the Express Pay account?"

He narrowed his eyes.

"Why would someone do that?"

"You tell me," I said. "Why would someone overpay on a government contract and then funnel the money through an account the county's CPA can't audit?"

Andy drew in a breath and sat straighter.

"Are you accusing me of something?"

"No," I said. "If I were accusing you of something, you would know. I'm not subtle."

He stood and then pushed in his chair. I didn't move.

"I don't know if I'm comfortable having this conversation."

"That's fine," I said. "I'll give you twenty-four hours to get your affairs in order and to turn yourself in to the police. We'll be arresting you for fraud, conspiracy to commit fraud, and probably embezzlement, too. If money from this fund was used to commit other crimes, I suspect we'll be charging you with those, too."

He didn't move for almost thirty seconds as he considered. Then he pulled out his chair and sat.

"But I didn't do anything."

"And that's the problem," I said. "You're a CPA who works for the county, and you know of a major county account that you've never audited. Furthermore, it looks as if that account has been used to embezzle money for years. At the very least, can't you admit this looks a little suspicious?"

He picked up his Manhattan and took a gulp. Then he set it on the table again.

"I did nothing wrong."

"I don't care about right and wrong. My job is to arrest people who break the law, and it looks like you did. Unless you talk to me, I will send you to prison."

His hand shook so badly he almost spilled his drink. Then he closed his eyes.

"Breathe and tell me what you know," I said. "Who has access to that account?"

He raised his eyebrows and shook his head.

"I don't know for sure."

"Let's start with who doesn't have access," I said. "How about your boss? If he wanted to buy a new, expensive chair for his office, could he cut a check from that account?"

"That's not how it works," said Andy. "If a department or agency wants to use money from any account in St. Augustine, their budgeting officer submits a purchase requisition request to procurement. Then someone in procurements looks to see whether we've got a comparable item in the county's inventory. If we do, procurement will send over that instead. If we had nothing comparable, they'd send the request to accounts payable."

He paused.

"I'm with you," I said.

"Accounts payable will determine whether the requesting department has enough money in its budget to cover the purchase. They'll either approve it or ask for more information. If they approve the purchase, they'll send the request back to procurement, and somebody from procurement will actually go out and buy the thing. They're supposed to look for the best deal they can. Afterwards, they'll send an invoice to accounts payable so they can deduct the money from the appropriate department's budget."

Our department had a similar procedure before buying anything, so I didn't bother to write the steps down.

"What do you do?"

"I look at the books and make sure everybody follows the rules," he said. "It's the most boring job in the county."

His assessment seemed correct, but I didn't want to say that aloud.

"What rules govern the Express Pay account?"

He shrugged but said nothing. I leaned forward and lowered my chin.

"Think hard and speak if you want to stay out of prison."

"I don't know anything about that account," he said. "It was above my pay grade. You want to learn about it, you need to talk to Darren Rogers. As I understand it, he established it when he became a county councilor in the early seventies. I don't know who else can touch it."

I picked up my drink and swallowed it in a gulp. The rye was dry and spicy, while the bitters added complexity and a deep herbaceous flavor. The vermouth was a pleasant, complex note in the background. It was a good drink, one I should have enjoyed. Instead, I barely tasted it.

I took my wallet from my purse and put three twenties on the table. It was more than enough to pay for our drinks.

"Thank you for your help, Mr. Bernstein."

"So I'm not in trouble?"

"Not at this time, but I wouldn't make any long-term

plans right now if I were you."

He swallowed hard and looked to the table.

"I do what I'm told, and then I go home."

"I had a colleague who used to say something similar," I said. "Somebody shot him in the chest six times and dumped his body in the river. Even if you are just doing your job, you ought to be careful. You overlook a secret long enough, somebody's bound to think you know more than you should. If I were you, I'd watch my back. And I'd get a lawyer."

He asked me to wait, but I had already heard everything I needed to hear. I left the bar and walked to my car and took out my cell phone. I had turned it off so I wouldn't be interrupted during my date, but now I called Marcus Washington. He answered immediately.

"Joe, where are you?"

"Café St. Clair," I said. "The Barking Spider was so busy that Andy and I couldn't get a table. And sorry to tell you this, but I'm not sure Andy's too happy with either of us right now."

"That's too bad," said Marcus. "We've been looking for you. We're at your house. You didn't answer your phone."

"I turned it off so Andy and I could talk," I said. "Who's we, and what's going on at my house?"

"No time to explain. Just get here."

He hung up before I could ask another question. I stared at my phone for a moment before slipping it into my purse. It looked like I was going to my old house.

24

I drove without knowing what to expect, but as I approached the house and saw dozens of flashing lights through the woods, my stomach began falling, and I knew something awful had happened. Kevin Owens—one of our uniformed officers—stood in the road about a quarter mile from the home with a pair of flashlights in hand. He flashed them toward a spot on the side of the road that drivers often used to turn around. Instead, I stopped and opened my window.

"Hey, Kevin," I said. "What's going on?"

Kevin hurried to the car.

"Hey, Joe, sorry," he said. "I didn't recognize your car. I thought you drove an old truck."

"I used to," I said. "A crazy person shot it full of holes with a high-powered rifle while trying to kill me. Now I drive this."

He nodded as if he had heard similar stories often.

"You'll need to park here completely off the road. The fire department has to truck in water because there aren't any fire hydrants around here."

I straightened. My skin tingled.

"What's burning?"

"Your house," he said, his voice low. "Sorry. They're trying to keep the fire from spreading to the woods."

I swallowed a lump that threatened to grow in my throat.

"It's that bad, huh?"

He hesitated before it was that bad. I thanked him and then backed up to park alongside the road. Once I was sure the fire department could pass without sideswiping my car, I grabbed the flashlight from the evidence collection kit I kept in back and walked a familiar path toward my house. The acrid smell of smoke was strong even half a mile away, but it grew more pronounced the closer I came to the house.

As the trees thinned, the orange glow grew brighter, and the sounds of men and women shouting to one another grew louder. A dull roar filled the air. Then I saw the house, or at least its remains. The west side, the one with my bedroom, had already collapsed on itself, while flames shot out the windows and licked the siding of the east side. There was no point in trying to save it. The firemen, instead, were trying to prevent the fire from spreading to the trees.

I stayed near the road a couple hundred yards away. Eventually, a fireman saw me standing there. He motioned to the man beside him, who turned out to be Marcus Washington. When he saw me, he broke away from his small group and came toward me with his hands held to his sides.

"We can't find Roy."

I furrowed my brow, not understanding what he was saying.

"I'm sorry, Joe," he said. "I know what your dog meant to you. We looked all through the woods, but we couldn't find him."

I shook my head and closed my eyes.

"He's not here," I said. "He's with my mom and dad. We moved out yesterday."

Marcus closed his eyes and drew in a breath.

"Good."

Neither of us spoke for a moment. I swallowed hard.

"I had a photo of my mom in there," I said. "She and I were together. I was about four. It was Christmas or Thanksgiving, but I don't remember which. She was smiling. Erin didn't smile much, so it was special."

Marcus nodded, but he didn't understand what I was saying. The words just tumbled out.

"Erin Court, my biological mother, was a prostitute, but she never worked on Christmas or Thanksgiving because her clients wanted to spend those holidays with their families. We'd stay in a hotel, and we'd open presents. I always got socks because Erin thought they'd keep us from getting sick. Socks were never the real present, though. For two days a year, I had a mom like every other kid."

"I'm sorry about the picture," said Marcus.

I swallowed.

"Thanks. Me, too," I said. Before he could say anything else, I cleared my throat and crossed my arms. "Anybody hurt?"

"Not that we know of," he said. "Your neighbors smelled smoke and sent their teenage son to check out what was going on. He called 911 when he saw a fire burning on the side of the house. The fire department came out, but there aren't hydrants out here, so the truck ran through its water tank pretty quickly. They had to call for a tanker truck."

I stayed on the edge of the property but walked to my left so I could see the backyard. The fire department had parked two trucks in the front lawn and then snaked their hoses down the driveway and beside the house to the back. The oak tree around which I had built Roy's dog run had turned black, and the branches that hung closest to the house looked charred and twisted, but the surrounding woods had yet to go up. Marcus followed but gave me a few feet of space.

The firemen were working hard, and I didn't want to get in their way, so I walked back to the road again, where the heat wasn't as intense. For a few moments, I watched the house I loved burn, but then I looked to Marcus.

"How'd this happen?"

He hesitated but then looked down.

"We don't know yet," he said. "You didn't leave any candles lit inside, did you?"

"No. I haven't been in the house since yesterday, anyway."

Marcus focused on the house.

"I know you were having some renovation work done. Any of that include electrical work?"

"It would have, but I didn't get to it. The county condemned the place before construction could start." I paused and then sighed. "I'm just glad no one was hurt."

Marcus started to respond but stopped himself

215

before saying a word. Then he looked over my shoulder in the direction I had parked.

"We've got company. You want me to stick around?"

I turned and saw Darren Rogers and Sheriff Kalil walking toward us. Both men had deep scowls on their faces. I turned back to Marcus.

"Is the fire your case?"

"If the fire department determines it's an arson," he said.

"So you've got to stick around until they do that?" I asked. He said yes. "If I kill Darren Rogers, promise you'll hire me a good lawyer."

He laughed.

"You kill Darren Rogers, I'll help you hide the body."

"Deal."

The sheriff and county executive reached us before either of us could say anything else. Rogers almost had a swagger to his step. The sheriff glowered and looked uncomfortable.

"I love jokes," said Rogers. "What are you two laughing about?"

"Nothing special," I said.

"You sure?" asked Rogers. "When Sheriff Kalil and I were walking up, you two looked like a bunch of kids caught sneaking into school after the tardy bell. You two weren't planning anything, were you?"

"No, sir," said Marcus.

"We were plotting a coup," I said, almost the moment he finished speaking. "Total government takeover. The revolution starts here in St. Augustine."

"I see," said Rogers.

"She's kidding," said Marcus.

Rogers looked to me.

"Given the situation, I wouldn't think you'd be in the joking mood."

I forced myself to smile at him even though I didn't feel like smiling.

"I'm tired, frustrated, and angry. Life sucks sometimes. You can either break down and cry, or you can laugh at your own rotten luck and hope for better days ahead. I choose the latter. Is that okay with you?"

"That's just fine," he said, looking toward the house and shaking his head. Then he looked at me and grinned. "I've got to hand it to you, Joe. I knew we upset you, but I never expected you to burn your house down. That's just downright spiteful."

I held my breath for a few seconds so I wouldn't tell him off. Then I shook my head.

"If I had burned the house down, I would have removed the furniture and valuables."

He tilted his head to the side and shrugged.

"Wouldn't it look suspicious if you had emptied the place out?"

"Maybe, but I wouldn't have taken everything. I used to have a picture of my mom and me, and now I don't. I'll miss that."

Rogers tilted his head to the side.

"I guess you'll just have to content yourself with

other pictures."

"I didn't have other pictures of her," I said. "That was it. Now it's gone."

Rogers furrowed his brow.

"What kind of girl only has a single picture of her momma?"

I didn't know how to answer that, so I didn't bother.

"What do you want, Mr. Rogers?"

Before Rogers could respond, the sheriff stepped in front of Marcus and locked his eyes on mine.

"Detective Washington, head home. You're a professional, but I understand that you and Detective Court are friends. To eliminate even the appearance of bias, I'll take over this case."

Marcus took a breath and glanced at me. I mouthed *thanks* to him, and he focused on the sheriff.

"Good luck, sir," he said. "Paul Cluney is the fire investigator. He's around somewhere."

"I've got this," said the sheriff. Marcus gave me a tight smile before turning and leaving. "Detective Court, you've done this job long enough to understand what comes next. We don't know if a crime has been committed tonight, but we'll operate on the assumption that this was an arson until we learn otherwise. Where have you been tonight?"

"On a date," I said. "I spent the afternoon getting ready at my parents' house in Kirkwood with my little sister. I then came here and spent the evening with Andy Bernstein at Café St. Clair."

"Café St. Clair," said Rogers, drawing in a breath. "I know Andy. You two are both public servants. Not too many public servants can afford a night at Café St. Clair."

I glanced at Rogers.

"I took out a loan. It's cool."

"Will Mr. Bernstein confirm that you were together tonight?" asked the sheriff, his expression neutral.

"He should, but if you can't get in touch with him, ask the bartender and waitress. I left a decent tip. After I left the restaurant, I called Marcus."

The sheriff considered me.

"Why'd you call Marcus?"

"Because he set me and Andy up. I wanted to tell him it wasn't a great date."

Rogers crossed his arms and narrowed his eyes.

"So you claim you have no idea why your house is burning," he said. "You didn't hire anybody to burn it? You didn't leave a candle burning inside on the off chance it'd catch the house on fire?"

"Nope," I said. "I'm pretty well gutted right now. I love that house."

"You don't seem gutted," said the sheriff. I glanced at him.

"I don't wear my emotions on my sleeve," I said.

No one spoke for the next few minutes. My lower lip started trembling, so I bit it to keep anyone else from seeing that I was on the verge of crying.

"Just so you know," said Rogers, "this changes nothing. Your house was county property this morning, and it's county property now. Our plans won't change. If you burned this place down, you gained nothing."

"Cool," I said, my voice low as I looked to the sheriff. "Am I free to go?"

He considered me and then nodded.

"Yeah. I'll see you at work tomorrow," he said.

I walked away. My legs felt heavy, but I forced myself to maintain an even, steady pace all the way back to my car. Even though I had already rented a house in St. Augustine, I didn't want to be alone tonight, so I drove north to my parents' place. Mom was in bed when I arrived, but Dad and Roy were on the couch in the living room. When he saw me, Roy raised his head but didn't get up from Dad's side.

"Traitor," I said, sitting on the other end of the couch. Dad looked at me.

"You look nice," he said. "Did you go out?"

"Yeah, sort of," I said. "It was kind of a date."

He glanced at me and then to the TV.

"It go okay?"

"My house burned down."

Dad chuckled a little and shook his head.

"That may be too much information for your old dad," he said. I didn't know what he was thinking, and I was too tired to ask about it. Instead, I watched TV in silence for a moment before yawning.

"I'm going to go to bed," I said. "You mind letting Roy out?"

"Not a problem," said Dad. "You sleep tight,

sweetheart."

I thanked him, headed to my room, and crashed on the bed without bothering to change. I just needed the night to be over.

25

Roy and I woke up early the next morning. He seemed happy, but even with eight hours of sleep, I felt weary to the bone. My arms and legs felt heavy, and my chest felt as if an elephant had sat on me. I didn't want to get out of bed, but I gently pushed Roy away anyway and then swung my legs over the side of the bed while he jumped to the ground.

"You want to go for a run?"

He panted hard and opened his mouth in a doggy grin, but I knew he didn't want to run. He probably liked the idea of going out, though. I changed into some clean yoga pants and a sweatshirt and brought Roy into the kitchen. Dad was reading a book at the kitchen table and drinking coffee, but Mom must have been in bed. Roy promptly sat at Dad's feet and gazed at him like a teenager mooning over his sweetheart.

"I think he likes you," I said. Dad reached down and petted Roy's head.

"He knocked my beer off the patio table yesterday and slurped it up from the ground before I could stop him," he said. "He's just looking for free booze."

"Aren't we all," I said, patting Roy's back. "If you don't mind watching him, I want to go for a run."

Dad smiled.

"Have fun."

I said I would and thanked him. My mom and dad

lived in an upper-middle-class neighborhood with lots of mature trees and big family homes but few sidewalks, forcing me to run on the side of the road. It was early enough that few people were heading to work yet, but if I had waited another hour, I would have had to dodge some morning commuters.

When I got back to my mom and dad's house, I didn't feel better, but I felt tired. So that was something. I plopped down on a chair at the kitchen table beside my mom.

"Nice run?" she asked. I nodded.

"Yeah. It feels good to move. Is there still coffee?"

Dad said there was and poured me a cup. I smiled and took it gratefully.

"You keep doing nice things like this," I said, "and I'll upgrade the three-star rating I gave your bed and breakfast on Yelp."

Mom drank her coffee and shook her head.

"Smartass."

"Yep," I said, smiling to her.

"So Joe had a hot date last night," said Dad. "He burned her house down."

Mom furrowed her brow. I brought a hand to my face and rubbed my eyes and sighed.

"Is that a euphemism?" asked Mom.

"I wish," I said. "And my date didn't burn my house down. That was somebody else."

"Wait," said Dad, reaching to touch my forearm. "I thought you were making a joke last night. Your house caught fire?"

I sipped my coffee.

"Yep. Whole place was trashed. Darren Rogers and the sheriff came out to question me. They seemed to think I lit the fire, but I had an alibi."

"I'm so sorry, honey," said Dad, pulling his hand back. "That was supposed to be a joke."

I forced myself to smile.

"It would have been funny."

Nobody said anything for a moment. I looked at my coffee and took a breath.

"Somebody burned my house down," I said, saying my thoughts aloud for the first time. "Darren Rogers said people in St. Augustine didn't want me, and apparently he was right. Roy and I could have been inside. We could have died."

"Roy was here, and you were on a date," said my mom. "Nobody got hurt."

I gave her a tight smile. Mom reached her hand out. I grasped it and held it tight.

"Do they know how the fire started?" she asked.

"Not yet," I said. "The house is gone, though. I shouldn't be upset. I was losing it, anyway."

Mom squeezed my hand tight. Dad reached over and put his hands on top of Mom's.

"You can stay with us as long as you want," said Dad. "We can even fix up the basement for you. It's got its own entrance, so it'll be like your own private apartment."

I smiled at him but shook my head.

"That's sweet, but I've already rented a temporary house in St. Augustine. Besides, my employment contract requires me to live either in St. Augustine County or one of the surrounding counties."

Neither Mom nor Dad said anything. I swallowed.

"I lost a picture of my mom," I said. "Erin, I mean. She and I didn't have many happy memories, but this was a good one. Every day that passes, there's less and less of her. She was a lousy mom most of the time, but she tried some days. Someone should remember that. She shouldn't just disappear."

My throat felt tight, and I had to fight to keep a tear from falling. We sat together for ten or fifteen minutes without saying anything. Then I stood and hugged my mom and dad and thanked them for making me part of their family. Dad squeezed me tight and said our family wouldn't be the same without me. I told him that was both literally correct and kind. He laughed. Mom just hugged me and said she loved me. It felt nice.

Since I had work to do, I dressed and left Roy with Dad for the day again. Instead of driving to my station in St. Augustine, I stopped by my old house in the woods. It had burned almost to the foundation, but the fire department had kept the fire from spreading to the trees. Considering how much timber surrounded the property, that was a victory. I parked in the gravel driveway and walked to the backyard, where I stood beside the oak tree and the grave of my old dog, Roger.

"Hey, dude," I said. "As you may have heard, I lost

225

the house. Roy and I won't be back, but the county's turning this place into an RV park, so you'll have company. They won't know you're here, but I will. I miss you."

I stayed for a moment but then stood to walk away. Before I could go more than a foot, I stopped.

"And, hey, Roger, if you see Darren Rogers around here, follow him home and haunt him. He deserves it."

In a story, the wind would have blown, and I would have heard a dog barking somewhere distant, but I heard nothing. That didn't matter, though. Roger had been my friend, and I'd care about him as long as I lived.

After my trip to the house, I drove to work, sat through a tedious morning briefing, and went to my desk to check my messages. Paul Cluney, the county's arson investigator, had emailed me to let me know he suspected the fire was an arson, but he couldn't prove it yet. I forwarded the message to Sheriff Kalil. The investigation was his problem. I had other shit to do.

Luke kept refreshing his browser, hoping for an update about the fire at Detective Court's house. It wasn't a big story, but the local newspaper had sent out a photographer to take pictures. Neither Detective Court nor her dog had been home at the time of the fire, but her house had burned nearly to its foundation. The story didn't mention anything about the fire's origins, which frustrated him.

He sighed and then left the local newspaper's website to browse the *St. Louis Post-Dispatch*'s front page. The Flamethrower—the media's nickname for him after he murdered the cowboy at the gas station—didn't even make the front page. Instead, the lead story that morning focused on an internecine squabble between the St. Louis Metropolitan Police Department and the St. Louis Circuit Attorney's Office.

Luke stretched and looked to Kendra, who was lying on her back in the Pack 'n Play in the living room and chewing on a squeaky toy.

"Hey, sweetie," he said. "It's almost time for tummy time."

If she had understood that, she would have groaned. Tummy time was important for her muscle development, so he made her do it even though she didn't like it. He set a playmat on the carpet so she'd have something to do, and then he picked her up and lay her on her stomach on the ground. At first she just looked around, but then she got her knees beneath her and planted her hands on the ground.

"Come on, honey," he whispered. "You can do it. Push up."

Slowly, she lifted her head and then her shoulders. Luke smiled wider and wider.

"Come on, baby," he said. "You're almost there."

He smiled at her. She rocked back and forth before

collapsing onto her stomach again.

"You did it," he said, lying beside her and stroking her back. "You're so strong."

She reached for his hand and tried to pull his fingers into her mouth. He wondered whether she was teething. He and Irene had some teething toys somewhere in their closet, so he left Kendra on her belly for a few minutes before picking her up and putting her back in her Pack 'n Play to keep her contained.

"Daddy'll be right back."

She smiled at him, but then focused on her hands as if she had never noticed them before. As he walked to the garage, he sang a song about a baby shark so Kendra would know he hadn't left. When he told people he designed theater sets for a living, most people assumed he sat at a desk and read plays and drew pictures of what those plays might look like all day. And he did that some, but set design—at least as he did it—was very specialized construction work. He had to know how to build and frame walls, how to install crown molding and baseboard, and how to engineer a scaffolding so that it would hold an actor and the set pieces on which he stood.

For the moment, he ignored his carpentry tools and picked up the hard case containing his soldering gun. Bigger theaters had dedicated lighting designers and electricians on staff, but Luke had always believed he should learn as many trades as he could. He couldn't rewire a house, but he had taken enough electronics courses to build complex circuits to control the lights during a theater performance.

It took three trips to get all the tools and equipment he needed, but he put together a soldering station on the granite countertop of the peninsula that separated their kitchen from the living room. Irene would scream if she saw him soldering in there, but he didn't care. Kendra giggled and cooed as she played.

He looked at her and smiled.

"Mommy made fun of Daddy," he said, his voice high and singsong. "She said Daddy was a loser, but he's not a loser. Now he's building a remote detonator that will burn her boyfriend's house to the ground. Yes, he is. Yes, he is."

Burn the bitch down.

Luke smiled.

"We'll play again once I'm done."

I love you so much, Daddy.

Luke's heart was so full of joy as he worked that he began crying. It was strange to think Irene could have produced a child so wonderful. He couldn't wait to kill his wife so that Kendra would be his alone.

26

It felt as if it had been forever since I last worked the Flamethrower case, so I reread some of my notes and rewatched the surveillance video. Luke Glasman's weird behavior made me suspect him still, but I didn't have any physical evidence or eyewitness accounts of him at the gas station. Maybe I could find some, though.

I printed pictures of the heavyset man on the surveillance footage and Glasman's driver's license photo and headed out. My team and I had already knocked on doors and talked to the neighbors, but time could do funny things to memories—especially memories of traumatic events. A witness too shaken by recent trauma to identify a suspect very well might recognize one from an image presented to her days later when she was in a better state of mind. If I got lucky, I might even find a witness who saw the murder but who wasn't available on our earlier visits.

For the next hour, I walked up and down the street outside the BP station, knocking on doors and talking to anyone who passed. Nobody could help. Finally, I stopped by a barbershop about half a block from the gas station. The barber probably could have retired at any moment and drawn a full Social Security check, but he didn't look frail. His olive-colored skin made me think his ancestors came from Greece or Italy, while his thin salt-and-pepper hair was swept to the right. An easy, good-natured smile graced his lips. The shop was empty. He patted his barber's chair.

"Have a seat, Detective," he said. "You're already gorgeous, so I can't guarantee I'll make you prettier than you are, but I'll be glad to give you a trim."

I smiled.

"I bet you say that to everybody who walks through the door."

"Only the women," he said, winking. "What can I do for you?"

I told him I was working the Flamethrower murder. That perked him up.

"I remember that day," he said. "Rob Dawson was in the chair. He comes about once a week, and I give him a shave and a trim."

"Did you see the murder?"

He shook his head, and my shoulders fell.

"Sure didn't," he said. "Gas station's too far, and my eyes are too old. I smelled it, though. Took me back to Vietnam when the Army, in its infinite wisdom, gave the dumbest private I've ever met a flamethrower. Poor idiot just about burned his leg off trying to cook some eggs for breakfast at our base camp."

I suspected he was a good storyteller, but I didn't have time for stories. I smiled anyway.

"Just for my own records, can I get your name and contact information?"

He was glad to oblige and handed me a business card on which he wrote his personal cell number. His name was Angelo Giancana, and he said he was seventy-two and lived with his wife—Rosie Giancana—about two blocks away. She worked in an upscale salon in a day spa overlooking the river, so she was at work about two miles away during the attack. I wrote everything down before looking at him and smiling.

"Okay, Mr. Giancana," I said. "What happened the day of the attack?"

"It was a typical morning," he said. "I drank some coffee with friends, complained about my wife and the rent, and then I cut some hair."

I showed him pictures of Luke Glasman and the heavyset man who'd murdered Laughton Kenrick.

"Are these two men familiar?"

He studied both pictures before covering his mouth with his hand.

"I've cut the skinny man's hair," he said. "Nice man, but quiet. He brought his daughter, but he had a cover over her the entire time. I've seen the other man, too. He's wearing a fat suit."

"Oh?" I asked, raising my eyebrows.

"Yeah," said Giancana. "He ran by the shop. Fat men don't run like he did. After he ran past, Rob and I came out to see what was going on. That's when I smelled the fire. Rob pointed up the street. The fat guy was taking off his shirt. That's what made him look fat. It was an outfit. Then he got in a big red SUV and drove off."

I asked him to repeat that from the beginning, so he told the story again. My heart started beating faster.

"So he wore a padded suit, which he took off before getting into a red SUV," I said. "Was it a big SUV or a small one?"

"Big," he said. "Real big. Like the kind you get when you've got a small penis or a lot of kids."

I smiled and wrote that down, growing excited.

"And you're sure it was red," I said. He nodded. "If you saw it again, could you identify it?"

He hesitated before tilting his head to the side.

"I don't know cars very well. My neighbor's kid gives me a ride to and from work."

Maybe his client Rob Dawson could help me, then. I'd visit him next. This was new information, but more important than that, it corroborated my earlier suspicions: Luke Glasman drove a red Chevy Suburban, which happened to be one of the largest SUVs on the market. Moreover, with Glasman's theater background, he'd know how to change his appearance. I had needed a break like this.

I thanked him for his time and made sure I got his correct contact information. As I walked to my car afterwards, I started to call the sheriff to let him know I had new information, but before I could dial his number, my phone rang. It was Miriam Staley, my little brother Ian's adoptive mother. She wouldn't have called me unless she thought it was important, so I needed to take this.

"Miriam," I said. "I didn't expect to hear from you."

"And I didn't expect to call you," she said. "I need your help, though. Ian has gone missing."

I stopped walking.

"What do you mean he's missing?"

"He went to school this morning, but then the school called and said he wasn't there."

I furrowed my brow as I started walking again.

"You called his girlfriend?"

"She's in school, and she doesn't know where he is, either. She's worried about him, which means I'm worried, too."

I said nothing until I reached my car a moment later. Once I sat down in the front seat, I spoke again.

"Frank Ross slammed your husband's hand in the car door. He threatened you, too."

"You don't know—"

"Stop talking," I said, interrupting her. "Ian is missing, so we're way past the point where you get to play damage control. I'll make some calls and do whatever I can to find my brother. Then we're going to talk."

"I'm not agreeing—"

I hung up before she could finish speaking. Then I dialed my mom's number. She answered right away.

"Hey, honey," she said. "Is everything okay?"

"No, I need a favor," I said. "Ian's missing. His parents are in some kind of trouble with a guy named Frank Ross. He's never been arrested, but the St. Louis police suspect he was involved with the murder of a physician. I think Ian may have gone after him to protect his parents. I need you to help me find my idiot brother."

Mom paused.

"Can I bring in some help?"

"Please," I said. "But you have to be discreet. That's why I'm calling you instead of the liaison office. If Ian's just being stupid, I don't want him to get into too much trouble. If he's going after this guy, though, he'll get hurt."

"I understand," said Mom. "I'll call some of my old colleagues and explain the situation. We'll keep it as low-key as we can, but every cop in the county will look for him soon."

"Thanks," I said. "I've got to go."

I hung up and turned on my car. My Volvo didn't have lights or a siren, but I drove to St. Charles as quickly as I ever had. Miriam and Martin Staley came out the front door as soon as I parked. I slammed my door and hurried toward them, feeling my temper build.

"Inside," I said. "I want the truth this time. If you lie to me, I'll arrest you for hindering prosecution."

Both Miriam and Martin stood and walked inside without saying a word. I followed them in. The Staleys owned a modern, clean home with an open floor plan. I followed them to their dining room, where we sat at a table with spaces for eight.

"So," I said, "how do you know Frank Ross?"

"If you love Ian, shouldn't you be out looking for him?" asked Miriam. I let my anger seep into my glare. Her face reddened, and then she sat back.

"Don't go there," I said. "How do you know Frank Ross?"

Miriam said something, but her husband cut her off.

"I don't know him," he said. "I knew his father, Henry Ross. He was a client."

I locked my gaze on Martin.

"Go on."

"When I was young and just starting out, I couldn't be too selective about my clients," he said. "Henry gave me consistent work. I couldn't tell him no."

I crossed my arms.

"Sure. Keep talking."

"About once a month, he'd bring me a suitcase full of cash. It was a mix. It wasn't just banded hundreds or anything like that."

I thought I knew where he was going with this, so I sighed.

"And your job was to deposit that money and make it look as if it were earned legitimately."

Martin shrugged but said nothing. Miriam leaned forward.

"We were broke," she said. "That was our income."

"When was this?" I asked.

Martin looked to his wife and blew out a slow breath.

"About 1980?" he asked. She nodded, and he looked to me. "Late seventies, early eighties. He wasn't my client long, either. Maybe five years. Then a lot of things happened in St. Louis, and I think Henry went to prison."

I wasn't alive in the late seventies or early eighties, but I knew enough about the history of crime in St. Louis to know what he was referencing. It was St. Louis's last big mob war. A gangster had died of cancer, and some of his followers fought one another for control of the remnants of their organization. They blew up each other's cars and shot up a few restaurants. In the end, everybody lost. They weakened themselves so much their organizations now barely existed except as memories.

"So you laundered money for a gangster, and now that gangster's son is extorting you."

Neither of them spoke for a moment. Then Miriam cleared her throat.

"He wants Martin to work for him, but Martin's retired."

I glanced at him.

"Good call. Money laundering's illegal," I said before pausing. "So you refused to help Frank out and, what, he threatened to out you about your past work for his father?"

"He threatened to kill us," said Miriam. "Me, Martin, and Ian. We were scared. Then he demanded money. We thought if we just gave him what he wanted, he'd leave us alone. He kept asking for more. We didn't know what to do."

And Ian, being full of testosterone and too little common sense, decided he'd solve his parents' problems for them.

"Have you tried tracking his cell phone?"

"Yeah, we've got an app on it," said Martin. "It's upstairs, though. He doesn't take it with him anymore."

I didn't believe that in the least, but I didn't want to

say it aloud.

"What's his girlfriend's name?"

"Jane Brodey," said Miriam. "She's a nice young woman, and she's just as worried about him as we are."

She was probably a nice young woman, and she probably was worried about her boyfriend. Still, that didn't mean she had told the Staleys everything. I called the school, introduced myself to the principal, and asked him to put Jane on the phone. He did as I asked.

"Jane," I said. "I'm Detective Joe Court. Ian's my little brother."

"Oh, hi," she said. "He told me about you."

"He told me a lot about you, too," I said. "He even asked me to let you two borrow one of my houses once so you could have sex without your parents walking in."

She paused.

"He asked that?"

"Yep. It was a while ago," I said. "Sorry I had to say no."

She said nothing, so I cleared my throat.

"What's Ian's phone number?"

She didn't hesitate before reciting the same number I had in my cell phone.

"That's not the number I want," I said. "Ian's in trouble. Give me the phone number his parents don't know."

"He doesn't have another phone."

"I know my brother, so I know that's a lie," I said. "Since you can't help, I'll call your mom and ask if she knows about it. And who knows? Maybe our conversation will stray to other matters. Like your sex life. It's none of my business, and I don't care, but I need his number. If I have to jam you up at home to get it, I'll be more than glad to do it."

"Don't call my mom," she said. "She'll kill me."

"Then give me his real number."

She sighed and gave me a new number. I wrote it down on my notepad. Then I read it back to her to make sure I had it right.

"Thanks so much," I said. "Have a nice rest of the day."

I hung up with her and then called the dispatcher's back line at my station. Trisha answered quickly.

"Hey, this is Detective Court. I need to find the location of a cell phone. It belongs to a minor who's in trouble."

"Of course, Detective," said Trisha. "What case is this for?"

I was pissed, so I didn't hold back.

"It's an emergency, Trisha. Just do your damn job."

She paused. When she spoke, her voice was flat.

"What's the number?"

I read her the number and then waited for about five minutes before she gave me an address.

"It's within two hundred yards of that. It's in south St. Louis County. Are you working a case in St. Louis or St. Augustine? Sheriff Kalil will want to know."

"Tell him I'm doing my job," I said, ignoring the

question. I hung up and looked to Martin and Miriam. "I know where he is. You two stay here. I'm going to find Ian."

27

I clenched my jaw and squeezed my steering wheel tight, unsure whether I was angrier with my brother or Trisha, my dispatcher. Ian was just a kid, and kids did stupid things, but he needed to learn how to control himself. Skipping school was one thing, but disappearing to go after the people who'd hurt his parents was stupid. Frank Ross would kill him, hide his body, and then go on with his life without missing a beat. Ian couldn't stop a guy like that, but he might die trying.

Trisha hurt for different reasons. I didn't have a lot of friends, but I cared about her, and I'd thought she had cared about me. We hadn't always agreed about everything, but we'd respected and trusted one another. Ever since George Delgado died, though, she had been cold and distant. She assumed I had killed him, but she hadn't even talked to me about it. I didn't know whether it'd be possible for a friendship to recover from a murder accusation, but I hoped we'd find out.

The address Trisha had given me belonged to an old red brick church with painted plywood where the windows should have been. It was in St. Louis's Fox Park neighborhood. The sidewalk outside the building was clean, and the old copper gutters with their green patina added a classic, aged look to the building. Even in its current abandoned state, it was pretty. A developer would eventually buy it and turn it into condos, but for now, it was gracefully decaying.

I parked in front of the building and walked around the back, where I found Ian's parked car. The engine still felt warm. He couldn't be far, so I called the phone number his girlfriend had given me. He answered on the second ring.

"Joe?"

"Yep," I said. "Where are you?"

"How'd you get my phone number?"

"Jane gave it to me," I said. "I threatened to get her in trouble with her parents unless she gave me your secret cell phone number."

"What the hell, Joe?" he asked. "That's not cool."

I sat down on the hood of his car.

"I don't care," I said. "Where are you?"

"Where are you?" he asked.

"Sitting on the hood of your car," I said. "We should talk. Your parents are worried, and the entire police force in St. Louis is looking for you."

He groaned.

"Why are you doing this?" he asked. "I didn't do anything wrong."

"You're not in school," I said. "Consider me the truancy police."

He paused.

"You'll ruin everything."

"Sorry to hear that," I said, looking around and hoping I could see him somewhere. "Where are you?"

He didn't respond, so I asked him again. Then he

gave me an intersection two blocks away. I told him I'd
see him soon and then hung up and started walking.
Restaurants, banks, bars, and shops lined the streets. The
area had crime, but few of the local businesses I passed
had bars over the windows, and nobody bothered me. It
was nice to see.

I found Ian sitting on a wrought-iron bench outside
an Italian restaurant. I sat beside him and leaned forward
so my elbows rested on my knees.

"What are you doing?" I asked.

"Watching," he said, his eyes never wavering from a
building across the street. It had a sign outside, but I
couldn't read it from across six lanes of traffic.

"Who are you watching?"

He glanced at me.

"You know," he said.

"Your parents are worried about you."

He shrugged.

"I'm worried about them," he said. "Dad's old and
has cancer. He can't take care of himself. Neither can
Mom. I've got to do it. This guy hurt them. Now, I'm
going to hurt him."

I smiled, but I didn't like where this conversation was
going.

"What do you plan to do?"

He sat straighter before reaching into his pocket and
pulling out the grip of a black semiautomatic pistol. I
held my breath so I wouldn't snap at him and tell him to
give me the gun right away. Dozens of questions flooded

my mind, but I could only ask one at a time. So I started with the obvious.

"What the hell are you doing with a gun?"

"I'm going to take care of a problem."

I closed my eyes and balled my hands into fists but couldn't get a word out for a moment.

"I don't know what to say," I said. "This might be the stupidest thing you've ever done."

He cocked his head at me.

"Nobody asked your opinion," he said. "You can leave now."

I considered him, but then I made a choice and stood.

"Sure," I said, looking at the street. Once I saw a break in traffic, I darted across. Ian watched and then followed a moment later.

"What are you doing?" he asked, grabbing my arm. "He'll see us."

I focused on the two-story brick building in front of us. The nameplate outside said it was Ross Investments, Inc., but it didn't include hours or any other information. I waved toward a security camera hanging above the door.

"The whole point of coming out here is for him to see us," I said. "Hard to shoot a guy if you can't see him. I'll just get him out here, and then you can blow him away and save your parents."

Ian brought his hands to his forehead and shot his eyes around the street again.

"What are you doing, Joe?" he asked. "We've got to

go."

"Why? You got stage fright?" I asked. "Now isn't the time for meekness. You've got to strike."

Before Ian could answer, the building's door opened, and Frank Ross stepped out. He smiled at us and then focused on Ian.

"You got my money, kid?" he asked. Ian said nothing.

"You want me to handle this?" I asked.

Ian said nothing. I looked to Ross.

"He's here to kill you," I said. "I'm here to stop him."

"I see," said Ross. "Thank you, but I can protect myself."

"I'm sure you can, but he's a kid. He's no threat. You are, though."

Ross looked me up and down. He wore a navy cable-knit sweater and dark jeans. He kept his hands behind him, which made me think he had a holster back there. I pushed my jacket back and put my hand over the butt of my pistol.

"How do you propose we resolve this impasse?" he asked.

"You assaulted Ian's father and caused serious bodily injury by slamming his hand in a car door," I said. "Because Martin is elderly, he's a special victim, which kicks your assault to a class-A felony. I'm thinking I'll just arrest you. By the time you're out of prison, you'll be so old you won't be able to hurt anybody again."

Frank considered me and then shrugged.

"It was an accident. Martin's clumsy."

I looked to Ian.

"Was it an accident?"

He looked to Frank.

"You should be careful about what you say, kid," he said. "The truth matters here."

"I appreciate your input, Mr. Ross, but shut up," I said. "It's Ian's turn to talk. Do me a favor, though, and put your hands in front of you where I can see them."

"Is it a crime to stand and hold my hands behind my back in front of my building?" he asked, smiling.

"Nope," I said, "but it makes me nervous. Nobody needs to get hurt today. Please just hold your hands to your sides."

He sighed and held his hands in front of him.

"Better?" he asked.

"Yep," I said. "Now, Ian, did this man slam your father's hand in a car door?"

"Yeah," said Ian, his voice low.

"Was it intentional?"

"Yes," he said. "He said he'd do the same to my mom next. He threatened to kill her."

"That's just one kid's opinion," said Frank, his lips thin.

"Maybe, but I believe him," I said. "Ian, call 911 and tell them where we are and that a police officer needs assistance."

Frank scoffed and shook his head. Ian stepped back

and started calling.

"You arrest me, my lawyers will have me out by dinnertime."

"That's often how it works," I said. "On the other hand, you could reach for the pistol behind your back. We could solve this right now."

"How do you think that'd work out for you?" he asked.

"Pretty well," I said, unbuckling the strap that kept my pistol in its holster.

He considered me and then put his hands on top of his head. I heard the sirens within thirty seconds and saw a marked police cruiser rocketing toward us moments after that. A single officer climbed out. He kept a hand over his pistol.

"What's going on?"

I pushed my jacket back so the officer could see my badge.

"I'm Detective Mary Joe Court with the St. Augustine County Sheriff's Department. I'm arresting Mr. Frank Ross for assault in the first degree. If you don't mind, please pat him down for weapons and take him into custody. I believe he's got a pistol in a holster on his belt."

Another cruiser pulled to a stop behind the first one. None of us looked at it.

"The weapon is behind me," said Frank. "And I've got a concealed-carry permit."

The St. Louis cops took over shortly after arriving. I

called my mom to let her know I had found Ian. We didn't talk long, but she said she'd call off her old colleagues, which I appreciated. Frank Ross refused to talk without a lawyer present, but Ian and I both gave statements. Since Frank had assaulted Martin Staley in St. Charles, detectives from that jurisdiction would have to do their own investigation, but they should have everything they needed.

About half an hour after they arrived, the St. Louis police left with Ross in the back of a cruiser. Ian and I walked back toward our cars. When he saw my Volvo, he gave me a tight smile.

"See you later," he said. "Thanks."

"You're not going anywhere until you give me your gun."

He hesitated and then stepped back.

"It's not mine."

"Then where'd you get it?"

He looked down.

"It's my dad's," he said. "He doesn't know I have it."

I pointed to the hood of my car.

"Give me the firearm and have a seat. We need to talk."

"I need to go home."

I put my hands on my hips.

"That wasn't a request. Give me the pistol and put your ass on the hood of that car now," I said. Ian complied. The pistol was a SIG Sauer P320, a nice gun. I pocketed the magazine and checked the chamber. It was empty. I sighed. "Do you understand the shit you would have brought on yourself if you had killed Frank Ross?"

He shrugged and looked down.

"I'm seventeen," he said. "I'm a minor. It wouldn't have mattered."

"Is that what you think?" I asked, lowering my chin. "You were lying in wait to commit a murder with your father's pistol. You're a minor, but the prosecutor would have charged you as an adult. If you had killed Ross, you would have gone to prison for the rest of your life."

"But he threatened my mom," said Ian, his voice high.

"That'd keep you from death row, but it wouldn't keep you out of prison. You're the smartest person I know, but if you had gone through with this, you would have spent the rest of your life doing the tax returns of your guards so they'd protect you from prison gangs. It isn't your job to protect your parents."

He looked at me, his face red and angry.

"Whose job is it, then?"

"Mine and people like me," I said. "Now get in your car and drive home. I'll meet you there."

He slid off the hood of my Volvo. I waited a moment, then got in my car and drove. Ian beat me to his parents' house but not by much. Immediately, Miriam and Martin rushed outside to hug him. He assured them he was okay and that he hadn't done anything stupid. The latter was debatable, I thought.

"Thank you for bringing him home," said Miriam. "We'll take it from here."

"No," I said, shaking my head. "Ian, go inside. I'm going to lecture your mom and dad."

"We don't need a lecture," said Miriam. I looked at Ian. He walked inside. His mom rolled her eyes, but then her face grew white as I pulled Ian's pistol from my purse.

"You guys recognize this? Ian says it's Martin's," I said. "I found it on him. He planned to use it to kill Frank Ross because he thought it was the only way to protect you two."

"Oh my God," said Miriam, covering her face with her hand.

"Thank you for stopping him," said Martin. "I'll talk to him."

"Not good enough," I said. "Frank Ross is in jail right now for slamming your hand in a car door, but they won't be able to hold him for very long without evidence. Detectives from St. Charles will come and interview you. Ian's already given a statement to the police in St. Louis, so I'd advise you to tell these detectives the truth."

Martin looked down.

"The car door was an accident," he said, almost mumbling it.

"No, it wasn't," I said. "Hire a lawyer and come clean or my little brother will die trying to protect you. If you love your son, do the right thing. If you don't, I'll move to have your parental rights severed for involving your teenage son in an ongoing criminal enterprise."

Miriam started to retort, but her husband stepped in

front of her.

"I'll call my lawyer and go to the police."

"Do that," I said. I turned and left, wondering whether I had just seen my brother and his family for the last time. I'd worry about that later, though. For now, I needed to focus on Luke Glasman.

28

It was almost midnight, and Kendra had been asleep for hours. Luke's eyes felt heavy, but he still had work to do. He had built dozens of remotely controlled light switches over the years for theater sets, but this was his first detonator. The theory was easy, but the prototype he had built at home hadn't produced a big enough spark to ignite gasoline vapors. After that, he and Kendra had driven an hour north to an electronics store in St. Louis for a bigger set of capacitors.

He had bought what he needed and then came home and built his new prototype. The larger capacitors had worked, but they had melted his circuit, which forced him to go back to the electronics store in St. Louis for additional components. By then, Kendra had been in her car seat for several hours, so she was getting fussy. To give them both a break—and since they were already in St. Louis—he had taken her by the zoo. She liked the sea lions and the hippos a lot, but she didn't seem too enamored with the other animals.

Thankfully, the zoo had tired Kendra out, so he then drove to Delmar Boulevard and rented a bench in a maker's studio for the rest of the afternoon. While his daughter napped, Luke built his detonator using his components and the studio's soldering guns. He finished his work at about six and then grabbed dinner and fed Kendra at a deli on Euclid Avenue.

Since he didn't want to go home and then drive back to St. Louis, he had parked in a lot near the Art Museum in Forest Park and watched the sun set. He must have fallen asleep sometime because Kendra woke him up at a little before midnight. He fed her the last bottle of powdered formula he had, then changed her diaper and set her back in her seat. She fell asleep again shortly afterwards.

He had waited for this moment all day. Irene and her lover would be in his bed, secure and safe and warm. Now he just needed to kill them. Irene's lover—an equity partner at her law firm—lived in Kirkwood, an upper-middle-class suburb in St. Louis County. It was a beautiful area with lots of mature trees, nice parks, and excellent schools. He and Irene would have loved to have bought a house there, but they couldn't afford the home they both wanted. Her boss, a single lawyer who made half a million dollars a year or more, had no such problem.

Luke left Forest Park and drove southwest on empty streets until he reached a Huck's gas station on Manchester Road near where Irene was staying. He worried at first that the gas station's bright overhead lights would wake up Kendra, but his SUV's windows had such a dark tint that she didn't even stir. He filled his five-gallon red gas can, paid with a ten-dollar bill inside, and then turned south down Dickson Street.

Irene's lover owned a beautiful two-story Victorian home with a wide front porch and white clapboard siding with black trim. Though her boyfriend was single, his home likely had five or six bedrooms and a yard big enough for a massive child's play set and every toy a little boy or girl could want. The homes nearby were of a similar size and age. Luke had followed his wife there a few weeks ago. He didn't care that she was having an affair, but he had wanted to see whether her boyfriend had looked like Kendra. He hadn't.

Eventually—after turning around twice because he made wrong turns—he neared the lawyer's street. Then his heart fell, and he gasped.

The flashing red and white lights from three massive fire trucks illuminated the night with pops of color like firecrackers, while marked Kirkwood police SUVs blocked drivers from turning down the road. Flames engulfed the lawyer's home and sent a plume of smoke into the sky. The acrid smell of burning insulation and other building materials filled the area. In the backseat, Kendra sputtered and then woke.

He slowed, then stopped and covered his mouth. A police officer walked toward his car. Luke was so taken with the fire that he didn't even think to open his window until the officer knocked and smiled at him. Luke fumbled with the button and then took a breath to calm himself.

"Evening, sir," said the officer. "Do you live around here?"

Kendra made a whiny noise. The cop shined his light back there but then pointed it down again when he saw the back of her car seat.

"No," said Luke, thinking quickly. "My daughter and I are out for a drive. The car soothes her when she's having a rough night. What happened?"

"A house fire," he said. "The firemen are working on it now. Since you don't live around here, why don't you head back home? I'd hate for your little girl to inhale smoke."

"Yeah," said Luke. "Thanks, Officer. Have a good night."

The officer said likewise and stepped away from the car. Luke drove home almost in a daze. When he got there, he parked in the garage and took Kendra inside. She fussed a little, but he rocked her until she calmed down. Then he put her in her crib, so she could talk herself to sleep. Afterwards, he poured himself a drink and sat in the dark in his living room, wondering what to do. Before he could decide anything, someone rapped on the front door, hard enough to make him jump.

He couldn't remember anyone knocking on his door in the middle of the night before, so he grabbed his cell phone in case he had to dial 911. As he walked, he flicked on lights. On his porch, he found two men in suits. Both of them held badges up as soon as they saw him.

"Yes?" he asked.

"I'm Detective Gabe Freshwater of the Kirkwood Police Department. My partner is Miguel Chavez. Are you Luke Glasman?"

Luke nodded, and the two detectives looked at one another. Chavez sighed. Freshwater gave him a tight, almost pained smile.

"I have some news to deliver, and I think it'd be best if we came inside and sat down."

"She's dead, isn't she?" asked Luke, his voice soft.

The tight smile left Freshwater's face, and he raised his eyebrows.

"Excuse me?"

"My wife," said Luke. "She hasn't been home for a few days. You wouldn't have come from Kirkwood to tell me she was alive. Was it a car accident?"

"It might be easier if we were inside, sir," said Chavez.

"My daughter's asleep. I don't want to wake her up," he said, gesturing to the patio set on the porch. "We can sit here and talk."

So the three men sat. No one spoke at first. Then Detective Freshwater locked eyes on him.

"We found your wife's car in the driveway of a home in Kirkwood this evening. Did she have family in the area?"

"No," said Luke. "I think her boyfriend lived there. They were both lawyers. What happened?"

"There was a fire," said Chavez. "The fire department found two bodies. Your wife's car was in the driveway. I'm sorry."

Luke swallowed. His eyes felt hot, and the world seemed to move slowly. He leaned forward and rested his elbows on his knees. Then Detective Freshwater cleared his throat. Luke looked up.

"This is difficult, we know, but we need to talk," said Freshwater. Luke's hands trembled, so he balled them into fists. "Where were you this evening?"

Luke thought and blinked.

"I was with my baby," he said. "She's asleep now. We went to an electronics store in St. Louis this morning, and then we went to the zoo. I had dinner at a deli in the Central West End in St. Louis and fed her a bottle there. After that, we drove around for a while because that helps her fall asleep."

"When did you get home?" asked Freshwater.

Luke shook his head and shrugged.

"I don't know. Kendra fell asleep in the car. I was afraid that if I went straight home, she'd wake up and be up all night."

Freshwater wrote that down on a notepad. Chavez leaned forward and rested his elbows on his knees, just as Luke had.

"Can you tell us about your wife?" he asked. "Would anyone want to harm her?"

"She was a lawyer, and she worked long hours," he said. "We didn't talk about her work. She was a good lawyer, though, and won more cases than she lost. She's got a lot of enemies. You'd have to talk to her coworkers about that."

Chavez looked him up and down, then leaned back and crossed his arms.

"You knew she had a boyfriend."

It wasn't a question, but Luke nodded anyway.

"Yes."

"How'd that make you feel?"

"How do you think?" asked Luke. "She was my wife, and she was having an affair. It hurt. Why do you ask?"

The two detectives looked to one another. Freshwater cocked his head to the side and gave Luke a neutral expression.

"There are indications that the fire was intentional," he said. "The arson investigator is still working, but he found what appear to be multiple ignition points outside the building."

Luke brought his hands to his face and rubbed his eyes before looking at the two detectives.

"I don't know anything, and I can't help you. Sorry."

Chavez stood. Freshwater did likewise. Then he reached for his wallet and handed Luke a business card.

"I'm sorry for your loss, Mr. Glasman," he said. "If you think of anything or have questions about your wife's death, call me. I've got my cell phone with me twenty-four hours a day."

Luke thanked both men. After they had left, he went back inside and pressed his back to the wall beside the front door. Gravity took over, and he slid down. Everyone Irene had ever met would have wanted her dead, but he hadn't killed her. As her cuckold husband, though, he was the obvious suspect. This could be really bad.

Then again, maybe not.

He hadn't killed Irene, but with her dead, he could

start over. The police would investigate and learn that Irene had enemies on every corner, and then they'd find her murderer. He might even get on TV. That'd be fun. He and Kendra could move to Chicago or New York, and he could get a decent job in the theater. Maybe he could even write again.

Before he realized it, Luke smiled.

"Ding, dong, the witch is dead," he said. A weight seemed to lift from him, and he laughed. It was over. He and Kendra were free.

29

I woke up in an unfamiliar bed in an unfamiliar home the next morning. It had been my first night in the place I rented in St. Augustine, and I wished I had just stayed in Kirkwood with my parents and my dog.

My afternoon after leaving the Staleys' house yesterday had been long, boring, and pointless. Angelo Giancano, the barber from St. Augustine, had said a client —Rob Dawson—had been with him when the Flamethrower ran past and removed his padded suit. He hadn't mentioned that this client was an elderly man who lived in the dementia unit of an upscale assisted living center in St. Augustine. Dawson was polite and tried to help, but I couldn't trust his memory. By the time I finished interviewing him, the sun had already set on a crappy day.

I yawned and stretched and sat up in bed. Roy was at my parents' house, so I had my rental home to myself. For a few moments, I just stayed still and enjoyed the quiet solitude. Then I stretched, changed, and went for a run around my new neighborhood. I got a few awkward waves from people who were probably wondering why a strange woman was running through their neighborhood at six in the morning, but they'd get used to me. And if they didn't, I didn't care. I didn't plan to stay in the neighborhood long.

After my run, I got ready for my day and went into

work, where I sat through a pointless morning briefing before going to my office. According to my voicemail, Detective Gabe Freshwater of the Kirkwood Police Department had called me in the middle of the night to ask about Luke Glasman. I called his cell phone and leaned back on my chair. After four rings, he answered with a tired hello.

"Morning," I said. "Sorry to call you so early, but this is Detective Mary Joe Court with the St. Augustine County Sheriff's Department. I'm returning your call."

The detective yawned.

"Yeah," he said. "I called your station last night to let you know we had a job in the county, and your dispatcher said you were already familiar with Mr. Glasman."

"Oh, yeah," I said. "We go back."

"Please tell," said Freshwater. "His wife died last night in Kirkwood, and we're wondering whether he's good for it."

I sat straighter and drew in a surprised breath.

"How'd she die?"

"Fire at her boyfriend's house," he said. "The fire department's arson investigator found two distinct points of origin. It looks like an arsonist placed a flammable substance in buckets outside two windows and lit them up. The fire crawled up the wall, broke the windows, and reached the building's rafters. The entire place went up fast. Somebody screwed the front door, back door, and first-floor windows shut, so the fire department had to break in."

"Huh," I said, leaning back again and thinking. "So it's a murder. You'd think the homeowner would have noticed somebody screwing the doors shut."

"The home was recently renovated, so it was well insulated. That would have dampened the sound. Plus cordless screw guns are a lot quieter than a hammer and nails. Mr. Glasman ever done any construction?"

I tucked a stray hair behind my ear and drew in a breath.

"He's a professional theater set designer, so he's probably a good carpenter," I said. I paused. "I can't prove it yet, but I'm building a circumstantial case tying him to the murder of a guy named Laughton Kenrick. There's a good chance Mr. Glasman is the Flamethrower, so burning his wife to death wouldn't be out of character for him."

"I'm glad you called," said Freshwater, his voice growing brighter. "How's your schedule today? We should meet and swap notes."

"Let me talk to my boss," I said. "He's prickly about things. I'll call you back in a few minutes."

Freshwater agreed, so I walked to the sheriff's office. He was on the phone with somebody, but he got off quickly. I filled him in on my phone call with Detective Freshwater, and he leaned back.

"You sure like to stick your nose in other people's business, don't you, Joe?"

"I'm working a case and following the evidence," I said. "If you don't want me doing my job, just say so."

He leaned back but said nothing. Then I raised my eyebrows and smiled. Finally, he sighed.

"Go on," he said. "If you don't find anything, though, don't bill the county for the gas you wasted getting there."

I wanted to remind him my employment contract required the county to pay me back for work-related expenses, but that wouldn't have helped anything. Instead, I left the room without saying anything and called Detective Freshwater to let him know I was on my way. The drive was easy, and I arrived at the police station—a squat brick building near a public park—a little over an hour after my phone call.

Freshwater came out a few minutes after I arrived. He was probably fifty and had thinning brown hair and a day's worth of growth on his chin. He carried a cup of coffee.

"Sorry about the wait," he said. "It's been a long night, and I was updating my lieutenant on the case."

I told him I understood. The detective and I then walked to his small office where I explained my investigation into the Flamethrower and how it had led me to Glasman. Freshwater took notes and asked a few questions, but mostly he sat and listened.

"You searched Glasman's house for the padded suit yet?"

"I didn't think I had enough for a search warrant, and I didn't want to tip him off by asking him to let me search."

"Gotcha," said Freshwater. He sighed. "We're still early in our investigation, but my partner and I talked to some of our victim's neighbors last night. Nobody seemed to see anything, but Miguel and I will recanvass the area later. It's a nice neighborhood, so somebody's bound to have surveillance cameras. Since you've seen fires you suspect Glasman has lit, I thought we could go by the fire here and see if there are any similarities."

I agreed, so we took separate cars to the former home of Jeff DeMille, Irene Glasman's lover. As expected, he had lived on a beautiful street with expansive yards, mature trees, and oversized historic homes. I had worn a thick sweater and coat this morning, and I was glad for both as I stepped out of my car half a block from the now destroyed home. Freshwater had parked in front of me.

I didn't need to go any closer to the house to know we'd likely find very little of value inside. A few blackened timbers protruded from the foundation, but most of the home was gone. Deep, muddy tracks crisscrossed the front yard from the firefighters' equipment, and an acrid smell hung heavy over the neighborhood. Freshwater's officers had strung yellow crime-scene tape across the sidewalk to keep civilians away.

We walked toward the remnants of the home without saying anything. It was an ugly scene made uglier by the knowledge that two people had died inside the home. When we reached the edge of the lawn, Freshwater held the crime scene tape for me so I could walk beneath. This was the second time I had approached a home burned to the foundation in recent days. It felt like a tomb.

"There's not a lot standing, but the western wall has two windows that are still intact," said Freshwater. "Both windows have a screw in them to hold them shut. There's a basement door around back that's still standing, and it has three screws in it holding it shut. My partner and I talked to the neighbors to the west, and they said Mr. DeMille's housekeeper liked to keep the windows open in good weather to air out the house. So the screws were new.

"Our forensic team extracted screws from other windows that had burned. If we find a screw gun in Mr. Glasman's possession, we'll see if they're a match."

I agreed and walked around the building.

"Why didn't Mrs. Glasman or Mr. DeMille break a window and escape that way?"

Freshwater followed me.

"Probably couldn't. Mr. DeMille renovated the home recently and installed impact-resistant windows. He could have hit them with a brick, and they wouldn't have broken. Homeowners don't typically put them in around here, but they're required by code in areas that get frequent hurricanes. The firefighters had a hell of a time getting in."

I glanced at Freshwater and then back toward the house.

"Why would he put those in?"

"He's a lawyer," said Freshwater, turning his head to the side. "Probably pissed a lot of people off and was afraid they'd break into his house. Or maybe they were more energy efficient. The neighbors said he had solar panels over his garage, so he might have been interested in that kind of thing."

That made sense, so I kept walking.

"Your arson investigator said there were multiple points of ignition?"

He nodded and led me to the foundation on the east side. The grass was scorched.

"We found melted plastic on the ground outside what would have been a window," he said. "We haven't analyzed it yet, but it looked it could have been one of those orange buckets you see at Home Depot. That familiar?"

I shook my head.

"In our fires, it looked like Glasman just tossed gasoline directly on the building."

"Maybe he learned how to do it better," said Freshwater.

"Scary thought considering he's potentially murdered three people already, but you might be right," I said, reaching into my purse for my phone. "I'll take some pictures. You ready to move on after that?"

He said he was, so I took a couple dozen photographs. None would make it to court, but I could reference them in my own notes. Afterwards, we started knocking on doors. I showed several people pictures of

Luke Glasman, but nobody recognized him. Luckily, though, we found a home about a block away with a surveillance camera built into the doorbell. The video didn't allow us to see Mr. DeMille's home, but it showed a major thoroughfare that led to DeMille's street.

Sure enough, the camera caught images of Glasman's red SUV, but it came about half an hour after the fire started. It looked like Glasman tried to turn down the street, but a uniformed officer stopped him. The camera's owner, an older man with a big brown dog, played the video three times on his iPad and then agreed to forward it to Freshwater.

We stepped away from the house.

"Why would Glasman drive by half an hour after the fire started?" I asked.

"To see his handiwork?" asked Freshwater.

He wouldn't be the first murderer to do that, so I nodded.

"Track down that uniformed officer and see what he has to say," I said. "I'm going to St. Augustine, and I'll get a search warrant for Glasman's house. We've got enough open questions. It's time we got some answers."

30

Luke didn't know what to expect when he opened his door and found three women in business clothes standing on his porch, but all three looked as if they had been crying. Kendra wriggled against him and smiled at the ladies. One gave her a tight smile back, but the other two couldn't seem to muster a grin. They looked uncomfortable.

"Can I help you?" he asked.

"Hey, Luke. We worked with Irene," said one woman. "I'm Lana."

"And I'm Destiny," said the woman to her right, giving him a tight smile. "We met at the Christmas party two years ago."

"I remember," he said, nodding, even though he didn't remember at all. He looked to the third woman. She looked familiar. "Are you Anne?"

"Anna," she said, smiling and holding out a hand toward him to touch his shoulder. "We're so sorry for your loss."

He didn't know what to say, so he said nothing. Then he sighed and shifted Kendra from one side to the other. She swiveled her head to keep a close eye on the ladies.

"Please come in," he said. "I'll make coffee."

"Sure," said Destiny. "And don't worry about the coffee. We'll make it. You just relax."

Luke held the door, still unsure what these ladies

wanted. Destiny and Anna went straight to the kitchen, where they started looking through the cabinets for the coffee, while he, Lana, and Kendra went to the living room. He tried to put Kendra in her play gym, but she clung to his neck so tightly he couldn't have put her down without prying her hands away from his shirt.

"Irene told us about your daughter," said Lana, looking toward the baby. "We never got to meet her."

"We don't take her out very often," he said. "I'm a germophobe with her."

Lana drew in a breath and blinked as she gave him a tender look. He hadn't met her before, but Irene had mentioned her name a few times. Irene hadn't thought highly of the woman's legal acumen, but Lana had brought a lot of business to the firm and would make partner one day for it. She seemed nice. He wondered whether Irene had been jealous.

"Evan, the firm's managing partner, told us about Irene and Jeff this morning," she said. "On multiple levels, I'm so sorry."

He looked at his hands, playing the role of the grieving, hurt spouse as well as he could.

"I want to remember Irene for how she lived instead of how she died. It'll be hard, though."

The coffeepot beeped in the kitchen, distracting Kendra, who was trying to put her hands in his mouth. He put the baby in the Pack 'n Play on her back, and she rolled onto her belly so she could better survey the room. With all the excitement, she was active today. Maybe they could play outside later to burn off some energy.

For another minute, neither he nor Lana spoke. Then Destiny and Anna came into the room, carrying cups of coffee, which they passed around until everyone had a mug.

"Thanks," he said before taking his first sip. They had used Irene's special Hawaiian coffee blend she bought online from a planation near Kona, Hawaii. It was about fifty dollars a pound, and she had never let him drink it. His palate, she had claimed, wasn't sophisticated enough—that giving him good coffee would be like taking a toddler to the Louvre.

"This is wonderful," said Destiny, leaning forward and looking at him with a furrowed brow. "What kind of coffee is this?"

"It's a hand-picked coffee grown on the slopes of Mount Hualalai at about twelve hundred feet. Irene liked fancy coffee. This was her favorite."

Destiny smiled and looked down. The room went quiet for a moment. Then Lana cleared her throat.

"We came to offer help," she said. "Our entire firm is at your disposal. I specialize in estates and trusts, Destiny is one of the best litigators in the firm, and Anna is our director of HR."

The way Irene had spoken about the cutthroat and hypercompetitive men and women in her firm, he would have more expected them to come and murder him in his sleep than help him after her death. It was touching that they'd drive all the way to St. Augustine to see him.

"Thank you," he said. "That's thoughtful. If I'm honest, I don't even know where to begin. Irene handled our will and insurance and things like that."

"We'll start at the beginning," said Anna, reaching into the soft leather bag at her side for a thick blue binder. She thumbed through a few pages looking to him. "First, Irene had a retirement account through a major mutual fund company, and you are the primary beneficiary. It's worth a little over three hundred thousand dollars. Since your name's already on the account, we'll take care of everything and make sure you have access to her funds.

"Second, Irene had the firm's standard life insurance policy. The payout is calculated based on her salary and comes to one point nine million dollars. You, again, are the beneficiary. Expect that check from the life-insurance company in the next month. Our firm believes in taking care of our associates and their families. We can't express how sad we are."

Luke closed his eyes and took deep breaths. If he and Kendra had been alone, he would have danced. Instead, he forced a somber look to his face.

"Okay," he said. "That's good. I'll pay off the house and her student loans."

"You'll still have to pay your mortgage, but upon Irene's death, her student loans are canceled, and the debt is discharged," said Lana. "I can take care of the paperwork for that."

He brought a hand to his face, wondering why he hadn't killed her years ago.

"I'd appreciate that," he said.

"This is probably best left for future conversations," said Destiny, "but if you'd like to consider filing a wrongful-death suit against your spouse's murderer, we can talk about that, too. That's far in the future, though."

"Okay," he said.

The ladies went quiet. Destiny and Lana looked to Anna. Luke wondered whether they had rehearsed this before coming over.

"The circumstances of Irene's death are difficult," said Anna before pausing. "This is unfair of us to ask, but the firm would be very appreciative if we could keep the nature of your spouse's death quiet."

At first, he didn't realize what they meant. Then he drew in a short breath.

"By the circumstances of her death, you mean that someone murdered her while she was in her boss's house in the middle of the night?" he asked.

Lana drew in a breath.

"Yes," she said. "If you'd be willing to sign a nondisclosure agreement about the affair, the firm would thank you with a check for two hundred and fifty thousand dollars."

"I see," he said before clearing his throat and standing. His three guests stood. Kendra cooed from the Pack 'n Play. "I'll consider your offer."

"Please do," said Lana. Before they left, Anna handed him the binder, and Destiny gave him her business card. Lana gave him a brief but awkward hug.

Once their car disappeared, he walked back to the living room and picked up his daughter.

"We're rich, honey," he whispered. She giggled and reached for his nose. "Yes, we are. Yes, we are."

In his hurry to kill Irene, he hadn't once given thought to how much money her death would bring him. With the insurance payout, he could buy a decent place to live in New York and send Kendra to private school, he could go back to school and work on a PhD...he could even write a new play and fund a performance of his own show.

Before he could start planning, though, he needed to check their bank and retirement accounts. He carried Kendra to the master bedroom and set her on the floor beside the bed. Irene had handled the household finances on her computer, but she hadn't had a great memory and had written her passwords on a piece of paper she'd kept in a filing cabinet in their closet.

Luke leafed through old tax returns and W2s before coming across a very thick hanging folder labeled *Life Insurance*. The size made him pause. Irene had a policy through work, but Luke made so little money as a freelancer that it made no sense to purchase a policy to cover the five to ten thousand dollars he provided the family each year. Irene would have some paperwork, but she shouldn't have had hundreds of pages.

He pulled the contents of the folder out and carried them to the bed. Kendra rolled on the floor toward him, so he picked her up and set her on his hip as he leafed through the documents. The more he saw, the more his heart pounded and the weaker his legs felt. This wasn't right. Something was wrong here.

He separated the documents into distinct piles and then stepped back. Kendra tried to stick her fingers in his nose, but he pulled her hands away and swore under his breath. If he could believe those documents, he had taken out five life insurance policies against his wife in the past six months. Kendra was the sole beneficiary in each policy. He flipped through the pages, his fingers trembling. He found a signature on each. It was his name, but Irene's handwriting .

"You witch," he whispered.

One life insurance policy was fine. Even two would have made sense. This was too many, though. He looked through the fine print and added the figures in his head. Between the five policies he had found and Irene's policy from work, he and Kendra were due fourteen million dollars.

No one would believe he was innocent. It was like that evil hag was reaching from the grave to strangle him. The police already suspected he killed his wife, so these policies would be like chum in the shark tank. He needed to talk to a lawyer. This was bad.

31

I drove back to my station and started writing a search warrant affidavit for Luke Glasman's house, but the more I wrote, the thinner my case seemed. I had some odd remarks he had made to me, video putting his SUV near the BP station around the time of Laughton Kenrick's death, and a disparaging letter Glasman had written to the Church of the White Steeple, but I had no physical evidence or witness statements tying him to the crime. That was a serious problem.

Aside from my lack of evidence, we had another problem as well. Even if I got a search warrant for Glasman's house, and even if we found a padded suit amongst his belongings, he'd claim he had it for theater productions and that we had only caught his SUV on video near the BP station because he lived a few miles from it.

I had investigated a lot of serious felonies over the years, and I had sent a lot of bad guys to prison. The more I worked this case, though, the more I doubted I'd close it. Whether through genius or dumb luck, the Flamethrower had chosen a murder weapon that was both effective and impossible to trace. He was also smart enough to wear gloves, to park outside areas with surveillance cameras, and to disguise his identity. Usually, I closed cases when criminals made stupid mistakes. The Flamethrower had made none.

I walked to the break room and got a cup of coffee, more to give myself time to think than because I needed a drink. My investigation so far hadn't gotten me anywhere, which meant I needed to start over and try something new. Maybe I could get the receipts from the gas station from the hours before Laughton Kenrick's death and interview the customers. The Flamethrower had planned his attack. Maybe somebody saw something suspicious.

Before I could return to my office, my cell phone rang.

"This is Detective Joe Court," I said, answering without looking at the screen first.

"Detective, this is Joey. You gave me your business card a few weeks ago."

The voice was breathless. I didn't recognize it.

"Okay," I said, pushing open my door and setting my coffee on my desk. "Remind me who you are, Joey."

"There's an emergency at the house," he said. "It's the one with the red brick and white columns in front."

He then read an address out. I didn't recognize it, so I scribbled it down.

"Okay," I said. "Slow down. What's the emergency and who are you?"

"Just come out."

The phone went dead. I pulled it away from my face and looked at the number, but I didn't recognize it. I couldn't remember anybody named Joey, either. Still, few people called me to report an emergency unless they truly thought they had an emergency. I left my office and hurried downstairs, where I asked Trisha to route a uniformed officer to the address in question.

"What case is this for?" she asked.

"I'm not sure," I said. "It's an emergency call that came into my cell phone."

She typed but then gave me an annoyed look.

"You should tell people to call 911 in cases of emergency," she said. "That's policy."

I wanted to ask her why she thought I'd tell people to call me in times of emergency, but instead, I forced a smile to my lips.

"Sure. See you later."

I jogged to my car, put the address into my cell phone's GPS, and then headed out. The drive took about fifteen minutes, and by the time I arrived, a marked cruiser had already parked in the long, sloping driveway of a two-story colonial-style brick home with white columns supporting an awning out front and a steeply pitched roof. The front yard was five or six acres, and the home was set back from the road on a hill.

I parked behind the cruiser and got out of my car. Sergeant Bob Reitz started walking when he saw me.

"Hey, Joe," he said. "What's the story? Why are we at Darren Rogers's place?"

I straightened.

"I didn't realize we were," I said. "You gone in yet?"

"I walked around, but the house looks secure," he said. "Are we at the right place?"

"This is the address the caller gave," I said. "I didn't recognize his name or voice, so this might be a prank. Let's knock on the door and see if anybody's home."

Bob and I walked to the portico. It was a beautiful, sprawling home with boxwoods and holly bushes along the foundation. Big mulched flower beds protruded into the front lawn, but at this time of year, no flowers grew. Azaleas flanked the front door. It would have been beautiful in the spring and summer, but winter had given it an austere look.

I knocked on the door and then rang the bell, but nobody answered. About thirty seconds later, I did it again.

"Sheriff's department," I said. "Anybody home?"

When nobody answered again, I looked to Bob.

"You sure this is Darren Rogers's home?" I asked. He nodded, so I took out my phone and dialed the only number I had for the county executive. His assistant answered and said Rogers had received a phone call an hour ago and then gone home. Since he had appointments backing up, she had called him fifteen minutes ago, but he hadn't answered. She was worried, but she hadn't called the police yet. I thanked her and hung up. "His assistant says he came home an hour ago and isn't answering his cell phone."

"Why isn't he answering the door?"

"That's a good question," I said, reaching for the doorbell. I rang it about ten times. Then I sighed, stepped back, and looked to Bob. "You said you walked around?"

"Yeah. None of the windows were open, and every door was locked."

I considered the door and sighed.

"If he's in there, and this is an emergency, we can't leave."

"He'll be pissed if he and his wife went out for brunch, and we kick his door down."

He was right, so I looked through my purse until I found the soft leather pouch in which I kept my lock pick set.

"Do me a favor and call Trisha. She might get an alarm at the house soon."

He agreed and called our station to let them know we were breaking into the home, and I knelt in front of the door and got to work. I didn't get the chance to pick locks on a day-to-day basis, but I did it often enough to keep my skills up. Where a trained locksmith could unlock a deadbolt within seconds, though, it took me a few minutes. Eventually, I got it open and stood.

"This will be embarrassing if we find him in the shower," said Bob.

"Yep," I said. "It'll be a lot worse, though, if he's had a stroke and we stay outside to save him embarrassment."

He pounded on the door.

"Sheriff's department," he said. "We're coming in."

We waited another thirty seconds, but nobody called out. I pushed open the door, gasped, and stepped back. Bob straightened and then reached for his phone.

"Check him out," he said. "I'm calling this in."

I strode inside. Rogers had an enormous two-story foyer with a curving staircase that led to a second-floor landing. The county councilor hung from the banister. His body was limp, and his face was gray. A foul odor filled the air. Even without touching him, I knew he was dead. If he had been alive, he would have been kicking and reaching for the rope.

I stepped back and brought my hand to my face. Then I remembered something. Darren Rogers hadn't come home to kill himself; he had come home because he received a call. I brought my hand down to my holster, but before I could draw my pistol, something heavy thudded into my back, knocking me forward. I would have fallen, but a cord around my neck held me on my feet. In an instant, it tightened, and I gasped.

Instantly, my training kicked in. I pivoted my hips and stepped back, trying to face my attacker and create some separation between us. Instead, he tightened the cord on my neck, wrapped an arm around my waist, and tripped me. I couldn't even brace myself. The side of my face thumped into the dark hardwood, and a knee pressed into my back. For a split second, my vision swam black and white. Then my head and torso were jerked upright by the force on the cord around my throat.

I couldn't breathe, so I acted on instinct and flailed my arms, hoping to catch my attacker with an elbow. With every move I made, though, my attacker gained leverage and cinched the cord tighter. My arms burned with exhaustion.

I kicked my feet hard and reached for the cord. It felt like nylon, and it dug into my skin so I couldn't even get a finger beneath it. My attacker's knee pressed harder against the small of my back as he wrenched upright. I tried to scream, but I couldn't draw in breath. Then, as if someone had flipped a switch, the strength started leaving my fingers and arms. They dropped to the floor. My mind screamed, but no sound left my lips. Then I tried kicking, but my feet barely moved. Black spots began forming in my peripheral vision.

As my eyes closed, shots rang out behind me, and then I heard footsteps. Something crashed above me, and the weight left my back. I couldn't draw in a breath. My lungs refused to work. Then I saw Bob's face above me.

"Joe!"

It felt like I was underwater. My eyes shut. I was floating in inky blackness. Then something pinched my nose, and air filled my lungs. I gasped and felt the weight leave me. My eyes fluttered open again. Bob knelt beside me. He had two fingers on my throat and stared at his watch. I drew in another breath of fresh air, and the fog left my vision. He took his fingers from my throat.

"You just stay there," he said. "Paramedics are already on the way. Your stomach is bleeding."

A lady named Nadine Kaiser had stabbed me in the lower abdomen just a little while ago. I must have torn the wound open.

"It's okay," I said, swallowing hard and closing my eyes again. I took a couple of breaths. "It's an old injury.

Are you okay?"

"I'm fine," he said. "The guy who attacked you is dead. I've got help coming. You stay where you are."

I said nothing. When I felt able to lift my head, I looked up but didn't move from my back.

"Who is he?" I asked.

Bob looked at me and then to the body near me. My attacker had worn dark coveralls, gloves, and covers over his shoes. A black hairnet covered his head. He looked ridiculous, but the outfit would have minimized the chances he'd leave forensic evidence behind.

"We'll ID him," said Bob. "Don't worry. You stay put until the paramedics come."

I took a breath. It'd take time to piece together what had just happened, but one way or another, I had the feeling it would come back to bite me. Little good came from murdered men.

32

The paramedics arrived about five minutes after Bob called them. They gave me oxygen in the back of their ambulance, but I wasn't too hurt. The wound on my stomach had broken open, but prior to this, I had been healing well. The EMTs re-dressed it as well as they could and suggested that I call my doctor when I had the chance. It was good advice, and I appreciated their help.

The sheriff and Marcus Washington arrived next. Bob Reitz had saved my life by shooting my attacker, but someone still needed to investigate, so the sheriff interviewed Bob and me separately and took pictures of the ligature marks on my neck and of the nylon cord still wrapped around my attacker's hands. I doubted Bob had even fired his weapon on duty before, so this would take something out of him. The station had a good counselor on retainer, though, and he had a support system. It might take him a while, but he'd be okay.

After interviewing me, the sheriff drove Bob back to our station. I walked to Marcus, who stood on the front lawn, taking pictures of the home and surrounding area with his cell phone.

"Hey, Joe," he said. "How are you holding up?"

"Shaky at first, but I'm better," I said. "Sergeant Reitz saved my life. I'm glad he was with me."

"Me, too," said Marcus. He looked down. "You still got that friend at the FBI? Since we've got a dead county executive, we might run into some interference on our investigation."

I considered and then sighed.

"We will, but we should work this on our own at first before we ask for help," I said. "Agent Costa can track down every link in a terrorist network and find every dollar a crooked accountant ever laundered, but murder isn't his specialty."

Marcus brought a hand to his mouth and looked toward the house.

"Okay. Let's see if we can ID this guy, then."

We went by Marcus's cruiser and picked up blue nitrile gloves so we wouldn't get our fingerprints on anything. Then we went back into the house. Our uniformed officers had already cleared the rest of the home, so Marcus and I were alone. We both took a couple dozen pictures of the entryway with our phones. Darren Rogers still hung from the second-floor landing. The guy who attacked me lay on the ground.

I snapped a couple pictures of his face and then stepped back.

"You recognize him?" asked Marcus.

I shook my head.

"No, but look at the knot around Darren Rogers's throat," I said, holding up my phone and then zooming in on the nylon cord. "It's a slipknot instead of a noose. It's the same knot that was around Nico Hines's throat."

Marcus looked and raised an eyebrow.

"You sure?"

"Yep," I said, flipping through the photos on my phone again until I found one of Nico Hines. He had been a physician who ran a pill mill in town. Supposedly, he had hanged himself from a tree in his backyard. Marcus looked at my picture and then to Darren Rogers.

"You might be right," he said. Skin all over my body tingled as I knelt beside the dead man. His blood had pooled on the ground around him, so I avoided stepping on that as I felt his pockets. I pulled out his wallet and handed that to Marcus and then felt his front pockets for a phone.

"He's got two hundred and sixty dollars cash but no credit cards, business cards, insurance cards, or ID."

"Cash but no credit cards or ID," I said. "That seems normal."

Marcus snickered as I pulled out his cell phone. I stood and powered it up.

"Phone's locked," I said, kneeling beside the body again. "Can you do me a favor and tell me if it's raining?"

Marcus furrowed his brow and then walked toward the front door. I grabbed the dead guy's hand and used his thumbprint to unlock the phone. Marcus came back as I stood.

"Did you just do what I think you did?"

I glanced from the screen to him and then back to the screen as I searched through the settings for a way to disable the lock screen.

"Do you think I just used the dead guy's finger to unlock his phone?" I asked. He nodded. "Then yep."

"That's creepy, Joe."

"He's dead, so I didn't think he'd mind."

Marcus shivered for effect but then walked to stand beside me.

"You find anything?"

"The call history has two entries. The first is to Darren Rogers's office, and the second is the emergency call to me," I said. I paused a second. "So he killed Darren Rogers and then called me to lure me out here, presumably so he could kill me, too. This guy's a dick."

"Yep," said Marcus. "Check out his text messages."

It was a good idea, so I opened the messaging program. Unfortunately, he hadn't texted anyone. He did, however, use the phone to send email. I opened the mail program.

"His email address a732334.3@gmail.com," I said. "That's a mouthful. It says his name is Carlos Danger. Wasn't that the secret nickname of a disgraced New York politician?"

Marcus looked to the body on the ground.

"So he's a murderer, and it looks like he stole a former congressman's secret identity," he said. "You know, the more we look into this guy, the more I think he wasn't on the up-and-up."

I smiled and looked through Mr. Danger's emails. Eventually, we'd have somebody in the state crime lab dump the phone's contents onto a computer so we could catalog everything, but for now we could search manually. In the past three weeks, Mr. Danger had sent forty-four emails to varied recipients, all of whom had unintelligible email addresses like his own.

As I searched through the phone, Stan Rivers, the coroner, came in and whistled.

"Oh, my," he said. Stan was a mortician, and I doubted he had any real forensics training. He didn't know what he was doing, but he was local, and he was cheap. That made him perfect for the coroner's job in the eyes of our county councilors. "I guess I'll just get started with Mr. Rogers, then. Can someone give me some background?"

I grunted and glanced at Marcus.

"Rock, paper, scissors?" I whispered.

"Keep working the phone," he said, smiling. "I'll deal with the coroner."

I took the phone to the front of the house. Officer Katie Martelle stood outside with a log sheet. She smiled when she saw me at first, but then she furrowed her brow.

"That wound on your neck looks nasty," she said, almost flinching. "You okay?"

"I will be," I said. "Paramedics checked me out, and I'm good to go. Bob got the guy before he could do any permanent damage."

She drew in a breath and then exhaled slowly.

"He was pretty shaken up at the station," she said. "I'm glad you're okay."

"Me, too," I said, smiling. I excused myself and then sat on the brick steps that led to the front door. None of the forty-four messages Mr. Danger had sent contained much information, but they all followed the same template. It took me a few minutes to get it, but then I looked at Katie.

"Hey, Katie," I said. She smiled at me. "Do me a favor and go to your cruiser and use your laptop to search for Clint Knight of Arlington, Virginia."

She cocked her head to the side.

"Should I look for anything in particular?"

"Just a basic background search," I said. "I'll stay here and maintain the log book."

"You got it," she said. I waited about five minutes for her to do the search, and she came back with a quizzical look on her face. "I found him right away, but he's dead."

"Hiking accident?" I asked.

"Yeah, he fell off a cliff in the George Washington National Forest," she said. "If you already knew about him, why'd you ask to search for him?"

"I was just checking something," I said, standing. "Thanks."

"No problem," she said, sounding confused. I smiled and walked back inside. They still hadn't moved Darren Rogers's body. Marcus walked to me.

"You find anything?"

"Yep," I said. "I believe Mr. Danger murdered Clint Knight by throwing him off a cliff in northern Virginia. According to his emails, that job cost sixty-five thousand dollars and was designed to look like an accident."

"Who's Clint Knight?" asked Marcus.

"I have no idea," I said, looking down to Mr. Danger. "I doubt he did, either. Knight was just a job. Mr. Danger is a contract murderer."

Marcus took a step back and then drew in a breath as he looked toward the body on the ground.

"How many people you think this guy's killed?"

"I don't know," I said, "but I think we can assume quite a few. Among his other emails, he's got one here with six names on it. Vic Conroy, Richard Clarke, Arthur Murdoch, Zach Brugler, Nico Hines, and George Delgado. Someone paid him a lot of money to knock off Darren Rogers's enemies."

Marcus considered.

"We've got Mr. Danger's phone, but we should be able to get the IP address of the person he emailed with a court order," said Marcus. "Assuming he wasn't using a virtual private network, that IP address should give us our murderer."

"We'll call that Plan B," I said, typing an email address from Carlos Danger's phone into my own. Then I hit the send button on a blank email. Within seconds, I heard a ding. Marcus, Stan Rivers, and I turned to look at Darren Rogers's body. "Mr. Rivers, can you get the cell phone from the deceased?"

Rivers looked at the body and then back to me, his brow furrowed.

"He's off the ground."

"I noticed," I said.

"I don't think I can reach it," he said. "Usually, the

bodies I work with are on the ground."

Marcus and I both looked at him, unsure how to respond. Then I lowered my chin.

"This is your job, Mr. Rivers," I said. "If you can't do it, find someone who can."

He considered the body.

"I'll have to get my assistants."

"Fine," I said, looking to Marcus. "So here's where we're at: Darren Rogers had multiple enemies around town and a fledgling real estate empire that couldn't get off the ground because of those enemies. Based on the messages on his phone, he contacted Mr. Danger via email and proposed murdering those enemies. Mr. Danger responded that he needed ten thousand dollars to research the crimes. Rogers agreed, and then, presumably, Danger came to town, looked around, and gave Rogers the price. Rogers agreed, and Danger murdered everybody."

Marcus crossed his arms.

"Why did Danger kill Rogers today, then?"

"We've got to speculate there, but we know Rogers has a lot of eyes in our station," I said. "I think Rogers learned we were looking into him and freaked out. Mr. Danger realized Rogers was a threat to him, so he came back to knock Rogers off and to kill me for good measure to stop the investigation."

Marcus considered and then blinked.

"So you think this was about money."

"It usually is," I said. "Rogers had investments all

over town, but he couldn't profit on those investments until he started bringing in more business to St. Augustine. He couldn't persuade more businesses to come to town as long as Vic Conroy, Nico Hines, and the others were operating their illicit businesses. So, Rogers hired Danger to solve the problem. There are still holes, but we're on our way."

Marcus gave me a half smile.

"You did it," he said. "You once told me Rogers was your white whale, and you got him."

I looked at Darren Rogers's body.

"I guess so."

"I thought you'd be happy," said Marcus. "You took out a bad guy who ordered at least six murders."

"I am glad about that," I said. "The county's safer without Rogers in it, but seeing him dead doesn't make me happy. I'm just glad it's over. He won't hurt anybody again. I guess that's something to celebrate."

33

Luke knew dozens of lawyers, but they had all worked with Irene and thought well of her. If they couldn't see through the facade she threw up to mask her vile nature, he couldn't trust their judgment. That had forced him to find one the old-fashioned way.

Luke parked his red SUV on the street in the first open spot he could find and then walked around back for Kendra's stroller. A moment later, he pushed his daughter up the sidewalk toward his new attorney's office. He had never met Eleanor King, but her reviews on the internet looked good. She worked out of an Italianate red brick building two blocks from the courthouse in downtown St. Augustine.

A big picture window overlooked the street, giving him a view into her small but neat office. A rainbow-colored welcome mat rested in front of her door. It was as far from the glass-and-steel skyscraper out of which his wife had practiced as he could get. Hopefully Ms. King knew what she was doing.

He knocked on the wooden front door and stepped inside. The interior was musty, and the floor creaked. Bookshelves covered the walls, reminding him of the old third floor of the library in college. It had held legal records, mostly, and nobody went up there except those looking for a quiet place to study or to have sex in the stacks. He and Irene had made liberal use of the space in college.

Ms. King stood from behind her desk, and he almost walked out. He was thirty years old, and he probably had five years on her. Luke had nothing against young women, but he had expected someone a little more... experienced. Before he could step out, she smoothed her black pencil skirt and smiled.

"Mr. Glasman?" she asked, holding out her hand. "I'm Eleanor King. We spoke on the phone."

He hesitated and then walked toward her desk to shake her hand.

"We did," he said. He paused. "Based on the reviews online, I expected someone a little more...mature."

She blushed a little and looked down.

"I'm young, but I'm a good lawyer," she said. "I graduated near the top of my class at Washington University. My grandmother's name was also Eleanor. You probably saw her reviews. I'm taking over the practice."

"Oh, good," he said, breathing a little easier. "Is she around?"

"Nope," said Ms. King, shaking her head. "She passed away. I inherited the practice."

He hesitated before responding. The area had tons of lawyers, but he didn't know how many knew his wife.

I like her. She's prettier than Mom. I bet she's smarter, too.

He looked down at Kendra. If she thought he could trust Ms. King, maybe he could.

"I'm sorry to hear about your grandma," he said.

"Like I said on the phone, I'm Luke Glasman. My daughter, Kendra, is in the stroller."

She looked at Kendra and smiled. Kendra giggled and kicked. That was a good sign.

"On the phone, you mentioned an inheritance."

"Yeah. My wife just passed away, and I've been going through our paperwork. Before she died, Irene took out multiple life-insurance policies. Kendra is the beneficiary."

Ms. King gave him a sympathetic look.

"I'm very sorry about your spouse," she said. "A minor can't inherit property in Missouri, so the court will place the life-insurance payout in an account and appoint a conservator. Since you're Kendra's daddy, that'll be you. Parents are always the court's first choice unless there are extraordinary circumstances. I'd be happy to represent you in court and answer any questions you might have."

"Thank you," he said. He paused. "The situation is complex, though."

Ms. King turned and looked toward her desk.

"How about we have a seat, then?"

He agreed, and the two of them sat down. He had expected her to sit behind her desk like a high school principal, but instead, she sat in front of it in the chair beside his. She smiled at him. He had almost forgotten what it felt like to have an adult smile at him.

"Irene was murdered," he said. "She was at her boyfriend's house. Someone burned it down. The police don't know who did it yet."

Ms. King straightened.

"That's awful," she said. She started to say something but then stopped, closed her eyes, and drew in a breath. "I'm so sorry."

"I didn't do it," he said. "But the police think I did."

The lawyer shifted her weight away from him. He wondered whether she regretted sitting near him now.

"Okay. Did you talk to the police?"

"I did," he said. "And I told them the truth. I didn't do it, and I don't know who did. She wasn't even in St. Augustine when she died. She and her boyfriend were at his place in Kirkwood. We had a big fight a few days ago, and she left town."

The lawyer brought her hand to her mouth.

"Did she have enemies, or did her boyfriend have a spouse?"

He looked down at the hardwood floor.

"I don't know," he said. "She was a litigator at a big firm in St. Louis. Her firm and clients liked her, but I don't think she made too many friends outside her firm. She was good at her job and had cost a lot of people a lot of money."

Ms. King considered him, then stood and walked to the other side of the desk.

"Okay. In the future, don't talk to the police without me present," she said, reaching into a drawer and pulling out a business card. She wrote something on the back and slid it across the desk to him. "That's my personal cell phone on the back. If the police contact you again, call me."

He took the card and thanked her.

"Now tell me about the life-insurance policies your spouse took out."

Luke had expected that line of questioning, so he had brought the paperwork with him. He showed it to her and explained how he had found it. The lawyer considered him and then swore.

"And you're telling me you had no idea that these policies existed?" she asked.

"That's exactly what I'm telling you," he said. "Kendra's the beneficiary, but I supposedly took the policy out and signed the contracts. That's not my signature on the paperwork, though. That's Irene's."

Ms. King leaned back.

"Why would your wife do that?" she asked. "If she wanted an additional life-insurance policy, why wouldn't she take it out in her name? And why would she keep it a secret?"

Luke didn't have an answer, so he shrugged.

"Would you have stopped her?" asked Ms. King.

"Of course not," he said. "If it made her feel comfortable, I would have encouraged it, but she never told me. I didn't know she had any life insurance outside of what work provided."

Ms. King considered but said nothing. Then she leaned forward and sighed.

"Was she sick?" she asked. Luke shook his head, and she sighed again. "These policies don't make sense. If she wanted to commit fraud, she'd take out an inflated insurance policy on your house and burn it down. Life insurance, though, only pays out if she's dead, and this one wouldn't even pay out to her. You and your daughter are the only persons who benefit from these policies."

He could see where she was going, so he shook his head.

"I didn't take them out, and I sure as hell didn't kill my wife."

"I'm not saying you did," she said. "The police will ask, though. Why did your wife go to all this trouble to take out multiple life-insurance policies?"

"I don't know," he said. "You'd have to ask her."

"I would if she were still alive," said Ms. King. She paused. "Kendra is the beneficiary of these policies. Suppose your wife dies, and it looks like you killed her. Who would get Kendra?"

"Shirley Decker. She's Kendra's godmother and Irene's best friend," he said. He paused. "If it changes anything, I recently found out I'm not Kendra's biological father."

"That does change things," said Ms. King. "Kendra's biological father will always have a strong claim on her. If he wanted her and was a suitable parent, I can't imagine the courts would even consider giving her to Ms. Decker."

"Why wouldn't he want her?" he asked. "She's wonderful."

"And she'd come with a fourteen-million-dollar trust fund," said Ms. King. She blinked and then looked down at her desk. "This will sound nuts, but is it possible that

Kendra's biological father murdered your wife and set you up?"

He shook his head.

"He was just some lawyer she met. He probably doesn't even know he got Irene pregnant."

Ms. King paused.

"How about Ms. Decker?"

He hadn't thought of that, but he should have.

"Shirley's a forensic pathologist. She has access to cadavers, medical records, and the St. Louis County morgue."

Ms. King narrowed her gaze at him and blinked.

"I'm not following."

"You were right. My wife's body was burned beyond recognition, so the police couldn't visually identify her. Irene's not dead. Her boyfriend's probably not dead, either. They set me up, all three of them. Irene took out the life-insurance policies, and Shirley provided a pair of bodies. They dumped them in Jeff DeMille's house and lit the place on fire. Now they're just waiting for the police to arrest me and for the courts to give Kendra to Shirley. Shirley will collect the life insurance, and then they'll all disappear."

Ms. King laced her fingers together and considered. Then she blinked and leaned forward.

"That's a strong accusation."

"Irene's quite a woman," he said, allowing the full measure of his disgust to enter his voice. "Shirley had access to medical records and the bodies. She had it all:

motive, means, and opportunity. And this is just like Irene. She'd run away with millions, and I'd go to death row. She's probably laughing her ass off right now."

Ms. King said nothing. Then she cleared her throat.

"You've given me a lot to consider and study," she said a moment later. "In the meantime, I'll get you a representation agreement. I want you to go home and keep your head down. Don't talk to anybody. If the police come to you, call me."

He seethed inside, but he tried to keep his voice calm and even.

"I will."

"Don't worry," she said. "If your fears are true, there will be a paper trail. We can follow that and find your wife. We'll bring in the police. They can take care of this."

He nodded but didn't feel enthusiastic. For the next twenty minutes, he completed paperwork and cut Ms. King a check for ten thousand dollars. If she kept him out of prison, it'd be more than worth it. By the time he left, he felt waves of nausea and anger course through him.

After his meeting, he and Kendra drove home, where they found a white Ford SUV in his driveway. The moment he parked, two men in suits stepped out. Detectives Freshwater and Chavez. They had driven to St. Augustine the night Irene had "died."

Luke got out of his car. His face felt hot and angry, but he tried to look calm.

"Detectives," he said. He left Kendra in the car,

mostly so she wouldn't see her father interrogated.

"I'm glad we caught you, Mr. Glasman," said Freshwater. "We need to talk to you about your wife."

Luke crossed his arms.

"Did you find her?"

The two detectives hesitated and looked at one another, clearly confused.

"We found her yesterday," said Chavez. "She died in a house fire. We spoke to you about that last night."

"I remember," said Luke.

"Some new information has come to light," said Freshwater. "Her friend Shirley Decker visited us this morning. Do you know Ms. Decker?"

Luke groaned internally.

"Yeah. I know Dr. Decker," he said, sighing. "Let me guess: she said I was a monster who eats children and beats the elderly."

The two detectives looked at one another again before focusing on him. Freshwater looked toward the home, his face impassive.

"Can we come inside and talk?"

"We might as well get this over with," said Luke. "I'll call my lawyer, and we'll figure things out."

34

I stayed at the crime scene long enough to watch Dr. Rivers and two assistants lower Darren Rogers to the ground. As much as I disliked Rogers, I couldn't feel good about his death. I hadn't expected it to end like this, and I couldn't shake the feeling that something very bad was waiting to happen.

For now, though, that didn't matter. The wound on my abdomen was bleeding, which meant I needed to see a doctor. I got in my car and searched through my phone's address book until I found the phone number of my primary care physician. Unfortunately, she couldn't get me in for another few days, so I drove to an urgent care center run by St. John's, our local hospital.

A nurse practitioner looked at the wound on my abdomen and said it looked healthy and uninfected. She also said I didn't need stitches, which I appreciated. Instead, she cleaned the wound up, put a big butterfly bandage on it to hold it closed, and then put more bandages on top. My entire side felt stiff, but I could deal with that. She warned me to take it easy, but my job didn't always allow that.

After my urgent care visit, I drove to Walmart and bought two inexpensive tops before driving to the house I had rented in St. Augustine. There I changed into fresh, blood-free clothes.

As I sat on the bed in the master bedroom, I took

deep breaths. It would take time for Darren Rogers's death to sink in, and I didn't know what would happen next. Rogers had been appointed to his position by the County Council, but the county ought to have held an election. I hoped the council would call for one instead of appointing one of its members. The police department would have to investigate Rogers and Carlos Danger, too. We had weeks of grueling work ahead of us, but I hoped we'd have answers at the end.

After ten minutes, I locked up the house and drove to my station to write reports. The moment she saw me, Trisha stood from the front desk.

"Hey, Joe," she said. "Can I talk to you?"

She hadn't called me Joe since George Delgado had died. My stomach tightened a little, but I forced a smile to my face as I walked to her.

"Hey," I said. "Something you need, Officer?"

She looked around. The lobby was empty, but she lowered her voice anyway.

"Bob Reitz told me what happened at Darren Rogers's house," she said. "I'm sorry you were hurt."

"I'll be fine," I said. "Bob's a hero, though. He saved my life."

She said nothing, so I gave her another tight smile.

"I'm going to head to my office. I've got reports to write."

"Please don't go yet," she said. "I owe you an apology. I haven't been nice to you lately. That was unfair of me. I thought you killed George Delgado, and I didn't know how to deal with that."

I looked at her and drew in a breath.

"You're right. That was unfair of you. And it hurt. I wish you had just talked to me."

She looked down.

"I should have," she said before pausing. "Did this guy kill George Delgado?"

"Yeah. It looks like Darren Rogers paid him."

She sighed and shook her head.

"This is awful," she said. She paused. "I'm sorry. You and George just fought so often…" She paused again. "I don't have an excuse. I was wrong, and I'm sorry. That's it."

Part of me wanted to tell her sorry wasn't good enough, but a much bigger part of me wanted my friend back. I considered my response carefully before speaking.

"Thank you for the apology," I said. "If you're sorry and want to make it up to me, buy me a drink after work. Probably not today because I'll be doing paperwork for the next hundred years, but soon."

She smiled.

"I'd like that," she said, looking down to her desk. "I have one more thing. Detectives Freshwater and Chavez from Kirkwood, Missouri, are in town to interview Luke Glasman."

I stepped away from the desk.

"Where are they?"

"Their plan was to wait in his driveway until he came home."

"Okay," I said. "Thanks. Glasman's still my primary suspect in the Flamethrower murder. I should talk to them."

She wished me luck, and I headed out. When I reached Glasman's home, I found two SUVs in the driveway, so I parked out front and jogged to the front door. Detective Chavez opened before I could knock.

"Hey," I said. "I miss anything?"

"Not yet. We're waiting for Mr. Glasman's attorney. She's on her way."

He held the door for me, and I stepped into the home. It was clean and modern and had nice hardwood floors. Someone had piled baby shoes and socks beside the front door, and there was a child's walker toy in the middle of the entryway. In addition, the home's electrical outlets all had clear plastic plugs in them, and little rubber cushions covered the sharp edges of the entry table against the wall opposite the front door.

"Where's Glasman now?"

"Putting his little girl down for a nap," said Chavez. "Gabe's in the kitchen. Come on. Mr. Glasman made coffee."

We walked down a short hallway to the eat-in kitchen. It was a nice use of space. The kitchen was open to the living room, allowing Mr. Glasman to watch his daughter play while he made dinner or cleaned. A huge bank of windows and French doors allowed copious amounts of light to fill the space from outside. Detective Freshwater sat at the kitchen table, watching birds eat at a feeder in the backyard.

"Good morning," he said. Then he paused and looked at his watch. "Or afternoon. Whatever it is."

"Long day?" I asked, pulling out a chair near his. He nodded and yawned. "So you guys got to meet Mr. Glasman's elusive daughter. Was she cute?"

"We didn't meet her," said Freshwater. "We waited for him in the driveway, and he pulled up, took his daughter's seat from the back of his SUV, and covered her up before we could see her. Then he carried her to her room. He said something about her having a heart condition."

I hesitated.

"He told me the same thing," I said. Then I paused. "Does it seem like he's hiding his kid from us?"

Chavez shrugged.

"Maybe he's afraid she'd be scared of us," he said. "Or maybe the kid's genuinely sick."

"That's probably it," I said. "It just seems weird to me. Anyway, you have new evidence against him?"

Before he could answer, the doorbell rang.

"That must be his lawyer," said Chavez. "I'll get her. You two stay here."

He disappeared and came back with a young woman wearing a cute pencil skirt and carrying a briefcase.

"Where's my client?" she asked, her eyebrows so high and angry they almost formed a V on her forehead.

"Putting his daughter down for a nap," I said.

"Oh," she said. She looked at the three of us. "Have

any of you talked to him since he asked for me?"

"No," said Freshwater. "He's been trying to rock Kendra to sleep since we got here. He said she was overly tired. It might take a while."

"Is the coffee for everybody?" she asked. Freshwater it was, so she walked to the kitchen, grabbed a mug, and poured herself a cup. When she got back to the table, she introduced herself as Eleanor King and laid the ground rules for our interview. She specified that this was a voluntary interview and that she could end it at any moment. If we asked questions that she thought were out of bounds or tried to mislead her client, she'd kick us out and refuse to cooperate with any future investigation. It seemed fair. We waited for about ten minutes in amiable silence until Mr. Glasman came to the kitchen.

"She's down," he said. "We've got a couple of hours if we need it. What can I help you with?"

"Thank you for agreeing to see us, Mr. Glasman," said Freshwater. He looked to his lawyer. "And thank you, as well, Ms. King. We're here, as we told Mr. Glasman this morning, because a woman named Shirley Decker called us early this morning. Ms. Decker was a friend of Mrs. Glasman."

"She was," said Luke, glancing to his attorney. Ms. King's eyes kept switching from Luke to the detectives. She was nervous. I wondered how many cases she had ever worked. "Shirley was my wife's best friend. She and I had a relationship as well. Irene and I went through a rough spot two years ago and split up. While we were split up, I slept with Shirley. Neither she nor Irene ever forgave me."

"I see," said Freshwater. "When did you last speak with her?"

"I don't know," said Luke. "And it wasn't as if Irene didn't sleep around. She had new boyfriends every week."

Neither Freshwater nor Chavez spoke. I kept quiet, too, but Ms. King leaned forward.

"We stipulate that Mr. and Mrs. Glasman had a difficult marriage that involved infidelity on both sides for a significant amount of time. Both partners knew what they were getting into when they married."

"Did it bother you that your wife spent so much time with other men?" asked Chavez.

"I got over it. It was part of our marriage."

"Did you ever hit your wife?" asked Freshwater.

"No," said Glasman.

Freshwater and Chavez both stared at him, unwavering. They wouldn't have driven all the way to St. Augustine and asked the question unless they had something. Ms. King fidgeted.

"I think we're done here," she said. "Unless Luke is under arrest?"

"He's not under arrest," said Freshwater. "I do have something to show him, though. I think you'll want to see it."

A more experienced attorney probably would have ended the conversation there. If they had evidence tying Glasman to a crime, she'd get access to it as part of the discovery process before a trial. Instead of telling us to leave, though, she swallowed. I kind of felt bad for her.

"Okay. What have you got?"

Freshwater reached to a briefcase beside him and pulled out a transparent evidence bag. He slid it across the table to Glasman.

"Ms. Decker gave us this letter this morning," said Freshwater. "Do you recognize the handwriting?"

Luke looked down and blinked.

"It looks like Irene's handwriting."

"That's what Ms. Decker told us," said Freshwater. "Do you want to read it aloud?"

Luke's eyes scanned the document, but he said nothing. Freshwater pulled it toward him, picked it up, and started reading.

"'Luke found out about my affair today and pushed me against the wall. He took off his belt, whipped me with it until I bled, and then forced me to my knees.'"

Freshwater glanced up from the document.

"Your wife claims you beat her with a belt until she had welts all over her back and rear end and then forced her to commit a sexual act," he said. "Afterwards, she went to Ms. Decker's home and asked her friend to take pictures of her wounds. Would you like to see those?"

Luke shook his head.

"This is over," said Ms. King. "I need to talk to my client."

"I never hit my wife," said Luke, glancing at his attorney. "We didn't always get along, but I've never hit her—or anyone—in my life. I wouldn't risk losing my daughter."

Freshwater nodded as if he believed that.

"Luke, please stop talking," said Ms. King. "Detectives, we're done here."

"Are we done?" asked Chavez, looking to Luke. "Or do you have more to say? Why would your wife say you hurt her unless you had?"

"Because she's an evil bitch. And she's not dead," said Luke. He looked to his attorney. "Tell them the truth."

"Not now," said Ms. King. "We need to stop talking and regroup."

"Why do you think your wife is still alive?" I asked.

Luke locked his eyes on mine. His entire countenance darkened, and when he spoke, his voice was low and throaty, but it had a sibilant quality to it, like a snake.

"Because you can't kill the devil with fire."

The change in his demeanor was so rapid and complete that I didn't know how to respond. Then Ms. King cleared her throat and shot to her feet.

"Everybody out. Luke, shut up. Detectives, please leave."

This time, Mr. Glasman seemed to agree with his attorney because he stood up. He was back to being the meek stay-at-home father again.

"You can see yourselves out," he said. "I have work around the house."

We thanked him for his time and left the home. None of us said a word until we stood behind the Kirkwood detectives' SUV in the driveway.

"That was interesting," said Chavez. "You think he's laying the groundwork for an insanity defense?"

Freshwater shrugged. Chavez looked to me.

"That's possible," I said. "Did you see his eyes change, though? I think he's genuinely nuts. Do you actually have pictures of Mrs. Glasman with bruises?"

Freshwater looked grim.

"Yeah. He hurt her pretty badly."

I sighed. Even if I couldn't prove he murdered Laughton Kenrick, at least he'd go to prison for something.

"How sure are we that Irene Glasman is dead?" I asked.

The two detectives looked at one another. Chavez raised his eyebrows and then looked to the ground.

"We'll talk to the medical examiner," he said. "We found two bodies in the home, both of which were burned badly. One had the bone structure of a male, and the other had the bone structure of a thirty-year-old female. Mrs. Glasman's car was in the driveway, and she was known to stay over in the house. We'll check her dental records."

I brought a hand to my mouth.

"Do we consider the possibility that Mr. Glasman is right and that his wife is still alive?"

Freshwater gave me a tight smile.

"It's an elaborate setup if she is," he said. "To make it work, she'd have to murder two people. If she was willing to do that, why wouldn't she just murder her husband?"

I shrugged.

"If she hates him, there are few better ways of getting back at him than to send him to prison forever."

"But she could have sent him to prison for assault already," said Chavez. "You didn't see the pictures Dr. Decker gave us. They were brutal."

I crossed my arms and drew in a breath, giving myself a moment to think.

"You're probably right, but I still feel like we're missing something," I said. "I guess that's your part of the case. I'm still working the Flamethrower murder, and I haven't got shit. Thanks for letting me tag along for the interview, but you've got your case in hand. If you need anything, call me. I've got a ton of paperwork to fill out."

They told me they'd call if they found anything. I wished them luck and drove to my station. I had a long, boring day ahead of me, and I figured I might as well get started.

35

Eleanor closed the front door and gave Luke a hard stare as she crossed her arms. She didn't look angry. The look she gave him was more disappointed than anything. He had seen similar looks every day of his married life, so her stare didn't bother him. It worried him, though. He swallowed.

"I should have expected that," he said. "She told me she was going to do something like that."

Ms. King opened her eyes wide and lowered her chin.

"And you didn't think to tell me that?"

"I've had a lot on my mind," he said, reaching into his pocket for his cell phone. He pulled it out and opened the app on which he had recorded his wife threatening him. Then he played it for his lawyer. Her shoulders fell as Irene's recorded voice called him a sweet, stupid man and recounted a plan to have dozens of her friends accuse him of beating her. When the recording ended, she crossed her arms and took deep breaths.

"We can use this, but we've got to be careful," she said. "Until we can prove otherwise, we have to act as if your wife is dead and that you're upset by this. That means we can't speak ill of her in public. You have to look like a grieving, confused husband. Otherwise, you look like you wanted her dead."

He crossed his arms.

"But she's not dead."

Ms. King softened her voice.

"We have to prepare for the possibility that we're wrong," she said. "In that case, you're back to being the primary suspect in her death. Your life will get much harder."

She was right. He hadn't killed her, but Irene was even more dangerous dead than alive. He brought a hand to his face and closed his eyes.

"I didn't want this," he said. "I just wanted to be a dad. That's it. I even tried to divorce her, but Irene wouldn't let me. She knew the courts would award me custody and that she'd be paying child support and alimony for years. Everything came down to money. But I didn't kill her, and I didn't hurt her."

Eleanor drew in a breath and blinked.

"I'm glad you didn't kill or hit her, but that doesn't make this easier to defend. Shirley Decker has pictures of your wife that she claims prove you beat her with a belt. The audio you played me is exculpatory, but only if we can prove it's Irene. That might be tough."

He opened his eyes and looked at his lawyer. Then he blinked.

"She's done things like this before," he said. "Irene's devious. She and a guy named Lamar were up for a promotion last year at her firm, so Irene made up a fake Facebook account and started sending Lamar nude pictures of one of the office assistants. I don't know how Irene got naked pictures of Denise, but she did. Then

Lamar's wife found Denise's pictures and confronted her husband in the office. It was embarrassing for everybody. Lamar got fired, and Denise's husband left her. Irene got the promotion, though."

Eleanor lowered her voice.

"Jeez. Does anybody else know about that?"

"Shirley, probably," he said. "Irene wouldn't have told anybody else. If the truth had gotten out, her firm would have fired her."

"The bar association would have gone after her, too," she said. She thought for a moment. "If she's dead, we can use the story and the audio file to establish reasonable doubt. We'll undercut the police's case by demonstrating that there are other people with a motive to kill her."

"But she's alive."

The lawyer locked eyes on him and lowered her chin and voice.

"I hope she is," she said. "For now, I need you to put together a list of people who might have serious grievances against your spouse. People like Lamar and Denise, people she's hurt. At the very least, the list will give the police other names to obsess over."

"I can do that," he said.

She told him to call her if he found anything interesting, and then she left. He stayed in the front room of the home and wondered what the hell he should do. Irene had been planning this for months, so he doubted Shirley Decker's pictures would be the only surprise. He wondered whether she had used makeup, or whether

Irene had let Shirley hit her with a belt to make the welts more realistic. He hoped it was the latter.

Once Ms. King's car left his driveway, Luke went inside and grabbed a clean sheet of paper on which he could write the names of people Irene had hurt over the years. He started by looking through their college yearbooks. Luke didn't know why his wife wanted to keep the yearbooks their college had sent, but they came in handy now. Irene had been in a sorority, which put her in close contact with several women who hated her guts now.

He wrote down five names of women he knew she had hurt. All five women were younger than Irene, and all five had been a little heavy. Their college had been small, so Luke knew them pretty well. They were wonderful, intelligent women, and most of them had great senses of humor. But Irene had made a habit of pointing out those areas on their bodies they were most bothered by.

One lady had arms that she thought were too large, so Irene gave her a ladle as a white elephant gift for Christmas and explained that she had a fine job ahead of her working in an elementary school's cafeteria. Two of the ladies carried extra weight on their midsections, so Irene had given them catalogs from a company that specialized in maternity clothes. She had hurt every one of them.

After flipping through his yearbooks, he opened his laptop and checked out Facebook. Immediately, he knew something was wrong. He had lost almost fifty friends since he last logged on, and he had almost two dozen messages, most of which mentioned a video and most of which expressed disbelief, anger, disappointment, or a combination of the three.

He didn't know what was going on until he found a message with a link to his spouse's profile. There, he found a video. Irene sat on a stool in front of a gray screen and stared at the camera. Her hair brushed against the tops of her shoulders, so this must have been taken before her most recent haircut. Her expression was somber, and she held her arms close to her sides. She had crisscrossed her feet and rested them on the stool's lower rung, making her look almost like a kid. He wondered whether she had practiced that.

"Hi. If you're seeing this, it's because I'm dead," she said. "So that sucks."

She paused. Her deadpan delivery was excellent and almost made it funny.

"I don't know what happened, but I know who killed me: my husband, Luke Glasman," she said before pausing. Her lower lip quivered, and she balled her hands into fists on her lap. Irene had been a good actress. She may never have gotten her big break and starred on Broadway or in movies, but she probably could have made a living in theater. He wondered how differently their lives would have gone if she had taken that chance. She looked down. "Luke is a sadist. He enjoys hurting me."

He pushed back from the table and crossed his arms.

"He calls me his little onion and says he has to peel my layers away. He uses a belt for that," she said, pausing long enough to dab at her eyes. Then she looked at the camera again. "He forced me to go to a sex club in Chicago, where he let strangers do things to me. That's why I applied for a job in St. Louis. The city was smaller, so I thought he couldn't hurt me the same way. Instead, he was worse."

She kept talking, but he tuned her out until she mentioned Kendra.

"I'm terrified for my daughter," she said. "I don't know what he'll do to her. She's a baby now, but she'll grow up to be a little girl."

Luke clenched his jaw so tight he thought his teeth would crack.

"I tried to divorce him," she continued, "but he was Kendra's primary caregiver. He said he'd kill her if I left. I couldn't let that—"

He slammed his laptop shut before she could say another word. He wanted to scream, but he didn't want to wake up Kendra. Instead, he balled his hands into fists and walked around the home, fuming. Waves of anger and revulsion washed over him. He'd never hurt Kendra. Even the thought disgusted him. His baby girl was his entire world, the one piece in his life that gave everything else meaning. He refused to let Irene take her from him.

He opened the laptop again and checked out his retirement account. Irene had tried to claim that he didn't need his own retirement account because he'd live with her for the rest of his life, but Luke knew he had to take care of himself. So, he had opened a Roth IRA account and siphoned small amounts from their joint checking account every month. In his boldest month, he had moved four hundred dollars to his account, but most months, he only took fifty or a hundred bucks.

The account had close to twenty thousand dollars, more than enough money to disappear. It'd take at least twenty-four hours, but he ordered his brokerage firm to liquidate his mutual funds. Once that was done, he could withdraw the cash and hide until things calmed down. He'd take a hit on his taxes, but he could deal with that.

Unfortunately, the money was just a holding maneuver to buy time. He needed a long-term plan, one that Irene wouldn't have expected. She'd had months to plan her death and pin it on him. To counter that, he needed to do something unexpected.

He needed to find her and kill her for real.

She wouldn't have gone to a friend's house because that'd be the first place he'd look. She didn't have siblings, so she wouldn't be there, either. Her mom was still alive, but she lived in a senior-care facility and didn't have room for overnight guests.

With her resources, she could be anywhere, but she was a lawyer, a litigator. A criminal defense lawyer or prosecutor might have contacts who could create fake IDs and other documents needed to disappear for real, but Irene didn't. What's more, she wouldn't have gone without creature comforts. Wherever she was, she was spending money, and the kind of money she needed would come with a paper trail for the right person to follow. Luke wasn't that person, but he thought he knew someone who was.

He picked up his phone and dialed a number from the call history.

"Detective Court," he said. "It's Luke Glasman. Thank you for seeing me this morning."

The woman paused.

"I shouldn't be talking to you without your attorney on the line."

"That's okay," said Luke. "I'll sign a waiver or something. Can we talk?"

She didn't hesitate.

"Sure. If you're willing to sign a waiver, come down to my station. We'll talk on the record."

He agreed and thanked her and hung up, wondering whether he had just made a huge mistake.

36

I hung up and leaned back in my chair to think. My morning meeting with Glasman had been a waste of time, but I had learned long ago to sit down and shut up whenever a suspect wanted to talk. More times than not, every word they spoke was a lie, but now and then, they allowed something truthful to slip in. I could use that against him in court.

I put my computer to sleep and reserved the second-floor conference room for the next hour. Glasman had told me he'd be by as soon as he woke up his daughter, but I figured I still had a little time, so I called Detective Freshwater to let him know what was going on. He and Detective Chavez were already half an hour away and didn't want to turn back, so I agreed to record the conversation for them. I doubted anything would come of it, but stranger things had happened.

After that, I grabbed some waters from the break room in case Glasman was thirsty and set the lights low in case his daughter was fussy after just waking up. As much as I wanted him to confess to something, I hated to think what would happen to his daughter if we had to arrest him. Hopefully he or his spouse had a relative who could give Kendra a stable home, but in the meantime, we'd have to put her in an emergency foster home. Her heart condition would add challenges, but we'd deal with that problem if we came to it.

Once I got the conference room set up, I brewed a fresh pot of coffee in the break room and walked to the front of the building to wait for my guest. The day was cool but clear, and we had plenty of parking on the street in front of our station. I sat on the stone steps out front. About ten minutes later, a red SUV drove past. Glasman was at the wheel. He gave me a half-hearted wave and then pointed up the street. I stood.

Glasman drove about half a block before finding a spot big enough to accommodate his massive car. As he set up his stroller and tenderly picked up his daughter from her seat a few minutes later, I couldn't help but feel conflicted. He may have hosed an obnoxious racist with gasoline and lit him on fire, and he may have murdered his wife and her lover, but he seemed like a good dad.

Then again, anyone willing to douse another human being with gasoline and light him on fire had something wrong with him. Irene and Laughton Kenrick may have coaxed the monster out, but Luke Glasman gave it life. Inside him, he had a little Dr. Jekyll and a lot of Mr. Hyde. That he could pass off as a conscientious single father made him even more dangerous. I needed to get him off the street before he murdered anyone else.

Once he got his daughter strapped into the stroller, he looked left and right before walking up the street toward us. I waved to him and wondered how we would get the stroller up the stairs. When the county renovated the building, they had put in a ground-floor side entrance and elevator for those with mobility issues, but the property didn't have enough room for a ramp near the main entrance.

As he crossed the street, I pointed toward the employee parking lot on the side of the building.

"We'll use the handicap accessible entrance," I said. "There's an elevator."

He paused before changing direction. I thought nothing of it when a car turned onto the road about a block away, but then I heard tires chirp. I glanced toward the car and held my breath. It was accelerating hard.

The world seemed to slow down. I stepped into the road and held up my hands.

"Luke, stop! Back up!"

Glasman furrowed his brow and gave me a quizzical look. Then he looked to his left. The car had changed its trajectory and barreled straight toward him. There were two people inside. One had a slight build and long hair. It looked like a woman. The driver was a man.

I wanted to sprint across the street and push Glasman and his daughter away, but it felt as if someone had encased my feet in concrete. I wouldn't make it. Glasman wrapped his arms around the stroller, lifted it from the ground, and pivoted his hips. The stroller landed on the hood of a late-model Honda Civic, well off the road. Glasman jumped onto the hood beside his daughter and pulled his legs up moments before the sedan hit and then careened away.

I ripped my phone from my purse and called up the camera to get a picture of the car as it sped away. It was a red four-door sedan, and it had looked relatively new. Our station had surveillance cameras pointed at the parking lot, but I didn't know whether any would be angled to get the license plates of vehicles that drove past the front of the building.

Luke slid off the car and then got his daughter from the stroller. She was crying. I covered my mouth and swore under my breath. Then Trisha came from the front door.

"Everybody okay?" she asked. "I heard the crash."

I looked over my shoulder at her.

"Yeah, we're good," I said. "I'll need the surveillance video from the parking lot, and see if Marcus is—"

"He's running!" shouted Trisha, interrupting me. I looked at the street and found Luke sprinting toward his SUV.

"Glasman, stop!" I shouted. "We can protect you."

Whether he heard me, I couldn't say. When he reached his SUV, he climbed in, clutched his baby, and drove away, leaving his stroller in the road. I walked to the middle of the street and held up my arms.

"Where the hell are you going, dude?"

He didn't even slow down before turning the corner a few blocks away and disappearing. I stayed in the middle of the street and shook my head, unsure what the hell had just happened.

Luke's stomach hurt, and his head felt light. Kendra squirmed in his arms and tried to push away, but he didn't let go. He didn't know where to go, but he needed to escape. A tremble passed through his arms and into his gut. If he had been near a toilet, he might have vomited. Everything about this was wrong. Nobody knew he had gone to the police station except Detective Court. He hadn't even told his lawyer.

He looked down to his baby.

"I'll take you somewhere safe, okay, honey?" he said. "I won't let anybody hurt you."

She struggled against him, so he started singing a lullaby she liked. It felt crazy to sing a lullaby as he ran from the police, but he didn't know what else to do. Nothing made sense anymore. He wished he hadn't gone to that gas station and murdered the cowboy. He wished none of this had happened.

Everything came back to Irene. She had caused all of this. Had there been a single kind bone in her body, they could have been happy. He could have overlooked her constant need for approval, her unwillingness to consider anyone else's needs, her inability to remain faithful. It wouldn't have been a perfect marriage, but it could have worked.

She was rotten to the core, though. He wished he had killed her. At least then he'd have the satisfaction of knowing she was dead.

Since he didn't know what else to do, he drove around for almost five minutes, watching in his rearview mirror to make sure no one was following him. He didn't like driving around with Kendra clinging to him, but it worked for now. When he figured he was alone, he headed home and slowed about a block before arriving. There was a black Jaguar in his driveway. It was a beautiful car, purchased by its owner just six months ago. He knew because she'd brought it by the house to show off.

He ground his teeth and parked in front of the home. Dr. Shirley Decker stepped out of her car and locked eyes on him as he and Kendra came toward her.

"Get out of here," he said. "You're not welcome at my house anymore."

She tilted her head to the side and gave him a tight, malevolent smile that reminded him of his wife. Both women were evil harpies. It was no wonder they had gotten along so well.

"Is it really your house, sweetie?" she asked. "You didn't pay for it, did you?"

He pointed to the Jaguar.

"Get out of here."

"Or what?" she asked, stepping forward. Dr. Decker was about thirty and had thick brunette hair that seemed to shimmer in the late evening sun. Outwardly, she was a beautiful woman with a first-rate mind and ambition to match. Luke knew she was a devil in disguise.

"Get in your car and drive away, or I'll call the police."

She stepped back but shook her head.

"No, you won't," she said. "Irene told me the truth. You're the Flamethrower. You killed that redneck in the gas station. I didn't think you had it in you, if I'm honest. It's a shame you found your balls so late in life."

He looked toward her car and shifted Kendra so she was on his other hip. She wanted to get down and play on the grass, so she kept pushing away on his chest so he'd put her down. Instead, he stroked her back. They'd play as soon as they got inside again.

"Get in your car and leave," he said, walking toward his front door. "I won't ask you again."

"You going to light me on fire like you did Laughton Kenrick?"

He closed his eyes and shook his head.

"Who's Laughton Kenrick?" he asked. "Honestly, how do you think I could have killed somebody? I'm pretty sure the police would have noticed the murderer pushing a stroller."

She stepped forward.

"You're going to prison," she said, her voice as sly as a snake's. "You might as well turn yourself in and admit what you did. Tell them how you burned Kenrick but then decided that wasn't enough. Tell them how you murdered your wife and her boyfriend."

"Irene is alive, and you know it," he said. He injected as much venom into his voice as he could. Decker straightened and cocked her head to the side, confused. "Don't play stupid, Shirley. Where is she?"

"Your wife is dead," she said. "One of my colleagues did the autopsy. She burned to death in her boyfriend's bathtub. They tried to escape the fire in it because you had screwed the windows and doors shut."

He screamed that he hadn't done anything to her, but then he noticed a neighbor in the front lawn of the home next door. For about six months out of the year, thick bushes full of green bushes separated their homes and gave them privacy, but those plants had dropped their leaves weeks ago. Luke waved. The neighbor glared.

"I've called the police," he shouted. "I'm sorry, Luke. You're a good guy, but I'm worried about Kendra."

Luke rubbed his eyes and waved.

"She's fine. Thank you," he said, before looking to Decker. "Just get out of here. I don't want you here, and now the police are coming. You're trespassing."

Decker started walking toward her car but then stopped before getting in.

"Keep my daughter safe," she said. "Kendra's mine. It's in Irene's will."

"Of course it is," he said. "That's how the two of you plan to steal her life-insurance money. I know all about it. Now get out."

Decker got in her car and left. Once her car disappeared, Luke waved to his neighbor again and went inside, where he leaned against the wall beside the front door and slid to the ground. Kendra was free, so she made happy noises as she rolled on the ground. Then she rolled to her belly and pushed herself upright to all fours before making a tentative move forward.

It was the first time she had ever crawled. He should have been overjoyed, but he could barely bring himself to smile.

"Good job, sweetheart," he whispered. "Daddy's proud of you."

We have to kill Aunt Shirley, too.

Kendra's reptilian voice seemed louder than usual. He sighed.

"I know, baby girl," he whispered. "But I'm tired. For now, let's just play."

37

As I had thought, our department had surveillance cameras filming the parking lot, but none of our cameras overlooked the street. My camerawork was equally unhelpful. One of my pictures sort of looked like a car, but the others were just red boxes. None would help us identify the vehicle that had tried to kill Mr. Glasman and his daughter.

Since neither my pictures nor the department's surveillance video would get me anywhere, I called Glasman over and over, but his phone went to voicemail every time. Still, I left him messages.

"Mr. Glasman, this is Detective Joe Court again. I need you to call me. I'm not sure what's going on, but you're safer in my station than you are out on the streets. For your daughter's sake, call me. She could have gotten hurt today. I can keep you both safe."

I hung up and waited a minute, but my phone didn't ring. Then I sighed and looked through my purse for the business card of Eleanor King, his attorney. She answered right away.

"Ms. King, this is Detective Joe Court. We've had an issue involving Luke Glasman, and I'm wondering whether he's contacted you."

She paused.

"What kind of issue, Detective?"

I explained that Glasman had called me and asked to

meet, but, upon his arrival at my station, someone in a car had tried to run him down. She paused when I finished.

"Have you seen a red four-door sedan lately?" I asked, finally.

"No, Detective, I have not," she said. Her voice was sharp and angry. "You knew my client had representation. Why did you agree to meet him without me present?"

"That's what you're angry about?" I asked. "Somebody tried to kill your client, and you're pissed that he tried to talk to me?"

She paused and sighed.

"I'm concerned that somebody tried to hurt Mr. Glasman, but I can't do anything about that. I can, however, do something about your illegal contact with my client."

"Neither my station nor I did anything improper," I said. "Mr. Glasman called, and I told him I couldn't talk to him without his lawyer present. He insisted anyway and said he'd sign a document agreeing that he had waived his right to counsel."

"You should have called me. You knew I was his attorney of record."

I shook my head and leaned back.

"I appreciate your position, but that's not my responsibility," I said. "People switch attorneys all the time. I didn't know if you had fired him, or if he had fired you. All I know is that your client understood his rights, and he waived them."

"Did you record the conversation?" she asked.

I paused and cocked my head to the side.

"You don't know me, and I don't know you," I said. "Since you're an attorney in town, though, there's a good chance we'll run into each other on future cases. Let's not poison our professional relationship by accusing each other of acting in bad faith now. But to answer your question, I did not record the conversation. Mr. Glasman called me unsolicited, and I spoke to him. I'm not in the habit of recording every conversation that comes my way."

She swore and then sighed.

"I warned him not to talk to the police without me present."

"I understand," I said. "You may not be able to answer this without violating attorney-client privilege, but has he mentioned that someone might be after him?"

She didn't hesitate before responding.

"He thinks his wife faked her death and is trying to kill him," she said. "Beyond that, I can't respond without being in breach of my attorney-client privilege."

"I appreciate your obligation, but Mr. Glasman and his daughter are in very serious trouble. Anything you can tell me would help."

"If I told you more, I'd be disbarred," she said. "I'll call him, but I don't know where he is or who would be after him. And if he doesn't want me around when you talk to him, he's not going to take my calls, anyway."

"If you talk to him, please ask him to turn himself in. I'm worried about his daughter."

"Me, too," she said. "I'll be in touch."

She hung up, and I sighed. Then I looked up when someone coughed from my doorway. Sheriff Kalil leaned against the doorframe, his arms crossed.

"I just spoke to Officer Marshall," he said. "What's going on with Luke Glasman?"

I filled him in on what happened and on my conversation with Glasman's attorney. He considered and then raised his eyebrows.

"So you're still after this guy even though you have almost nothing connecting him to Laughton Kenrick's murder?"

"I'm still working the case, and he's still my best suspect. I've not found anything that points fingers at anyone else, and I've not found anything that clears him."

He brought a hand to his face and then sighed as he shook his head.

"If you're not making headway, you're off the case," he said. "I'll give it to Marcus."

"Marcus is already working a major case," I said. "If you take me off the Flamethrower case, you're putting it on the shelf. It's a horrible crime, and you'll be giving up on it."

"No," he said, shaking his head, "I'll be giving a second experienced investigator a crack at it after the first one failed to produce anything."

I leaned back on my chair and crossed my arms.

"Marcus is a good detective, and I'd normally say that's a good plan, but he's working a major felony right now. We don't even know how many people Carlos

Danger killed."

The sheriff squinted.

"Who's Carlos Danger?"

"The contract killer who murdered Darren Rogers. We got the name from his cell phone. It's fake, but it's what we've got. From what I've seen, that case could take months to unravel. If you put Marcus on this one, too, you'll spread him thin. It's your call, though. You're the boss."

He straightened.

"I am the boss," he said. I didn't know how to respond, so I said nothing. "Fine. You want the Flamethrower case to yourself, you've got it. If you don't close it, though, you'll be cleaning out your desk."

He couldn't fire me for failing to close a case, and we both knew it. He was posturing.

"I'll follow the law and our department's procedures," I said. "If you wanted a guaranteed outcome, you got into the wrong business, Boss."

He narrowed his eyes at me, grunted, and left. I sighed and picked up my phone to call Mr. Glasman again. As before, it went to voicemail.

"Mr. Glasman," I said. "It's Detective Court again. Since you're not returning my phone calls, I'm coming to look for you. When you get this message, call me. Let's make this easier for everybody."

I hung up and waited for a call that didn't come. Then I stood, grabbed my jacket, and headed out.

Irene had made sure Luke didn't have many friends, but despite her best efforts, she had never driven a wedge between him and his sister. Valerie and her husband lived in a beautiful old house on two hundred acres outside Mount Vernon, Illinois, a small town about eighty miles east of St. Louis. Luke hadn't visited them as much as he would have liked in recent years, but they were family. Kendra had never met her aunt and uncle, but he couldn't imagine a safer temporary home for her. Valerie hadn't even hesitated to offer to give her a home for as long as he needed.

He packed three duffel bags full of clothes, diapers, burp cloths, her favorite toys, blankets, and even her Pack 'n Play. The Pack 'n Play wouldn't be as comfortable as her crib, but she could sleep in that for a time. It took a couple of trips, but he filled the back of the SUV and then put Kendra in her car seat. She had fussed a little, but he knew she'd fall asleep once he got on the highway.

As he drove toward Illinois, he wondered whether should just keep driving to Canada or Mexico. Once his brokerage firm sold his mutual funds, he'd have enough money to get by for a while. He could change his name, and they'd disappear. He could wait tables like he did in college, and he could watch Kendra grow up.

Then again, Irene had worked too hard to destroy him, and Kendra was worth too much money to let him go. She and Shirley would hunt him to the ends of the earth. He'd never be free until they were both dead. That decided things for him. It was him or them. They had both made their choices.

Valerie had agreed to meet him in O'Fallon, Illinois, in the parking lot of a Walmart near the interstate. After more than an hour of driving, he found her maroon minivan at the edge of the parking lot near a Panda Express. His sister was younger than him, but she had always seemed older. She had three kids, a loving husband, a dog, and a beautiful home. She was happy, and he was happy for her.

When he parked, Valerie stepped out of the driver's seat of her car and threw her arms around him the moment he opened his door. He hadn't realized how tired he was until that moment.

"Okay, honey," said Valerie a moment later. "What's going on? I haven't heard from you in weeks, and now you want me to take Kendra?"

He looked down.

"The police think Irene is dead," he said. "They think I killed her."

"Oh my," she said, covering her mouth. He didn't tell her about the things he had done, but he told her about the life-insurance policies, the statement Shirley Decker had given to the police, and the video posted to Irene's Facebook feed. He also played her the audio file of Irene threatening him. Valerie went quiet for a moment. "You need a lawyer."

335

"I've got one," he said. "For now, I need a friend and someone who can take care of my baby while I figure this out."

"Yeah, of course," she said. "Can I meet Kendra?"

He smiled and took the baby from her seat. She was a little fussy at first because she was just waking up from a nap, but she warmed up to her aunt Val pretty quickly. While they got acquainted, he moved Kendra's clothes and other bags from the back of his SUV to the minivan. Valerie already had a car seat in the back of her van, so he put Kendra inside and gave his sister another hug.

"You'll be okay," said Valerie. "Just remember that. You did nothing wrong."

"I know," he said, looking down at the asphalt so he wouldn't lie to his sister's face. "Please just take care of my baby."

"We will," she said. "Jarrod and I will treat her as if she were our own for as long as she's with us. What are you going to do?"

"Whatever my lawyer tells me," he said. "That and pray."

"Okay," she said, holding out her arms for another hug. He held her tight for a moment and then looked at his baby through the window. He hoped he'd see them both again. As he watched Valerie drive home, he felt as if someone had just scooped out his insides with a spoon. He wanted to shout, scream, cry, and hit something, but none of those actions would have accomplished anything.

This would never end until he killed Irene.

He put the car in gear and headed toward the interstate. Dr. Shirley Decker lived in Fenton, a suburb southwest of I-270 in St. Louis County. He and Irene had been to her house dozens of times over the past few years for parties and other social events. Luke hadn't enjoyed a single gathering, but Irene knew how much he hated them and hadn't allowed him to stay home. If Irene was anywhere, she'd be there, laughing her ass off at him.

He drove past big commercial districts and into a neighborhood full of two-story homes and small but well-kept yards. Shirley owned a colonial home with cream-colored siding and a two-car garage. He parked in her driveway and then walked around to the rear of his SUV for a weapon. He didn't keep much in the car, so he lifted the carpet to expose the spare tire and small tool set there. The jack was in pieces, but the tire iron would do.

As he stepped back from the SUV to shut the door, he heard another car's tires on the road behind him. Then the noise stopped, and a door opened. He turned around and found a Volvo station wagon and its owner, Detective Court. She smiled, but he didn't think she meant it.

"You're a hard man to find, Mr. Glasman," she said. "Do me a favor and put down the tire iron."

He looked at the tire iron and then her and sighed as he made his decision.

"Sorry about this," he said, swinging the weapon as hard as he could.

38

The moment he swung his arm, I lifted mine to keep him from hitting my head with the tire iron. Glasman was bigger than I was, but he didn't twist his hips or get his back into the swing. His power came from his arm and shoulder. That was probably the only thing that kept me from breaking my forearm. The moment the tire iron connected, pain shot through me. I gasped and staggered to a knee, disoriented.

Glasman didn't waste time. He tossed the tire iron down and ran to the front of his car and climbed in. With seconds, the rear end of the big SUV was hurtling toward me. I vaulted forward and onto the grass. The hard-packed earth hit my now quite bruised arm, and I gasped again as pain lanced through me. As I looked up and saw Glasman through the front window of his monstrous SUV, it almost looked like he mouthed *sorry*.

Then he hit the front end of my car with a crash of metal on metal. With the weight of Glasman's massive SUV on the front quarter panel, my car slid across the asphalt as if it were on ice. Then he put it in gear and drove off. The whole encounter took, maybe, thirty seconds, but he had committed so many felonies in those thirty seconds that he'd never walk free again once we arrested him.

I rolled onto my back, sat up, and rotated my forearm. It hurt, but nothing felt broken. For a few moments, I stared at my car. The front headlight was shattered, and the front panel had pushed against the front driver's-side wheel. The car might drive, but I couldn't chase anybody in it anytime soon. That dickhead.

My purse was on the grass, so I grabbed that and called Detective Freshwater from Kirkwood to tell him what had happened. The moment I finished speaking, he said he and Chavez were on their way and that Chavez would call the county dispatcher for help and to alert them to look for Glasman's SUV. That left me sitting and waiting.

A uniformed St. Louis County police officer arrived about two minutes later in a marked cruiser. I showed him my badge, and he walked around Dr. Decker's home to make sure it was secure. Every officer within five miles was now looking for Glasman's SUV, but St. Louis County had about a million residents and a lot of roads, giving Glasman a lot of hiding spots. Another uniformed officer arrived a few minutes later. He had cross-trained as a paramedic, so he checked out my arm and made sure I wasn't in shock. I was fine, though.

About fifteen minutes after I placed my call, Detectives Freshwater and Chavez arrived. They parked in front of the home and jogged toward me as I sat on the grass.

"You okay, Detective?" asked Chavez. "If you're hurt, we can get you to a hospital."

"Nothing's broken. I'm fine," I said. "The fucker hit me with a tire iron and then tried to run me down with his car."

"We can pick him up for attempted murder now," said Chavez. Freshwater looked to me.

"Why were you at Dr. Decker's house?"

I told him about my call with Glasman and my attempt to meet him at my station. Then I showed them pictures I had taken of the car that tried to hit him. They agreed that my camera work was subpar and that it was unfortunate my station didn't have cameras pointed toward the street out front.

"Did you know Glasman would be at Dr. Decker's house?" asked Chavez.

"No, but it was an educated guess," I said. "Glasman's lawyer said he believes his wife is still alive. Dr. Decker was his wife's best friend. From what I gather, she wasn't close to many other people. I figured he'd assume she was here and come to look for her."

Both of them looked toward the house.

"Dr. Decker's on her way home from work," said Freshwater. "We had planned to see her today, too. She's been posting videos of Irene Glasman on Facebook and Instagram."

I raised an eyebrow.

"What videos?"

"The kind that allege her husband beat and sexually assaulted her and that she feared for her life," said Chavez. "She's got bruises in many of them. I've seen a lot of bruises over the years. These don't look like makeup. They're real."

I couldn't help but furrow my brow at that. I had worked enough domestic violence cases over the years to know that domestic abusers came from all professions, races, and social classes, and that there were few common patterns. In most cases, though, the abuse came because one partner wanted to control the other.

I had only seen Irene and Luke Glasman together once, but Irene had seemed to be the dominant partner in that relationship. She'd had the power, and he had cowered in front of her. It was hard to believe he had hurt her behind closed doors, but it could have happened. I wished she had come to the police. We could have helped her.

"I guess you never know what secrets people keep behind closed doors," I said.

"In this case, that may be doubly true," said Freshwater. "We've had multiple life-insurance companies contact us about Mrs. Glasman's death. One of those policies had been taken out by her firm when she was hired, but the others were taken out by Mr. Glasman in the past six months. Kendra Glasman is the beneficiary and is due fourteen million dollars. Since she's a baby, her father will control the money."

I sighed and felt my shoulders drop.

"So he killed her for the insurance money."

"Oh, there's a twist," said Chavez. "The policies were paid for by a bank account in Mrs. Glasman's name, and the signatures on the life-insurance policies don't match Mr. Glasman's handwriting."

I furrowed my brow.

"Why would Mrs. Glasman take out fraudulent life-insurance policies?"

"You already know the answer," said Freshwater. "To make it look as if her husband killed her."

"But she'd have to die to benefit," I said, lowering my chin.

"Or, it'd have to look as if she died," said Chavez.

I brought a hand to my mouth and almost chuckled.

"You've got to be kidding me," I said. "Now you believe him? You think she faked her death to frame her husband?"

Chavez shrugged.

"It's wild, but the theory fits the evidence."

"Then who died in the house fire in Kirkwood?" I asked.

"We're still trying to figure that out," said Freshwater. "The bodies were badly burned, so the medical examiner's office is trying to look for dental records of potential victims. It's possible Irene Glasman and her boyfriend are dead, but it's also possible she set up her husband for murder."

I said nothing as I thought. Then I laughed.

"Most people would have just gotten a divorce."

The two men smiled but said nothing as a black Jaguar drove past and then parked about half a block away.

"I believe that's Dr. Decker," said Chavez. "Let's see what she has to say about her friend."

Freshwater and I agreed, so the three of us walked toward the black sedan. Dr. Decker wore a black polo-style shirt and dark jeans. A tie held her hair from her face. Presumably, she wore some kind of gown to protect her clothes at work because they looked spotless. Even standing a few feet away from her, I couldn't help but notice a disinfectant smell wafting on the breeze.

"Thanks for coming out, Doc," said Freshwater. "We hate to tell you this, but you might be in some danger. Luke Glasman might want to kill you."

She opened her eyes wide.

"Is that why there's a broken station wagon in front of my house?"

"The Volvo's mine," I said. "I came out here because I suspected Mr. Glasman might try to contact you. Then I found him in your driveway with a tire iron. He attacked me and fled."

She looked me up and down.

"Are you all right?" she asked. "I'm a forensic pathologist, but I'm a physician, too."

"Just bruised," I said. "We need to find Glasman. I don't know a lot about him, but he loves his daughter. He wouldn't have rammed my car with her in the SUV. Who would he trust with Kendra?"

She paused and looked from me to Freshwater and then to Chavez. Finally, she lowered her chin and raised her eyebrows.

"You guys don't know, do you?"

"Don't know what?" asked Freshwater, narrowing his

eyes.

"Luke Glasman doesn't have a daughter."

I didn't know how to respond, so I looked to Freshwater and Chavez. They looked as confused as I felt.

"What do you mean?" I asked.

"Have you ever seen his baby?" she asked, raising her eyebrows. "I'm sure you've seen him pushing a stroller, but have you seen the baby inside it?"

"I never gave it much thought."

"Six months ago, Irene gave birth to a beautiful little girl with a complex congenital heart defect. A team of doctors performed surgery, but Kendra wasn't made for this world. She fought for a week, and then she died. Luke couldn't handle it. Irene needed a partner, but he lost himself in his own world. Then, one day, he brought home a doll from somewhere, and he started pushing it around in a stroller as if it were real.

"Irene tried to take care of him. They went to therapy together and tried to process what happened. On the doctor's advice, she even pretended that stupid little doll was a real little girl. She even got her friends and family to pretend, too. The doctor thought that if we treated Luke gently enough, he'd process his daughter's death in his own way. If we kept telling him the doll wasn't real, though, he'd only retreat further into his imaginary world."

I crossed my arms, unsure what to say.

"That explains why we never saw the kid," said Chavez. Freshwater and I both nodded.

"Irene tried to help him, but he kept getting worse," said Decker. "Then he got violent. He started hitting her because he thought she'd take his doll away. She couldn't divorce him because she thought he'd crack further and kill himself. And she couldn't go to the police because she didn't know how he'd react. If he attacked a police officer, they'd shoot him.

"I know it sounds terrible, but this was why she had an affair. She needed somebody in her corner. She started seeing her boss."

Dr. Decker paused.

"Irene was the best friend I ever had. She just wanted to be happy. I know Luke was sick, but he had no right to kill her. It was an impossible situation. I guess she's free now."

It'd take time to investigate and process all this, but the story made sense of much of what had happened.

"Did you know she took out multiple life-insurance policies?" I asked. Dr. Decker closed her eyes and sighed.

"You don't have kids, do you?" she asked.

"No," I said.

"Before she gave birth, Irene went a little stir crazy and got nervous. She was the primary breadwinner in the house, and she was afraid she'd die in childbirth. So, she took out a bunch of life-insurance policies in case something bad happened. The money would go to Kendra, but Luke would manage it. She wanted to take care of her family. That was before they knew how sick Kendra really was."

Freshwater cocked his head to the side.

"Why would she sign them in her husband's name?"

"I don't know," she said, shrugging. "You ever heard of pregnancy brain? A lot of pregnant women show significant declines in memory and executive functioning during their third trimester. We don't know why, but it's a real thing. She probably just got the paperwork mixed up. She was under a lot of stress."

I stepped back and looked to Freshwater and Chavez. Both of them had eyes wide open and perplexed looks on their faces.

"Can we have a few moments, Dr. Decker?" asked Freshwater.

She smiled and looked at her house.

"Can I just go home?"

"Sure," said Freshwater. We watched her go in, and then I looked to my two colleagues and blew a slow breath out.

"Did that story make sense?" I asked.

"My wife talked about pregnancy brain," said Freshwater. "I called them senior moments and thought I was funny."

"You think it's plausible?" I asked.

"Honestly," said Freshwater, lowering his chin, "I don't know what the hell to think except that we need to find Glasman."

I agreed and walked to the front door of Dr. Decker's home. She opened the door as soon as I knocked.

"You know Luke Glasman better than we do," I said. "Where do you think he'd go?"

"His sister's house," she said. "She lives in Mount Vernon, Illinois, and she's as crazy as he is. She and her husband live on a farm and have an arsenal big enough to arm the Illinois National Guard. Watch out for Luke, too. He killed that guy in the gas station in St. Augustine and told Irene he planned to burn her alive, too."

"He told his wife he was the Flamethrower?" I asked.

"Yeah, and she told me," she said. "She was too scared to tell anyone else, though. He was sick. She was afraid he'd kill her or somebody else."

"Okay," I said. "Thank you. Stick around. We might have to ask you more questions soon."

She said she didn't have any plans to leave, which I appreciated. Then I turned to Freshwater and Chavez.

"You guys want to go to Mount Vernon with me?" I asked. "If this doll is as important to Glasman as Dr. Decker says, he's bound to come for it."

"None of us has jurisdiction in Illinois," said Chavez. "We'll have to call the Illinois State Police."

"We'll do it on the way," said Freshwater. "Let's get this guy before he kills somebody else."

39

I didn't bother calling Sheriff Kalil before heading to Mount Vernon, mostly because I didn't want to argue with him. Instead, I helped Freshwater and Chavez push my Volvo to the curb so it wouldn't block traffic in front of Dr. Decker's home, and then I got in the back of their cruiser and called a tow truck to pick up my car. As we headed to the interstate, I then called the Illinois State Police and told them we planned to talk to a resident in their jurisdiction. They promised to keep a pair of troopers nearby in case we needed to make an arrest, which I appreciated.

We planned our surveillance as we drove, which made the almost two-hour drive seem quicker than it actually was. Valerie and Jarrod Brockette's farm lay well beyond the outskirts of town on a back country road. The landscape was flat, and it stretched for miles in every direction. The wind would have rolled across the flat earth like a wave and crashed into everything in its path, so the family had planted evergreen trees and shrubs around their home, creating an almost park-like feeling in the middle of a field of winter wheat.

Freshwater drove past the home and its front lawn. A gravel driveway meandered across the property, around a pond and play set, and to a very pretty brick Federalist-style home with white columns out front. A pair of young boys played on the play set outside. Detective Freshwater parked on the side of the road maybe a quarter mile from the driveway. Then he turned and looked at me.

"Okay, Detective," he said. "You know the deal. We're looking for information, but your safety is our priority. If you find guns, or if you feel threatened, back off. We'll call in the locals then."

"Agreed and understood," I said, reaching for my phone and setting up the walkie-talkie app we planned to use. I had two steady bars of connection, so I expected it to work fine. "Can you hear me through this?"

An ear-splitting feedback squeal filled the car, so I covered my phone's microphone with my thumb. Freshwater covered his ears.

"The phones work," said Chavez. "Let's not test them again."

They both looked at me.

"You ready, Detective?" asked Freshwater.

"I am," I said. Since I was sitting in the back of a police cruiser where suspects typically sat, Freshwater hopped out and opened my door. Both of the detectives wished me luck and reiterated that they'd be seconds away if I ran into trouble. I appreciated the sentiment, but we all knew their backup didn't matter. If I had an emergency, it'd be over well before they could arrive. My job was to recognize potential threats and de-escalate them before they exploded. That was easier said than done.

Before getting out of the car, I grabbed a clipboard and notepad from Freshwater's evidence kit and the small copy of the New Testament that Detective Chavez carried in the inside pocket of his jacket. As long as I stayed in character, the Brockettes shouldn't have any reason to believe I was anything but a churchgoer out to share her faith. I walked about thirty feet away.

"Can you guys hear me?" I asked.

"Five-by-five," said Chavez, his voice loud and clear. "I've got three bars, so we should continue to have a good connection."

"Good," I said, continuing to walk. I set my phone on top of the clipboard. It only took a few minutes to reach the driveway. When the boys on the play set saw me, they jumped down and ran toward the house, so I lowered my chin. "The kids saw me and ran inside. I'm going to have a welcoming committee. Be ready to move."

"I'll turn on the car and inch forward," said Freshwater. "Dr. Decker said these guys were twitchy, so be careful."

"Understood," I said. "My emergency word is 'bananas.' You hear me say that, come and get me."

"Gotcha," said Freshwater.

Instead of following the meandering driveway, I walked straight across the lawn toward the home, the front door of which now hung open. As I approached, I heard voices inside, and my footsteps slowed without conscious thought. The boys were telling somebody—their mom, if I had to guess—that they saw a lady walking up the drive. Within seconds, a woman in her late twenties stepped into the doorframe.

"Can I help you?" she asked.

"I hope I can help you," I said. "Were those your boys who ran in earlier?"

She hesitated.

"Yeah."

"Children are one of the greatest blessings God can bestow on his people."

She snickered.

"You don't have any, do you?"

A smile sprang to my lips unbidden.

"Not yet. Maybe one day."

She crossed her arms.

"I'm sure you're a lovely person, but I don't want to talk about my kids," she said. "What can I help you with?"

I smiled.

"I wanted to tell you about the new church we plan to build in town."

She said nothing, but then the door opened wider, allowing me to see the entryway. Luke Glasman stood right behind his sister with a very live baby in his arms.

"I thought that was your voice," he said. "I'm not going to let Valerie lie to protect me. You're here to arrest me, aren't you?"

Valerie Brockette closed her eyes and sighed. Her entire body seemed to slump. I ignored her and focused on Glasman.

"Is that your daughter?" I asked. He looked at the

little girl in his arms.

"Yeah. This is Kendra. If you come near me, please wash your hands. She's got a compromised immune system. I don't know if I told you that."

"You did," I said, plucking my cell phone directly from my clipboard. "Guys, call your station and tell them to arrest Dr. Decker. Then call the State Police and tell them we need some officers to make an arrest. Glasman's here, and his baby is very much alive and well. We got played. Oh, and bananas. This whole thing is bananas."

"We're on our way," said Freshwater. I looked toward the porch.

"Mr. Glasman, please hand your daughter to Mrs. Brockette and step forward. I'm taking you into custody for trying to kill me with your car this afternoon."

He handed his sister his baby but then shook his head.

"I wasn't attempting to murder you," he said. "I was just trying to get away."

"I don't think that distinction matters a whole lot, but thanks all the same," I said, motioning him forward. "You got any weapons on you?"

"No," he said. "And I'll answer any question you've got, but I need you to promise me something first."

"I'm not sure either of us is in the position to bargain, but sure," I said. "What do you want?"

"I want my sister to get custody of Kendra."

I looked to Mrs. Brockette and then back to him.

"I'll see what I can do," I said, speaking honestly and

looking toward the driveway. Freshwater and Chavez had parked and were walking toward us. I looked to Mrs. Brockette. "Do you have firearms in the house?"

"Of course not," she said. "I've got boys. If I kept guns around the house, they'd shoot each other. My husband keeps his hunting rifles in a gun safe in a locked room in the barn."

"Good," I said. "Your brother hit me with a tire iron and tried to run me down with a car. We'll take him into custody. Before we do that, Illinois state troopers will walk through the house to make sure everybody's safe. Then we need to talk. Sound good with you?"

"I won't argue," she said, looking down and then to her brother. "And I'm sorry if Luke hurt you. He's a good man, and he's trying his best. He's not been in his right mind lately."

"I'll bear that in mind," I said, forcing a measure of softness into my voice. "Now ask your children and anyone else inside to come out. And call a lawyer if you've got one. This is going to be a rough day."

40

We put Glasman in the backseat of Freshwater and Chavez's cruiser and waited for the Illinois State Police to arrive. Since we were out of our jurisdiction, he wasn't technically under arrest. We were just holding him. Thankfully, he didn't run off. At first, he said nothing, and we didn't ask him anything. Then, he started telling us about his daughter and how proud of her he was.

About ten minutes after we placed the call, the first troopers searched the Brockettes' home and took Glasman into custody. Chavez and a uniformed officer stayed at the house to interview Mrs. Brockette and her family formally, while Freshwater and I drove with the state police back to their station with Glasman.

It had been a long day, but Freshwater and I finally sat across from Glasman in an interrogation booth an hour later. Freshwater and I sat on one side of a metal table with Glasman on the other. He looked haggard and tired but almost relieved somehow. Freshwater smiled at him.

"Okay, Mr. Glasman," he said, "I'm Detective Gabe Freshwater with the Kirkwood Police Department. With me is Detective Mary Joe Court with the St. Augustine County Police Department. Before we start, let me reiterate that you are under arrest for the attempted murder of a police officer. You may remain silent, but if you speak to us, we can use whatever you tell us against you in court. You have the right to an attorney. If you can't afford one, the court will provide one for you. Do you understand all that?"

"I do," he said, looking to me. "And sorry, Detective Court. I'm glad I didn't hurt you."

"Me, too," I said. "You sure you don't want us to call your lawyer?"

He looked down at the table.

"She can't help me," he said. "I'm in trouble."

He wasn't wrong, so neither Freshwater nor I corrected him.

"You mind if I record this?" I asked, reaching into my purse for my cell phone. He said it was fine, so I put the phone on the table between us and started a recording app. The state police had their own surveillance system, but I liked having my own recording as well. "Do you know anyone named Jason Kaufman?"

Glasman gave me a confused look and shook his head.

"He had big sideburns and drove a white Pontiac Grand Am," I said. "You had an altercation with him at the BP station in St. Augustine."

"Oh, yeah," he said. "I burned his house down. I was hoping to kill him, but I didn't see anything about it on the news."

"Why did you want to kill him?" asked Freshwater.

"He was an asshole. When he got to the gas station, he was playing music so loud it rattled my teeth. I asked him to turn it down. He did, but then he knocked on the window of my car to wake up Kendra from a nap. It was just mean. Then Kendra told me I should spray him with gasoline and light him on fire. I didn't have any matches on me, so I couldn't, but I thought about it."

I leaned forward and cocked my head to the side.

"Kendra—your infant—told you to murder him?"

"Yeah," he said, glancing at me. "She whispers to me sometimes. I don't think other people can hear it."

Mrs. Brockette had said her brother wasn't in his right mind lately. If he'd heard his infant daughter tell him to hose people with gasoline and light them on fire, she may have been on to something.

"I see," I said. "Did you kill Laughton Kenrick? He drove a white truck."

"He was a racist," said Glasman. "And yeah. I lit him on fire and watched him burn. I liked hearing him scream."

His matter-of-fact tone was unnerving, making me grateful that handcuffs strapped him to the table.

"Did Kendra tell you to kill him?" asked Freshwater. Glasman looked at him.

"Sort of," he said. "She just told me to fuck him up. She didn't say I should burn him. I just thought that'd be fun."

"I see," said Freshwater. "Did she tell you to kill your wife, too?"

He shook his head.

"I didn't kill Irene. Kendra and I drove to her boyfriend's house to kill them both, but it was already on fire when I got there. I would have killed her if I'd had the chance, but you know…"

"If you didn't kill your wife, who did?" asked Freshwater.

Glasman furrowed his brow and lowered his chin.

"She's not dead," he said. "Irene's a lot of things, but she's not stupid. She and Shirley Decker have been working for months to set me up. They took out insurance policies against Irene to make me look suspicious, and then they changed Irene's will so that Shirley would get custody of Kendra at her death. Shirley worked in a morgue, so she had access to bodies. Nobody died in that fire. You understand that, don't you?"

Neither Freshwater nor I reacted, so Glasman kept talking.

"You want the truth?" he asked. "Here's the truth. Shirley got the bodies from work, dumped them in the house, and made it look as if Irene and her boyfriend were dead. Their plan was for the police to arrest me. When that happened, Shirley would gain custody of Kendra and her inheritance. Once Shirley had Kendra and the inheritance, she'd disappear. Irene and her boyfriend would probably meet her in Mexico or Thailand or somewhere like that, and they'd live out the rest of their lives with millions of dollars in insurance money. I, meanwhile, would sit in a prison cell.

"Irene was evil, and she loved planning elaborate revenge plots. This was her masterpiece. When you arrest her and tell her my sister has Kendra, please take a picture of her face. I want to see it. Irene's disappointment will make everything worthwhile."

I didn't know how to respond, but Freshwater leaned forward.

"Your wife is dead, Mr. Glasman," he said. "The St. Louis County medical examiner checked the dental records of the bodies we found in Jeff DeMille's home. He and your wife died in the fire. They probably tried to open a window, but they couldn't because the windows were all screwed shut. Then they went to the bathroom and tried to wait it out in a cast-iron bath tub. They died of smoke inhalation. Afterwards, their bodies were burned beyond recognition."

Glasman's shoulders fell a little.

"Oh. That's sad."

"So you didn't light that fire?" I asked.

He shook his head and looked at the table. The story was wild, but I didn't know how much of it was true. It didn't matter because we had enough to send him to prison for the rest of his life already. I looked to Freshwater. He shrugged as if he didn't know what to ask next. Then I looked to Glasman.

"I've got one last question," I said. "Did you burn my house down?"

He gave me a blank, confused look for a moment, but then he drew in a breath and closed his eyes.

"Yeah. Sorry. I forgot for a moment. I've had a lot going on lately," he said. "You were mean to me, so I wanted to kill you."

"That seems reasonable," I said, unsure what else to say. I looked to Freshwater. "You have anything else to ask?"

"No," he said and looked at Glasman. "We'll take you back to St. Louis soon, but in the meantime, the officers here in Illinois will take care of you. You have everything you need?"

Glasman said he did, so Freshwater and I left the room. After closing the interrogation booth's door, the detective considered me.

"You ever tire of working in St. Augustine, give my boss a call. I'll put in a good word for you. We could use you."

I smiled.

"I appreciate that, but St. Augustine's home."

He said he had expected that answer. Freshwater and Chavez had work ahead of them, but my cases were mostly closed. After filling out a lot of paperwork in Illinois, we drove back to their station in Kirkwood. Glasman would stay overnight in Illinois while the lawyers arranged for his transfer, but he didn't concern me anymore.

It was well after dark when we arrived in Kirkwood. Since my car was in a repair shop and my dog was at my parents' house, I called my mom to pick me up and then borrowed her car and drove back to St. Augustine, where I filled out reports and then emailed the prosecutor to let him know what was going on. At a little after two in the morning, I drove back to my rental house and crashed on the bed.

For the next twenty-four hours, the world spun into fast forward, as it often seemed to do after we'd closed a major case. Glasman had confessed to Kenrick's death, but he was mentally ill and wouldn't end up in prison. The state would send him to a secure mental health facility, and he'd get the help he needed. He'd never walk free again, but he wouldn't die behind bars, either. Kendra Glasman would live with her Aunt Valerie and Uncle Jarrod, just as Luke Glasman had wanted. It was the best outcome we could have asked for.

A day after we arrested Glasman, Border Patrol agents caught Dr. Shirley Decker and Jason Kaufman trying to cross the border from North Dakota into Manitoba, Canada. Decker refused to cooperate, but Kaufman spilled everything in exchange for a plea deal.

According to Kaufman, Decker showed up at his house shortly after Luke Glasman tried to light it on fire. She offered him a plan to make millions and to get revenge on the man who'd tried to kill him. All he had to do was screw a few windows and doors shut and then burn down a house in Kirkwood, Missouri. It seemed easy enough, and she slept with him, so even if he didn't get the promised millions, he still got something.

After the fire, he and Decker watched Luke Glasman from a distance, expecting him to be arrested for murder any moment. Only Glasman was never arrested.

Decker and Kaufman needed him out of the way so they could get Kendra's inheritance, so Decker rented a red four-door Toyota Camry from a rental car place near the St. Louis airport and persuaded Kaufman to run Glasman down with the car. Unfortunately for them, they missed, and Glasman escaped with his daughter. Luke Glasman was the Flamethrower. He murdered Kenrick Laughton, and he tried to kill Jason Kaufman and me, but he didn't murder his wife. This entire case was bonkers.

As it turned out, Luke Glasman was right about one thing: his wife and Shirley Decker had been planning to frame him for murder and run away with the insurance money. They might have gotten away with it, but Shirley got impatient and greedy.

As best we could tell, Irene told Shirley that her husband was the Flamethrower and that he had tried to kill Jason Kaufman, and Shirley decided it was time to put their plan into motion. She seduced Jason and made him a deal he couldn't refuse. They killed Irene and her boyfriend. Nobody was innocent except the baby.

In the end, I lost a house I loved, and the St. Louis County prosecutor charged Jason Kaufman and Shirley Decker with capital murder. The tradeoff wasn't worth it, but at least neither Shirley Decker, Irene Glasman, Jason Kaufman, nor Luke Glasman would ever hurt anyone again.

Besides, I had my health and my dog, and eventually, we'd have a home of our own once more. For now, that would be enough.

41

The next week was slow, mostly because I had little to do at work. Marcus Washington was busy with Darren Rogers's murder and the investigation into Carlos Danger, which meant I picked up every other major felony that came into the station. It wasn't much. We got a call one morning for a stolen vehicle, but I closed that case when I found the car at the high school and learned that the owner's son had taken it without permission to impress a girl.

I also picked up a felony theft case in which someone had stolen several thousand dollars' worth of power tools from a locked box at a construction site. The thief then tried to sell them back to the owner on Facebook. Since the thief had contacted the contractor from his own Facebook account, it wasn't a hard case to break.

And that was pretty much it.

I read through a lot of cold cases and certified that we didn't have any new information that might help us close the cases, I worked a few traffic accidents, and I caught a pair of teenagers having sex in the bed of a pickup at a local park. By Friday morning, I was bored out of my mind and browsing local real estate listings on my work computer when somebody knocked on my door. I looked up and smiled at Special Agent Bryan Costa.

"Hey, Joe," said Bryan. "You busy?"

"Not really," I said. "Just hanging out and waiting for

somebody to shoot his neighbor so I have something to do. How about you?"

"Today's the day," said Costa. "You want the honors? We wouldn't be here without you."

I minimized my browser window and sighed. This was it, then. I had known this day was coming, but I hadn't expected it so soon. It was almost bittersweet.

"Okay," I said, standing. "Let's go."

Bryan and I walked into the hall outside my office, where I found Detective Marcus Washington waiting for us. The three of us then walked down the hall to the office of Sheriff Dean Kalil. Normally, we would have knocked, but today Kalil couldn't refuse us. Agent Costa had an arrest warrant. The sheriff was on the phone as we walked in. Kalil's expression soured when he saw us, and he held the receiver against his chest.

"I hope there's a reason you barged into my office."

Marcus said there was, walked around the desk, and took the phone from the sheriff's hand.

"Mr. Kalil is unavailable," he said before hanging up. Kalil opened his eyes wide, but I spoke before he could say anything.

"Dean Kalil, you're under arrest for conspiracy to commit the murders of Darren Rogers, Vic Conroy, Richard Clarke, Arthur Murdoch, Zach Brugler, George Delgado, and Nico Hines. We plan to add to those charges, too, by the way."

The sheriff stared at me, his eyes wide. Marcus, meanwhile, had shifted so that he stood behind the sheriff, just out of Kalil's reach.

"Mr. Kalil, put your hands flat on the desk in front of you and stand up," said Marcus. "I'm going to take your pistol and pat you down. You have anything in your pockets that could hurt me?"

Kalil cocked his head to the side and looked over his shoulder.

"You're fired, Marcus."

Marcus didn't respond. Agent Costa dropped a leg back and put a hand over the holster at his hip.

"I've got six federal agents downstairs collecting case files and records, but I can call them in if you're uncooperative," said Costa. "I've also got agents visiting the homes and businesses of most of St. Augustine's county councilors. Nobody's walking away from this."

Kalil stood but kept his hands on the desk.

"I've never killed anyone in my life. Hell, I've never even fired my weapon in the line of duty."

"That's why it's called conspiracy, buddy," I said. Agent Costa nodded to Marcus, who removed the sheriff's pistol from his holster. Then the detective began patting him down.

"You have the right to remain silent, Mr. Kalil, but if you choose to speak, anything you tell us can be used against you in court," said Marcus. "You have the right to an attorney. If you can't afford one, the court will appoint one. Do you understand that?"

Kalil glared at Marcus and then at me.

"I'm not saying a word."

"Then shut up and listen," I said. "We know who you are, and we know what you've done. We also know about the St. Augustine Express Pay account."

The sheriff cast his eyes to me and then to Agent Costa. Marcus straightened and handed Kalil's service pistol to Agent Costa. The FBI agent removed the magazine and round from the chamber and pocketed both.

"I don't know what the hell you're talking about," said Kalil.

"Yeah, you do. You were a frequent user of the Express Pay account," said Agent Costa. "In fact, you used the account to hire Victor Komenski—you knew him as Carlos Danger—to murder an awful lot of people."

Kalil narrowed his eyes at the FBI agent.

"This is ridiculous. I don't know anybody named Carlos Danger or Victor Komenski, and I sure as hell didn't hire a hitman to murder anyone."

"Tell me about Surety Building Maintenance," said Costa. Kalil straightened but said nothing. "If you don't want to talk, that's your right. The Express Pay account wired twelve thousand dollars a month to Surety Building Maintenance's bank account. Surety Building Maintenance wired that twelve thousand dollars a month to a bank account you control in the Cayman Islands. A lot of criminal organizations use similar corporate structures to hide the sources of their money."

Kalil closed his eyes and shook his head but said

nothing.

"Komenski murdered Darren Rogers and planted a phone on him," I said. "You gave Komenski that phone. You wiped the exterior of the phone well, but you left your fingerprint on the back of the battery. I'm guessing you changed the SIM card and didn't think to wipe the internal components down. That phone contained every email you sent to Komenski. He surveyed the area, planned these murders, and then executed more than half a dozen people on your orders. You wanted us to think Darren Rogers was the man in charge."

Kalil crossed his arms.

"My fingerprint is on a phone, and I own a building maintenance company," he said. "So what? I switch phones every few months because I like to keep up to date with technology. When I upgrade, I sell the old ones. Is that a crime now?"

"No," I said. "But hiring a contract murderer to kill your boss is."

Kalil considered me and then sighed.

"Darren Rogers was my boss, and I'm sorry he's dead, but I wasn't in business with him. I'm an honest cop."

"No, you aren't," I said. "Rogers recruited you for this job. He spent a quarter of a million dollars to get you elected and paid you very well to do his dirty work. You paid Komenski over three hundred thousand dollars from the Express Pay account to murder Darren Rogers's enemies. Then you paid Komenski to kill Rogers and try to kill me. We've got the emails from Komenski's phone and the financial documents from the banks involved. Rogers recorded every conversation you two had. We've got it all."

For a moment Kalil stood straight. Then he gave a slight shake of his head.

"You can't trace any of that to me."

"You wired payment to Komenski with a phone call," said Agent Costa. "The Express Pay account's bank recorded the conversation. They gave us the recording at the request of the Treasury Department, ostensibly for a tax evasion case. By the way, the IRS plans to audit you soon. You owe taxes on all your income, even illegally sourced income."

Kalil looked from me to Costa and then over his shoulder to Marcus.

"This is ridiculous," he said. "I should sue you for defamation."

"Cool," I said. "Since you don't seem to grasp what's going on, I'll bottom line it for you. Darren Rogers needed a tool to complete his work and decided you were the biggest tool he knew. We've got your emails, your phone, and a voice recording of you authorizing payment to a contract murderer. Good luck with your defamation lawsuit. You'll be filing it from federal prison."

In the movies, he would have shouted *You'll never take me alive!* and then reached for a gun he had hidden on his desk or in a secret pocket of his uniform. Instead, he just sort of deflated. I looked to Marcus and then Agent

Costa.

"You guys mind if I go back to my office? I found a house I kind of like, and I need to call my realtor to see if I can set up a showing."

"Go ahead," said Marcus. "We'll take care of Mr. Kalil."

I thanked him and wished them both luck before walking down the hall. For a few moments, I sat on my chair and spun around, but then I grabbed my purse and took the stairs to the lobby. Trisha smiled at me from the front desk, but she was on the phone and didn't stop me. I waved to her and left the building.

I hadn't planned this moment, but I knew where I needed to go. The roads were empty, so the drive to the cemetery took little time. I parked about a hundred yards from Susanne Pennington's grave and drew in a breath. My chest felt heavy and tight. Susanne had been my friend when I needed one most. I loved her. She had been kind and sweet and gentle. She had also been a murderer.

Well before I was born, Susanne's husband had raped and murdered a young woman. He had been wealthy and powerful, and his victim had been neither. The police refused to consider him as a suspect, but Susanne knew the truth. She murdered her husband to keep him from hurting anyone else, and Darren Rogers helped her get away with it. In exchange, Susanne gave up nearly everything she owned. The Penningtons' money provided the seed capital that became the St. Augustine Express Pay account.

Darren Rogers had planted a poison tree when he'd extorted my friend. That poison spread and corrupted everything it touched. From the outside, St. Augustine County looked bucolic and safe and beautiful. It was all a facade, though. The county had a per-capita murder rate higher than nearly every county in the state, we had drug use higher than all but a handful of locations in the Midwest, and, until his very recent death, we had the biggest pimp in the state operating out of a truck stop and hotel on the edge of town. Now, maybe those old wounds could heal.

I walked to my friend's grave and sat on the ground. My throat felt tight.

"Hey," I said. "I just came by to tell you it's over. Darren Rogers is dead, and FBI agents are arresting most of the County Council. I know that's not what you wanted, but I had to do it. I don't know if you care or if you can even hear me, but you're free now."

I paused.

"You were the first real friend I ever had," I said, blinking. "I miss you."

I hadn't been to Susanne's grave since her funeral, so I stayed a while and told her about Roy and my family and my half brother, Ian. I wished she had met him. She would have liked him. She would have said he had spunk.

After half an hour, I stood and walked to my car. St. Augustine had work ahead of it. We needed a new sheriff, a new county executive, new County Council members, new accountants…maybe an entirely new county charter.

I didn't dwell on any of that, though. The past was the past, and I had my entire life ahead of me. I planned to live it to its fullest.

Epilogue

Moving usually sucked, but, since everything I owned had burned in a fire a few weeks ago, it wasn't so bad today. I now owned a two-story brick colonial mansion in the middle of town. The previous owner had used it as a successful bed and breakfast, but that would change very soon. The building had a big commercial kitchen, beautiful living rooms, and ten bedrooms, each of which had an ensuite bathroom. The fenced rear yard even held a play set.

The moment I crossed the threshold and heard those old pine floors creak, I knew what I needed to do. I made an offer on the property before I had even finished the tour.

Now, three weeks later, Linda Armus and I sat on the patio out back and drank coffee. I didn't know Linda well, but people I knew and respected spoke very highly of her. She was about my age, and she had been the assistant director of a shelter for homeless teenagers in St. Louis. Now, she was the inaugural director of the Erin Court Home for Women. She leaned back in her chair and looked toward the main house.

"You know, it's not too late to back out," she said. "We don't have any clients yet. We could remove the sign, and you could move into the master bedroom and live like a queen."

It wasn't the first time she had said that. As before, I

shook my head and smiled.

"I don't want to be a queen," I said.

"What do you want?" she asked. "Usually, women like you just make a donation and go home. They don't buy a building and start a charity. And when they do start charities, they usually want to be in charge."

I cocked my head at her and picked up my coffee cup.

"What do you mean women like me?"

She smiled and shook her head.

"I didn't mean any offense," she said, "but you know what I mean. Rich women."

"I'm not a rich woman."

She looked behind her toward the home and raised her eyebrows.

"You sure about that?"

"I had some money, but it wasn't mine," I said. "My mom deserved a place like this. If she'd had somewhere to go, I might not have lost her when I did."

"You want to tell me about her?"

"I loved her. I think I still do," I said. "That's all that matters."

Linda smiled. We sat in silence for a few more minutes and drank our coffee. The shelter wasn't open yet, but today was a big day, anyway. My entire family was coming out. Mom called it a housewarming party, but it wasn't a party. It was just a get-together. We'd drink some wine, I'd give some tours, and then we'd sit around and enjoy each other's company. It'd be a nice day.

Ian and his parents arrived first, and I met them near the parking lot. My brother stepped out of the back seat of his car and nodded appreciatively as he opened the wrought-iron gate and walked toward me.

"This place is nice," he said. "I'm going to enjoy visiting you here."

I lowered my chin and pointed toward the garage.

"That's my place. It's a two-bedroom apartment above the garage," I said. "The big house will be for residents."

He looked over his shoulder at my little apartment.

"I guess that's nice, too."

We said nothing until Miriam and Martin, Ian's parents, joined us.

"This place is beautiful," said Miriam. "Congratulations, Joe."

I started to thank her, but Ian spoke before I could.

"So where's the wine?"

"On the patio out back," I said. "You can have some when you're twenty-one. In the meantime, there's root beer in the fridge. Follow the hallway to the kitchen at the back of the building."

He grumbled and left. I looked to his parents.

"We owe you an apology," said Miriam. "We hired a lawyer to deal with Frank Ross. The US attorney thinks Martin might have some information pertinent to a few ongoing investigations. We're taking care of things. We shouldn't have put you and Ian in the situation we did."

"Are you two safe now?"

"Yeah. And our attorney says the statute of limitations has passed on any financial crimes I committed," said Martin. "I'm more embarrassed than anything now."

"Good. Ian's a good kid," I said. "He needs his family."

"And you're a good sister," said Miriam. "I'm sorry I didn't see that before."

"Thank you," I said. Miriam smiled and stepped closer to me.

"Can I ask you something personal, Joe?" she asked. I smiled and said yes. "Why is your name spelled J-O-E instead of J-O?"

I looked down to the ground and blinked.

"My biological mother said I was named after my father, but I suspect she just couldn't spell very well."

Miriam laughed and squeezed my arm. Before she could say anything else, my parents pulled into the parking lot and honked their horn. Mom jumped out and hurried toward the gate. My dad, sister, and brother followed.

"This place is gorgeous," said Mom, staring at the house with her eyes wide.

"Yeah, I got lucky," I said. "The owner needed to sell, and Roy and I needed to buy."

"So this is home now, huh?" asked Dylan.

"Yeah. Linda's the director. You'll meet her inside. I'm going to live above the garage."

"But you're still a cop, right?" he asked.

"Yep. Why?"

Dylan exhaled a long breath and seemed to relax.

"Good, because I've got a ton of speeding tickets, and I need you to take care of them. Mom refused."

I laughed and shook my head.

"Even if I could fix your speeding tickets, I'd tell you you're on your own, dude," I said. He looked as if he wanted to protest, but our mom stepped between us before he could.

"How's your department?" she asked.

I groaned and looked down.

"A mess," I said. "The elected sheriff is in jail, the former sheriff is dead, the county executive is dead, and the FBI has arrested most of the County Council on corruption charges. Oh, and lawyers from a good-governance group have sued the county over the county charter. They think it was forced through without a proper election."

"So who's in charge?" asked Dad.

I shrugged and smiled.

"Don't ask me. The county scheduled an emergency election in January for county executive, council, and sheriff, so we're doing our best until then. Bob Reitz has the most seniority among our uniformed officers, so he's making the schedules for everybody in uniform. Marcus Washington and I split detective duties. Trisha Marshall's in charge of the front desk. Theoretically, the prosecutor might be my boss at the moment, but he doesn't know anything about police work and hasn't stepped foot in the station in weeks. I don't want to talk about work, though."

"Then give us a tour," said Mom.

For the next hour, I showed my family around the house and the garden out back, and I introduced them to Linda. Linda told them about the charity we were creating and the community we planned to serve.

As a police officer, I did my best to help people, but I always showed up after someone had been hurt, and I left before the victim could recover. This house was different. We were creating a home to provide transitional, safe housing for the victims of domestic violence and abuse. Our residents would feel loved and supported here, maybe for the first time in their lives. The world needed more places like this home.

After the tour, we sat around in the garden and drank wine. Linda had to leave early, but I was glad she came out. Eventually, Dylan, my brother, walked to me.

"Hey," he said.

"Hey, dude," I said. "How's college?"

"It's good," he said. "Just to warn you, don't let Mom corner you. She's going to ask you fifty questions about grandkids. It's all she's been talking about since she found out Amber York was pregnant."

"Okay," I said, laughing. Amber and I hadn't been friends, but she was my age and had lived a few houses down from us when I was in high school. "How is Amber?"

Dylan shrugged.

"Pregnant, so, you know," he said, shrugging again. "She's getting laid."

I laughed again. He considered me.

"You're different than when I last saw you," he said.

"What do you mean?"

"You're smiling," he said. "You didn't use to smile that much. And you just laughed. I can't remember the last time I heard you laugh. I think I got used to you looking angry all the time."

My chair creaked as I leaned back.

"I guess I am smiling and laughing more often now."

He looked toward my house.

"This is a nice house. You're doing something good here. You deserve something that makes you happy."

I smiled and thanked him but not because he was right. Not entirely, at least. This house didn't make me happy. True, the apartment above the garage was perfect for me and Roy. It had a modern kitchen, two good-sized bedrooms, a bathroom, and a living room. Maybe one day I'd meet somebody and start a family, but for now, I didn't need anything else. Roy and I could live happily there for a lot of years.

Though it was important, it wasn't the charity that brought a smile to my face, either. It was my brothers, my sister, my mom and dad. It was Miriam and Martin, Ian's parents. It was my dog, Roy. It was my friends and colleagues. My past had made me who I was, but for the first time in my life, I had somehow unyoked myself from its weight.

I had done my job. The bad guys were in jail, the good guys were mostly safe, and I had my family. I had found those things that made me happy, but even more than that, for the first time in my life, I had found peace.

AUTHOR'S NOTE

As most of you knew before picking this book up, *The Man in the River* is the last book in the Joe Court series. I've spent the last several years writing Joe's books, so it was surreal and more than a little bittersweet to write this one. Joe Court has grown and changed over the course of nine books, and I think she's finally in a place where she's well and truly happy. I hope her books have brought you as much joy to read as they've brought me to write.

My next series will involve an ex-police officer from the St. Louis area and her faithful dog George. The protagonist will have the tenacity and resourcefulness of Lee Child's Jack Reacher and the investigative abilities of Michael Connelly's Harry Bosch. Though the protagonist will come from the St. Louis area, the stories will take place across the US. I'm still in the planning stages, but I think this'll be a great series.

If you'd like to keep up to date with the new series, consider joining my mailing list or following me on Facebook. You can find more information about my mailing list by turning the page, and you can follow me on Facebook here:

https://www.facebook.com/ChrisCulverBooks

No matter what, I hope you and those you love are well.

All the best,
Chris Culver
9/2/2020

Stay in touch with Chris

As much as I enjoy writing, I like hearing from readers even more. If you want to keep up with my world, there are a couple of ways you can do that.

First and easiest, I've got a mailing list. If you join, you'll receive an email whenever I have a new novel out or when I run sales. You can join that by going to this address:

http://www.indiecrime.com/mailinglist.html

If my mailing list doesn't appeal to you, you can also connect with me on Facebook here:

http://www.facebook.com/ChrisCulverbooks

And you can always email me at chris@indiecrime.com. I love receiving email!

Enjoy this book? You can make a big difference in my career

Reviews are the lifeblood of an author's career. I'm not exaggerating when I say they're the single best way I can get attention for my books. I'm not famous, I don't have the money for extravagant advertising campaigns, and I no longer have a major publisher behind me.

I do have something major publishers don't have, something they would kill to get:

Committed, loyal readers.

With millions of books in the world, your honest reviews and recommendations help other readers find me.

If you enjoyed the book you just read, I would be extraordinarily grateful if you could spend five minutes to leave a review on Amazon, Barnes and Noble, Goodreads, or anywhere else you review books. A review can be as long or as short as you'd like it to be, so please don't feel that you have to write something long.

Thank you so much!

About the Author

Chris Culver is the *New York Times* bestselling author of the Ash Rashid series and other novels. After graduate school, Chris taught courses in ethics and comparative religion at a small liberal arts university in southern Arkansas. While there and when he really should have been grading exams, he wrote *The Abbey*, which spent sixteen weeks on the *New York Times* bestsellers list and introduced the world to Detective Ash Rashid.

Chris has been a storyteller since he was a kid, but he decided to write crime fiction after picking up a dog-eared, coffee-stained paperback copy of Mickey Spillane's *I, the Jury* in a library book sale. Many years later, his wife, despite considerable effort, still can't stop him from bringing more orphan books home. He lives with his family near St. Louis.

Made in the USA
Coppell, TX
12 May 2023